SECRET OF THE FAMILY TREE

DIGGING UP OLD ROOTS

TORRY ROSE

ISBN: 979-8-218-72726-0 (paperback)
ISBN: 979-8-218-79162-9 (hardback)
ISBN: 979-8-218-72727-7 (ebook)

CONTENTS

<h2>CHAPTER I</h2>

AMEARA

The fresh scents of grass and evergreens floated on the rhythm of a spring breeze over Hearthshire, Vermont. Enjoying these sweet melodies, Ameara Muaura Fairland knelt in her front yard beside her eight-year-old daughter, Anna, as they eased their hands into the moist soil, preparing the ground for planting fairy roses.

"That's right, Anna. Dig deep," Ameara instructed. The flowers were for Terrance, a massive old tree that grew so close to the Fairlands' stone home that its armlike limbs appeared to wrap around the dwelling.

"Why can't I use a shovel like Megan's mom does?" Anna asked. "Megan's mom even lets us use gloves when we help."

"Aw, but then you miss out on all the fun of getting really messy," Ameara explained while using her dirt-covered finger to draw a smiley face on a giggling Anna's forehead. "Isn't that right, Sam?"

Looking around for her youngest daughter—six-year-old Sam—Ameara found her stretched out on the grass, flat

1

on her belly, face to the earth, whispering with her eyes closed.

"What are you doing there, Sam?"

With one little finger, Sam jabbed at the ground. "Momma, can you tell those people down there to not take me?"

Glancing back at Anna, Ameara asked her, "Now, why would you tell your sister something like that? Are you trying to scare her?"

"No," Anna said, staring down at her shoes.

"Sam, the core people are not coming to take you. If they did, you'd be one lucky little girl. Remember? I told you the story about the core people and their room filled with colored rocks. You can even hear the Earth singing in their world."

"Oh, that's right." Sam sat up, pulling grass from her wild, bushy hair as the family's Irish wolfhound, Gypsy, licked her face from chin to temple.

Ameara patted the ground beside her. "Come here, Sam. Help me plant these flowers for Terrance."

Wiggling across the ground like a snake, Sam squeezed between her mother and older sister.

"Speaking of Terrance, Anna, I thought he said he wanted tulips this spring," Ameara said.

"Yeah, well, that was before a barn swallow told Terrance about fairy roses. So now, that's what he wants."

"I guess a tree as old as Terrance has a right to change his mind." Putting the tiny purple blooms to bed in their newly dug home, Ameara sat back on her heels, admiring their handiwork. "There. That should do it." As she stood and dusted off her pants, her thoughts wandered back to the phone call she'd received from her mother earlier in the day. "I wish I could brush away that conversation," she said under her breath.

"What'd you say, Momma?" Anna asked.

"I said, 'Let's get ready for dinner.'"

WITH ANNA and Sam tucked in for the night, Ameara finally settled down into her own bed with her diary. She didn't get far in her journaling before her husband, Innis, entered the room holding an orrery, a mechanical device that shows the rotation of planets around the sun. She watched as he cranked a little metal lever on the orrery's wooden base, making the spherical planets revolve around one another.

"What do you think?" he asked.

"So that's what you and Kitchet dug out of the attic. Very nice. I am impressed."

"Yes, and fitting all the pieces back together was a pretty daunting task," Innis said, placing the orrery on his nightstand. "It's not quite done yet. But when it is, I'll put it in Anna and Sam's room."

"They'll love it."

Staring down at the blank, lined pages in her diary, Ameara tried to concentrate on anything except breakfast with her mother in the morning.

"What time are you leaving tomorrow?" Innis asked, as if reading her mind.

"Oh … around seven, seven thirty, I guess. Mom said she'd be in her office early."

"What's the matter? You seemed anxious all during dinner."

"I'm worried, Innis. I'm afraid the news Mr. Lin brings concerns the Maskhim tracking Mom's movements."

Nanna Fairland, Ameara's mother, was a professor of historical geography at Eastern Vermont University. After Ameara's father died, Nanna decided it was time to leave the confines of the university to do field research, which was common for geographers to do. What was uncommon was the data Nanna gathered. She was mapping out locations across the globe that she knew stored knowledge of humanity's true past—information that a small group operating within every government, known as the "Maskhim," wanted to get their hands on. And this had Ameara worried.

"We don't know that's what Mr. Lin has come to tell your mother. We don't even know who Mr. Lin is," Innis said.

"Isn't it enough that this Mr. Lin knows who the Maskhim are? Innis, you know how these people work. They'll do anything to keep humanity in the dark about their lineage. And if the Maskhim suspect that our family has this knowledge, I don't want to think what could happen to us!"

"But you're forgetting that it's part of Nanna's job to study different cultures. She's not exactly setting off any alarm bells by visiting these areas. Let it go for the night. I bet by tomorrow, you'll be laughing at yourself for getting all worked up about nothing."

"I hope you're right," Ameara said with a sigh. Turning back to her diary, she made a small notation under the date, March 19, 1987:

Mr. Lin, Maskhim. What does he know?

CHAPTER 2

A MOTHER'S SACRIFICE

Ameara heard a door close, followed by rapid footsteps somewhere on the upper level of the faculty building at Eastern Vermont University. She imagined it was another professor catching up on paperwork this early hour. On the other hand, it could be Mr. Lin. On her arrival, she had seen a car parked near her mother's Jeep Wagoneer. With this thought in mind, she quickened her pace, her shoes scuffing against the steps and echoing down the empty halls.

The marbled doorknob to Nanna's office felt cold in Ameara's hand. The hinges shrieked abnormally loud when she entered. She found the room dimly lit and the heavy cloth curtains shut. *Something's wrong*, she thought. Her mother didn't stand to greet her. Instead, she sat motionless. Something was very wrong.

Rushing to her side, Ameara called out softly. "Mommy?" Her words were reminiscent of younger years, when she'd lingered in her parents' doorway as they slept. This time, her mother didn't open her eyes and smile at her; Nanna's glassy stare looked right past her daughter.

Absently, Ameara stroked her mother's hand while swallowing back the ball of emotions forming in her throat. "Mom, please—"

The slow whine of the door drew her attention. Turning, she saw a tall blond man in a dark suit walking deliberately toward her.

Ameara could hear his labored breathing and see the sweat glistening on his pale skin as it ran from his brow into his gray eyes. Halting a few feet from her, he looked past her to Nanna. He said nothing.

"Are you Mr. Lin?" she whispered. "I think something has happened to my mother."

"You are Professor Fairland's daughter?"

She thought his voice was surprisingly steady for someone who appeared to have run a footrace. "Yes. Can you help me? I need to get my mother to a hosp—"

"She's dead. There's nothing you can do for her now."

No! she thought. Ameara clenched her eyes shut, not wanting to absorb the truth. It was too late; the impact of his words stung like a slap to the face, forcing her to admit what she'd sensed from the moment she'd entered the office. Her mother was dead. However, her mind had no time to adjust to this realization as, without warning, the pale blond man seized her by the wrist.

"You need to come with me," he said.

"What— No!" Clawing at his fingers, she tried to loosen his hold as he dragged her through a door behind her mother's desk. "Help … someone help—" She tasted the salty sweat of his palm as he pressed it over her mouth while wrenching her arm behind her back. She stiffened her legs at the top of the stairwell but almost tumbled as he swiped his foot underneath her and proceeded to carry her down.

Emerging from a side entrance, Ameara found herself ushered to the dark-blue vehicle she'd noticed on her arrival. A stocky young man was pacing beside it.

"Simms?" she heard him call out to her captor, who was shoving her into the back seat.

Ameara tried to keep her hands from shaking by clasping them between her knees. *The Maskhim know about us*, she thought as Simms climbed into the driver's seat. "Where are you taking me?" she asked. He gave her no answer. Her thoughts churned like a blender trying to process what she needed to do next. That's when she remembered the woods adjacent to the university grounds —an area she'd walked through before. Ameara knew what she needed to do. She felt she had no other choice. Focusing on the back of Simms's head, she held her breath and watched as the car neared her mark. Adrenaline at full tilt and with all her might, she raised her leg and kicked him. His forehead hit the steering wheel, the car swerved, and she jumped out, running as fast as she could into the woods.

The moist leaves muffled Ameara's feet. Her once neatly pinned curls hung about her shoulders. Her heart thundered, threatening to burst from her chest, but she couldn't stop. She had to reach the densest part of the forest, where she knew she would find *the one* who could deliver her message.

Daring a quick glance behind her, she saw no sign of Simms. She hurried along, knowing she was closer to the one she sought as the trees' clear whispers encouraged her to "Run this way." Following the whisperers' directions, she dashed past tree after tree, finally ending her flight in an area thickly walled by pines. Sheltered in the midst of them stood a gnarled old tree.

She threw herself at the ancient one's feet, then wrapped her arms around its trunk, saying, "Help me. I need your assistance."

A light breeze blew across her face as an old woman stepped forth from the tree and stood before her. Then Ameara delivered her message to the crone.

"My mother, Nanna Fairland, is dead." As she spoke those words, a picture of her mother sitting lifeless behind her desk flashed into her mind. She shook her head, not wanting to dwell on the image. "The Maskhim have discovered our secret. I, Ameara Fairland, cannot return home. Please tell my husband, Innis, that he *must* protect our daughters."

"Child, don't lose hope," the crone replied. "I will send a message to my elder sister. Help will come."

Somewhere nearby, Ameara heard footsteps and knew her time was up. "It's too late for me now." Turning back onto the path, she walked away slowly. There was no more need to run.

Tears spilled over from Ameara's large brown eyes as memories of her mother came to her mind. Her thoughts then turned to Innis, Anna, and little Sam. She allowed herself to escape within these images until they were interrupted by a figure that blocked her path, wiping her cherished memories from her mind forever.

CHAPTER 3

INNIS'S DECISION

Sitting alone in his workshop, Innis held a picture of Ameara. It was his favorite photo of his wife, with their daughters on each side of her. He remembered exactly when he took the picture. It was at their last spring festival, a time that celebrated the season of rebirth. But this year, spring brought the news of death.

Slumping forward onto his workbench, Innis used his hands like metal vices, squeezing out Ameara's words, which ran through his mind: "I'm worried, Innis. I'm afraid the news Mr. Lin brings concerns the Maskhim tracking Mom's movements."

With only the four stone walls to hear him, he wailed openly at the thought of his wife's last words to him. Why hadn't he listened to her? Raking his hands through his straight, black hair, he'd asked that question of himself over and over again.

As he stood quickly, his chair slammed into the back wall. If only he had gone with her that morning. He would've protected his wife and mother-in-law from Mr. Lin, the Maskhim, or both. "But I didn't," he said to himself.

"They're ready," Samuel Kitchet said, entering the workshop. "My Bess says little Sam is starting to fall asleep."

Still clutching Ameara's photo, Innis pushed his chair back under his workbench. He stood for a while, seemingly studying the back of his hand.

"How are you doing, old friend?" Kitchet asked.

"Kitchet, do you think I am doing the right thing, taking the girls away from their home? Do you feel this is what Ameara wanted me to do?"

"I feel, Innis, that this is the best thing to do right now. They'll be safe with their Aunt Mayra. And you know how she loves to travel. Maybe seeing other parts of the world will help the little ones ... heal."

"I'll try to come back as much as I can, just to check in."

"Don't give it a second thought. The girls need all of your attention now."

Taking one more look around his workspace, Innis locked up and handed the keys to Kitchet. Both men walked in silence back to the main house.

Entering his daughters' bedroom, Innis found Sam fast asleep on her bed and Anna cuddling Gypsy in the window seat.

"Why can't Gypsy come too?" Anna asked as Bess gathered the girls' things.

"Your aunt's apartment in New York doesn't have room for a big dog like Gypsy. Besides, who will Terrance have to tell stories to until you come back?" Innis asked as he gathered Sam into his arms.

"Bye, Terrance," Anna said. "I'll hear the rest of the story later."

"Good night, Anna," the old tree responded while reaching a leafy limb inside to shut the window.

It was ten p.m. when, after a few parting words to the Kitchets, Innis tucked his girls into the back of his station wagon and headed down their hidden, tree-lined driveway. Under a new moon in the sky, the car's headlights guided them onto their new path.

CHAPTER 4

A FAIRLAND RETURNS TWENTY-FIVE YEARS LATER

A fresh layer of snow greeted a red four-door sedan carrying the Keen family as they made their way along a hidden driveway. Large tree limbs reached out to embrace each other, forming a canopy on either side of the lane. Wrapped warmly in her pink fleece jacket, eleven-year-old Samantha Muaura Fairland-Keen looked out the window from the back seat.

"Mom, I don't see the house," she said.

"You'll see it once we reach the top of the driveway," Anna said, smiling from the passenger seat.

That was the first sign of happiness her mom had shown since they'd boarded a plane from Australia, but Samantha understood. Her mom was returning home to bury her father, Samantha's Grandpa Innis. His passing was the reason they were moving to Vermont.

Staring back down the long driveway, Samantha could almost picture her mom as a child, playing with her sister, Sam, and their dog, Gypsy. Seeing all the trees that surrounded the property, she now knew why her mother always sought out woodsy areas to take walks.

Samantha had known her Grandpa Innis was ill, but he had assured her he would be just fine. "Not to worry," he'd said. "It's only a bout of the flu."

Two days earlier, her parents had received a call from the Kitchets, friends of the family. Mr. Kitchet said Grandpa Innis had suddenly passed away. His flu had turned into pneumonia. The pneumonia was too much for his heart.

Closing her eyes, Samantha formed a picture of Grandpa Innis in her mind. As if waiting to be summoned, he appeared just as she'd last seen him, his broad smile showing the lines that creased each side of his bronze cheeks and the corners of his eyes. She remembered him telling her that the lines on his face told of a well-lived life. His eyes were as black as his hair, which had streaks of what Samantha called silver stardust because of the way the gray in his hair twinkled.

Though she saw her grandpa only on his yearly trips to visit them, Samantha would miss him dearly. He had been the only grandparent she had left.

She turned and faced the path up ahead just as a three-story stone home came into view. Her dad pulled up to the front door, and, almost instantly, an older couple rushed from the home to greet them.

"Saints alive, Anna, it's so good to see you. Welcome home, welcome home," the older man said, grabbing Samantha's mom by both hands and shaking them fervently. "Anna, you remember my Bess?"

The small woman beside him threw her arms around Samantha's mom's waist. "Oh, Anna, we are so happy you're home. We're just sorry it had to be because of your dear father's passing."

Samantha stood back and watched the couple squeeze

and kiss her mom repeatedly as if she were their long-lost daughter.

"This must be the famous Mr. Kitchet and his lovely missus Innis spoke so much about," Samantha's dad said as he stepped up to shake the man's hand and kiss Mrs. Kitchet on her cheek. Samantha couldn't help but notice how tiny the Kitchets appeared as they stood next to her dad's six-foot-three-inch frame.

"Indeed I am, sir. And please—it's just Kitchet or Samuel. I prefer just Kitchet. Innis spoke fondly of you also. Tell me, Mr. Keen, did you have any trouble finding the place?"

Waving his hand in the air, her dad said, "No trouble at all. Your directions were perfect. Now, none of this Mr. Keen stuff. Mr. Keen was my dad. I'm just Craig."

"Kitchet, Bess, this is Samantha, our daughter," Anna said.

Extending her hand, Samantha hoped they'd accept that instead of bear hugs and kisses. She never understood why adults grabbed at other people's kids, smothering them with affection without even asking. Yet kids were told, "Don't let strangers touch you." *Talk about mixed signals*, she thought.

"Well goodness, Anna. She looks so much like your own blessed mother, except for all those beautiful curls," Bess said. Then she turned to Samantha. "Did anyone ever mention that you look like your Grandmother Ameara?"

"Yes, ma'am. Grandpa Innis told me I have my grandma's smile," Samantha said. She was used to remarks about her hair, which looked like long brown springs. After commenting on her hair, people usually next looked from her mom to her dad to see which one she favored. Her mom, with her black eyes, dark hair, and mocha complexion? Or was it her dad, with his light-brown hair, blue-gray eyes, and fair skin? Samantha felt she was a perfect blend of both her parents, like her favorite ice cream—vanilla fudge swirl.

"And look at the legs on her, Samuel. She's going to be as tall as Nanna. That would be your great-grandmother," Bess said to Samantha. "But can she help it, with a big fella like him for a papa? Can you give us a hug, Samantha?"

Well, at least she asked, Samantha thought as she allowed them to squeeze her until she thought they'd cut off her circulation.

Maybe it was the snow-covered evergreens in the backdrop, but to Samantha, the Kitchets looked like a Mr. and Mrs. Claus she'd seen on a greeting card, with their rosy faces and blue button eyes. Mr. Kitchet had a white beard with traces of black hair. He wore a heavy blue peacoat and lace-up boots. Samantha spied golden hair peeking out from under Mrs. Kitchet's wool hat. Mrs. Kitchet wrapped herself in a long gray wool coat, and a pair of fur-lined boots covered her feet.

It had become second nature for Samantha to notice people's clothing, their facial appearances, and how they carried themselves. She then assigned them to familiar characters from literature or movies or to people she had met before. This helped her remember things about them just in case she had to refer to someone later. She did this as part of her training to be a detective. Her goal was to become the real-life version of Nancy Drew.

"Okay, I am going to wimp out and just say I'm freezing," Craig said. "Does anyone mind if we take this reunion inside?"

Placing her coat on one of several hooks in the foyer, Samantha had a good look around at what would be her new home. A fire burned in the living room, which was off to the left of the entrance, making the house warm and toasty. She got a whiff of something good cooking that made her stomach growl, reminding her it was time to eat. A woven rug hung on a wall, depicting in its center a tree surrounded by a midnight sky with silver thread mimicking stars. Below the wall hanging was a simple wooden table with a basket of pine cones and pine branches. Samantha noticed that her shoes were wetting the nicely polished floors and thought that maybe it was best to remove them.

"Oh, don't feel you have to do that. These old wood floors can handle a little dirt," Bess assured her. "Just a quick whisk of a broom and a damp rag will clean it up." Then, giving Samantha a wink and a light squeeze of her hand, Bess whispered, "But this is your home now. So do whatever makes you feel more comfortable."

"Yes, ma'am," Samantha said, deciding to go ahead and remove her shoes.

"Bess. Call me Bess, dear. I want us to be good friends, Samantha—like your mom and I were when she was a young girl."

Samantha felt like she was returning home after a long trip. Which she thought was odd, since her family had never actually owed a home—or lived anywhere, for that matter—for more than a year.

Samantha's dad was a computer engineer whose office was the open road. When Samantha and her mom weren't traveling with him for work assignments, which was very rare, they lived in a small rented apartment in her dad's native Australia. This move to Hearthshire would give them the first home Samantha could truly call her own.

The small group moved on into the living room, where a stone fireplace took up most of a wall. There were two small overstuffed sofas with a wooden table between them and a larger sofa that faced the fireplace. A window seat was underneath a wide bay window, which looked out the front of the house.

"Can I be excused to look around upstairs?" Samantha asked.

"I bet you want to see your bedroom," Bess said. "I've made up your mom's old room for you. It's at the top of the stairs. First room on your left."

Slowly walking up the steps, Samantha ran her hand along the mahogany railing. Through the floor-to-ceiling windows at the top of the landing, she could see rows of trees stretching out into the distance. To the left of the stairs, she found her bedroom.

A full-size sleigh bed, which was against the far back wall, greeted Samantha as she entered. A white quilt with scalloped edges covered the bed, and a pale-blue eyelet bed skirt ran along the bottom. Four pillows lay comfortably at the head of the bed, neatly tucked inside pale-blue-and-white embroidered eyelet pillowcases. *This bed would never fit in my room back in Melbourne*, Samantha thought.

Built-in shelving lined half a wall on the right side of her bed. Samantha felt the shelves would be perfect for her books, which she normally stacked on the floor next to her bed after reading each night.

A fireplace burned at the foot of the bed, giving the room a nice woodsy smell. There was a window seat adorned with two midnight-blue pillows and a matching blanket folded neatly on top. This was where Samantha came to sit, peeking out the diamond-pained window just in time to see the Kitchets hurrying across the snow.

There were stones stacked in a row to form a low-lying fence. The couple passed through an opening in it and headed for a small one-story stone cottage a short distance away. *That must be where they live*, Samantha thought.

As they approached the house, something large caught her eye. It looked like a butterfly and was at least seven inches long, with black wings and red spots. It fluttered down between Mr. and Mrs. Kitchet, who struck up a conversation with it. Then Bess gestured for the butterfly to enter before she shut their front door.

It couldn't be a butterfly out this time of the year. It must be their pet bird or something, Samantha thought.

Getting up to explore her new room further, she came to stand in front of an unusual-looking mirror on the wall next to the fireplace. She ran her hand over symbols that someone had carved into the oval wooden frame. On the left side of the frame was a crescent moon, and on the right, a cluster of three large stars. Carved into the very top was a single star looking down onto a sphere etched into the bottom of the frame. The mirror's glass was black, making it difficult for Samantha to see her reflection. She reached out and touched it, when ... *Huh?* she wondered. The darkened surface shimmered, followed by what she thought was a flash of silver light shooting from the bottom toward the top. "What was that?"

"What was what?" her dad asked, entering the room with her luggage.

"A light just shot across this mirror, and the glass moved like water."

"It's just the light reflecting off the surface," he pointed out. "It's a poor choice of glass for a mirror. You can't really see yourself in it."

"This mirror has been hanging here ... since I was a child," her mom said, joining them. She ran her fingers along the wooden frame. "You know, I've seen this same crescent moon and stars somewhere else. But I can't remember where. Anyway, I think we should go down and enjoy the dinner Bess made and turn in early. It's been a long day for all of us."

Samantha let her parents go on ahead of her while she darkened the room. Standing in front of the mirror again, she touched it. The glass rippled, and a second later, the streak of silver emanated from the bottom of the frame and shot up toward the star.

"It's not a reflection from light. It's an image coming from inside this mirror!" she said.

CHAPTER 5

TAPPING IN THE NIGHT

The flames in Samantha's fireplace did their job of warming the room for its new occupant. A few embers lay on a bed of ashes, whispering to one another in their crackling, popping language. The only other sound in the peaceful abode was ... a tapping.

Whose bed is this? Samantha wondered as she woke up. Running her hands over the soft white quilt, she remembered: She was in her new bedroom in her mom's childhood home. Sitting up, she looked for the source of the tapping, but it had stopped. Normally, bumps and thumps in the night didn't bother her, especially in old houses like this one. Her mom told her that houses needed to stretch. "Houses pop their bones sometimes after their day of supporting the family they shelter," she'd explained.

Flipping her pillow over to the cool side, Samantha scooted back under the covers. But, before her head hit the pillow ... *There it is again* ... The tapping had returned. Leaning over on her elbow, she listened more carefully this time. She determined that it wasn't the sound of an old house. This was the rhythmic tap of a knocker. And there was something else. Samantha sensed that the shadowy stillness had been teeming with inaudible sounds just behind the tapping.

Climbing out of bed, she tilted an ear toward the air, trying to tune into the barely there sounds. But she couldn't make them out, and the tapping had stopped again. *Strange.* As she stood beside her bed, listening for the tapping to return, the bottoms of her feet started to tingle. "Ah, great. They've fallen asleep," she said. But the sensation didn't stop at her feet. It continued to travel quickly into her legs and along her spine. Her body vibrated as though set off by a tuning fork. Then, *pop!*

What the— Samantha thought. Stunned, she wasn't sure where the popping sound came from. But she did notice that after the pop, the tingling feeling flew out of the top of her head as if a cork had been removed. Timidly, she reached up and ran her hands through her thick curls. There were no holes or gaping wounds. Nothing was out of place, but something had changed. She could now make out the inaudible sound—it was a rich melody played on some sort of instruments. Then, again came ... the tapping.

It's coming from outside my window! Peeking through the partially closed curtains, she saw that it was a branch knocking up against the glass. *Ha! It's only a tree. Another mystery solved by Samantha, the great detective.* She giggled as she picked up a log to toss onto the fire. *But what was that strange tingling feeling?*

"Hello." A muffled voice of a man came from outside her window. Then ... three taps. "I say hello."

Samantha spun toward the window, the log falling from her hand. "Who's that?" *Oh, it must be Dad!* she decided. *He must've locked himself out.* Pressing her nose and hands up against the cold glass, she called out, "Dad, are you out there?" Peering out into the darkness, she looked through the tree's branches for signs of him down below, but no one was there.

"Oh, there you are. Why is there snow on my head? Have I been sleeping that long?" came the voice.

"Dad?"

Instead of answering Samantha's question, the male voice this time asked, "Should I finish the story now?"

With that, Samantha bolted from her room and ran smack up against her dad's chest in the hallway.

"Whoa, cherub," he said. "Slow down. What's on your tail?"

"There is ... someone ... outside my window. I heard ... a man talking. I thought ... it was you!"

Her dad quickly moved to her window as she stayed put in the open doorway.

"I don't see anyone," he said.

"Oh, hello," the voice said again. "Has she gone to sleep?"

Samantha came to stand behind her dad. "You don't hear a man talking?" she asked.

"Nope. I can see that the Kitchets still have their lights on. Maybe you heard them."

Was I hearing the Kitchets? she wondered. "But ... did you hear them talking a minute ago?"

"What's going on, Samantha?"

In one long breath, she told her dad how she woke to a tapping sound and felt a tingling in her body when she got up to investigate. And then how she heard a man's voice outside her window.

Placing his hands on her shoulders, her dad led her back to her bed. "It was a long flight, Samantha. You know, we've taken that trip from Melbourne to the States many times before. After these trips, you, your mum, and I have often had a nasty case of jet lag. Remember that time I woke up in the middle of the night, screaming in pain from a charley horse in my legs?"

She did remember that time. It had scared her. He'd screamed so loud. She thought her dad was seriously hurt.

"Your body is just trying to release the tension that came from sitting in one position on the plane. Add to that Grandpa Innis's passing and waking up in a strange room. Give yourself time. All of this is a lot to absorb."

He flattened her pillow and tucked the blanket around her. "Your mum is fast asleep. But if you like, I can sit with you, maybe sing our favorite song. Or are you too old for that now?"

"No, I don't think I'll ever be too old for our favorite song."

Sitting on the edge of her bed, Craig began to sing, his deep voice whispering the the lyrics of "Hushaby Mountain."

Samantha used to beg her dad every evening to sing "Hushabye Mountain." She'd heard it while watching his favorite movie, *Chitty Chitty Bang Bang*, when she was six years old. The movie became their favorite movie and the song their favorite song. That is, until the age of eight, when she discovered she preferred curling up to a Nancy Drew book. But tonight, their favorite song lulled her back to sleep.

CHAPTER 6

AUNT MAYRA EXPLAINS

K nock, knock. Can I come in?"

Recognizing the voice on the other side of her bedroom door, Samantha leaped from her bed, flung open the door, and threw herself into the arms of her mom's younger sister.

"Aunt Sam!" she cried out.

"Let me take a look at you," her aunt said. "Zen is going to be absolutely jealous. He's been complaining that he hasn't grown at all, and here you've grown a full inch or two since we last saw you." Alexzender, or Zen for short, was Samantha's older cousin by just thirteen months.

"Here, sit next to me," Sam said, making herself comfortable in Samantha's bed.

"When did you get in from Hawaii?" Samantha asked.

"About two hours ago. It's nearly ten a.m."

"Gosh, I better hurry. I haven't even thought about what I should wear."

"Don't worry. The service isn't until noon. I actually came up to help you get ready and see my old room. So, do you think you'll like living here?"

"Oh, yeah. I think it'll be great." Samantha felt she wouldn't tell her aunt about her strange experience the night before. In the light of day, she agreed with her dad that she'd just been overly tired. "Does it look the same as when you and Mom slept in here?"

"I think so. I was so young when we left."

"Do you ever wish you had grown up in this house instead of moving away to New York?"

"It was an adjustment, but Aunt Mayra made it into an adventure. We'd catch a plane, sometimes in the middle of the night, and just travel off to different places. It was great fun for me as a kid. It was because of a visit to Hawaii that I decided to attend college there and eventually settle. But my best memories are of Hearthshire as a child. Here is where I remember Mom."

Samantha thought Aunt Sam sounded just like her mom when she talked about her childhood home.

"Dad always told me and Anna that if we held onto the happy memories of Mom, she'd be with us always, wherever we made our home," Sam said. "I hope you do that today, Samantha, as we say goodbye to your Grandpa Innis. He would want you to think of only the happy times with him."

"I will."

"Now, let's get you dressed."

Studying her aunt, Samantha admired how she never bothered to tame her wild hair and the way she mixed and matched her clothes—like now. She was wearing black-and-white wool stockings with a snowflake design under a knit gold dress with an interlocking pattern of green and blue squares.

The most daring item of clothing Samantha owned was

a pair of purple high-top Converse sneakers with an All-Star emblem on the sides.

"I really like your stockings," Samantha said.

"I'll send you a pair."

As they made their way into the kitchen, Samantha made sure the white pearl buttons on her pink cardigan sweater all lined up and the ribbing at the bottom nicely hit the top of her pink-and-purple plaid wool skirt.

"Here's our sleeping beauty," her dad called out from the kitchen table. She thought he looked quite handsome in black dress pants and a black crewneck sweater. He was sharing tea with her Uncle Junzo, Aunt Sam's husband, who got up to give Samantha a hug.

"I think all that sleeping has made you taller," Junzo said as he gently stretched out one of the curls her aunt had piled high on top of her head with a pink ribbon. "Or maybe it's the hair that's giving you height."

Junzo wore his straight, black hair a little past his shoulders. He was an artist. And because he was an artist, Samantha supposed he had to wear his hair long and have a goatee. Most of the time, he also wore a mustache. But not today. His upper lip was clean-shaven. Besides illustrating his wife's books, he also taught art classes at his local high school on Oahu, Hawaii.

"Now, don't tease, you guys," Sam said. "I told her there was no rush. Besides, I wanted to have some private time with my favorite niece."

"Uh, Mom. Samantha's your only niece," said Zen, coming into the kitchen. "It's about time you got up, Samantha. We thought you were going to sleep forever."

"I'm still catching up from our long flight," she said, giving him a playful shove. She was glad Zen was there because he was someone her own age to talk with. Both she and Zen were homeschooled. But unlike Samantha, Zen didn't pack up and travel every year. He had opportunities to make friends in his own neighborhood.

"I was just kidding. So, it's gonna be weird not having Grandpa around, isn't it?" Zen said.

"Yeah, I'm really going to miss him," Samantha replied.

"It seemed like he'd live forever, you know. He just never seemed old to me."

Samantha realized this was the first time she'd seen Zen in anything other than board shorts with a surfboard tucked under his arm. "You're just like Mowgli from *The Jungle Book*," she'd always said to kid him. She took a good look at him now, all dressed up in long pants and a dark-blue sweater. He'd even combed his thick, wavy, black hair. *Boy, this sure is a different look for Zen!*

"Samantha," her mom said. "This is your Great-Aunt Mayra."

"Hello, Samantha."

Beaming from the kitchen doorway was a small woman with dimpled, round brown cheeks. Just looking at her, Samantha guessed this was where her Aunt Sam got her fashion sense. Mayra wore a royal-blue silk top over purple silk pants. And a pair of flat metallic gold shoes sparkled on her feet. Her hair was pulled back into a bun, which let Samantha see that she did have on a pair of earrings. But they didn't match. This made Samantha chuckle to herself as she remembered the stories her mom told her about the woman who'd raised her.

"Aunt Mayra is fluent in several different languages," Anna had said. "A very intelligent woman, really, who never fully learned to operate her own kitchen and has a habit of misplacing things. Mainly her earrings."

"Just call me Mayra. Or Aunt Mayra will do. 'Great-aunt' makes me feel utterly ancient." Then, twirling on her heels, Aunt Mayra turned to face everyone in the kitchen. "All right, everyone. We're about to leave. We'll be walking to the cemetery. That means wear sensible shoes," she said while kicking off her gold slippers and pulling on a pair of rubber boots.

"Your dad tells me you had a rather rough night," Anna said to Samantha as they put on their coats.

"Yeah, I think I was just tired. That's all."

"Samantha, you and Alexzender will walk with me," Mayra interrupted. She was now wearing a long black coat and already had Zen by the hand. Linking her other arm with Samantha's, she dragged them both out the door.

The tree-lined path was cleared of snow, making the walk much easier. Samantha even felt the weather was a bit warmer than the day before. Her mom and Aunt Sam walked together with the Kitchets while her dad and Uncle Junzo followed them. Samantha and Zen brought up the rear with Aunt Mayra between them.

"See these glorious life forms standing here?" Mayra asked, pausing to point toward the trees that formed the canopy along the path.

Samantha and Zen looked up at the giants towering above them.

"Every time I come back here," Mayra said, "I stand in respect of these ancient beings."

"What type of trees are they?" asked Zen.

"They don't belong to one particular species. However, all variety of trees on this planet can trace their genetic materials back to them. I cannot give you a suitable name like 'oak' or 'maple' because their names are lost to this world, lingering in the higher frequencies outside what most humans can hear. These trees are some of the true originals of this planet. But if you need a name to call them, Zen," Aunt Mayra said, continuing her trek down the path, "you can call them 'The Keepers.' That's how all Fairlands address them."

"Did she say, 'The Keepers'?" Zen asked Samantha as they walked over to stand in front of one of the trees while leaving Mayra to walk on ahead.

"Yep, that's what she said."

"Well then, The Keepers you are." Zen reached out to pat the tree's massive trunk. "Ouch!" he exclaimed, then immediately drew back his hand as though he'd been stung.

"What's the matter?" Samantha asked.

"I felt a spark or— Wait. My hand feels funny. You think I got stung by a bee?"

"Bees aren't out this time of year. Let me take a look." Samantha examined Zen's hand. "I don't see anything. How do you feel? Should I get your mom?"

"No," Zen said, flexing his hand. "It stopped. That was weird. For a minute, my hand got all tingly."

"Tingly?" *That's what I felt last night*, Samantha thought. "Come on," she said then, grabbing him by the arm. "I want to ask Aunt Mayra something."

They caught up with Mayra as she stood off to one side of the path. "I was just recalling all the wonderful times I've had here," she said, staring dreamingly back at the house. "I think I'll open up the old guesthouse this spring. It'll be good to just stay put for a while. You know? Reenergize."

"That sounds great, Aunt Mayra. I was wondering if I could ask you a question." Samantha said.

"Sure, go for it."

"You said most humans can't hear the names of these

trees. If you could hear them, would they sound like music, maybe?"

"I've heard it interpreted that way."

"Really? Well, last night, I heard music. But before I heard the music, I felt this odd tingling all over my body."

"Well, look around you, Samantha. You're in a cocoon of nature. You were probably hearing and feeling the vibrant nature essences that live here. And, of course, there's Terrance," Mayra said.

"Terrance?" Samantha asked.

"Yes. The tree next to your bedroom window is known as Terrance. His roots extend right under the house's foundation."

From Zen's knitted brow, Samantha knew they were thinking the same thing: *Aunt Mayra is a bit eccentric.*

"Sounds like a story from one of my mom's books," Zen said.

"You should pay attention to your mother's stories. You may learn something valuable," Mayra said.

"I will, I will. But when you talk about hearing nature, do you mean like the noise animals make at night?" Zen asked.

"What you call animal noise isn't noise to them. They're communicating with each other in their own language. Flowers, plants, and trees do the same thing."

"So, what you're telling us is that the music Samantha thought she heard was actually trees and animals talking to each other?"

"Zen, your dad speaks Japanese, right? If he were to greet someone in his own language, what would he say?"

Bowing with his arms tight to his side, Zen said, "Konnichiwa, ogenki desu ka?"

Samantha and Mayra couldn't help but laugh at Zen impersonating his father.

Mayra said, "Which basically translates into 'Good afternoon. How are you?' Now, Samantha, your dad is from Australia. How does he greet his fellow Australians?"

Not as animated as her cousin, Samantha slackened her jaw and did her best to mimic her dad's accent. "How ya goin', mate?"

"We just heard in both Japanese and Australian ways that people greet each other," Mayra said. "They sound completely different, right? Think of all the types of music there are in the world. Musicians string together an array of tones to convey how they want their songs expressed. Language is music. They both have a rhythm, but they sound different. This is the same with animals, trees, plants, and even water."

"I think I get it," Zen said. "It's like that dog whisperer guy on TV. He totally understands what the deal is with dogs. I'm like that with dolphins when I surf. I sit on my board, and the dolphins swim around me, and we talk. They tell me what the waves are doing that day or if it's safe to surf. They say other stuff like ..." Zen paused, glancing from Samantha to Mayra. "Well, I understand all their clicking sounds anyway."

"Zen, I haven't had the pleasure of communicating with dolphins, but I wouldn't dream of dismissing that you have," Mayra said with a smile. "Now, what's unfortunate is that most people will dismiss sounds they cannot understand outside their own native tongue. Why is that? It's because they're not in tune with that particular tonal pattern. If people are dismissing sounds from their fellow human beings, it follows that they are dismissing the musical language of nature too. And this also applies to the planets, who express their own special songs."

"That's what the Greek philosopher Pythagoras talked about—music and the celestial spheres. I read about him when I was learning geometry," Samantha shared. "I also came across *Harmonice Mundi* by mathematician Johannes Kepler. Kepler, who was also an astronomer, wrote—"

"Stop it! You're making my head hurt, talking about philosophers and mathematicians," Zen said, covering his ears.

"You're correct, Samantha," Aunt Mayra said. "But I'll have to side with Zen. The theories of these great thinkers, though valuable, are overcomplicated. When things are too complex, it turns people away. And we don't want that. What's important is that you both keep an open mind and a pliable ear. Keep it simple. Don't dig too far into the minds of men. Listen to the trees, whose roots are firmly planted in terra firma."

Samantha found her Great-Aunt Mayra quite interesting, but she put all that aside as they turned off the path from Fairland property and into the village of Hearthshire.

CHAPTER 7

A GATHERING TO SAY GOODBYE

A sign placed next to an old stone fireplace in the village center welcomed visitors to Hearthshire. A clock embedded in the chimney displayed the time for its residents. Traveling through the village, Samantha and her family passed a cluster of small shops—including a post office, a police station, and a library—that surrounded the square.

"Wow. Don't blink, or you'll miss the whole town," Zen said as they crossed the corner where Maple Street ended and Evergreen Street began.

Samantha didn't share her cousin's impression of Hearthshire. "I like it, and this is a village. It's smaller than a town. Hey, did you see the used bookstore? It's over there on the corner, next to the antique dealer's shop."

"You would notice a bookstore." Zen didn't even bother to turn and look. "I don't get the point of used bookstores. Why not just go to the library if you want to read an old book? Aren't bookstores supposed to sell new books?"

"Used bookstores sell hard-to-find and out-of-print books," Samantha informed him.

"This place feels old," Zen said, screwing up his face. Trailing behind their parents, Samantha stopped to look at a storefront window with a painted logo of a man holding a boot between his knees, a hammer in one hand, and a nail in the other. Under the drawing, it read, "The Cordwainer Shop." The shop reminded her of the story "The Elves and the Shoemaker."

"I think Hearthshire feels quaint," Samantha said before walking off.

"If *quaint* is a code word for *old*, then okay. It's quaint."

She didn't bother to argue with him. She knew he became disagreeable when he was nervous about something. The nearness of the cemetery was that something. Neither of them had ever been to a funeral. She tried to keep in mind Aunt Sam's words about remembering the happy times with her grandfather, but Samantha was starting to feel as nervous as Zen was acting.

The cemetery sat among an array of fir trees at the end of Evergreen Street. Several people stood in front of an octagonal building not too far from the cemetery's gated entrance. Mayra and the Kitchets stopped to speak with them while the rest of the family entered the building.

Inside, Samantha took a seat in the front row, sandwiched between Zen and her dad. Candles burned in mounted holders, which gave the room an intimate, peaceful feeling. Looking up, she could see the roof had been made from eight triangular pieces of stained glass adorned with trees.

"They sure take their trees seriously around here," Zen said, also making note of the roof.

A few feet directly in front of her, Samantha saw her grandfather's closed casket, with white and pink roses entwined in a fir wreath placed on top. If it weren't for the casket, she would have thought she was in the middle of a large conservatory.

"I think we should start now," Mayra said, standing in front of the casket. When everyone was seated, she began the ceremony.

One by one, friends and neighbors stepped forward to say kind words for the man they knew—Innis Moor. Samantha was listening intently until close to her ear, she heard someone say, "Psst, Samantha. Look at that guy over there."

A little annoyed that her cousin had taken this time to people-watch, she tried her best to ignore him.

"Samantha, look."

He's not going to let up, she thought. "What am I looking at?" she whispered back.

"That guy over there."

Standing near the entranceway, an Asian man, maybe in his mid-fifties, clutched a backpack to his chest. He reminded Samantha of Mr. Tan, a computer programmer who'd hired her father in Beijing.

"Yeah, what about him?" she asked.

"Don't you think there's something odd about him?"

Glancing over again, she appraised the man, this time with her detective eyes, and thought she noticed what Zen felt was strange about him. *He seems uncomfortable in his own skin*, she thought. Samantha watched as the man rapidly blinked his eyes and touched his face several times, as if making sure everything was in its place. He studied his hands, fussed with his hair, and tugged at his clothes. *Oh, that's it!* she realized. In his jeans and well-worn shoes, he wasn't as well dressed as the other attendees.

"I don't think he had time to change before coming to the funeral," she whispered to her cousin, who was now having a staring contest with the man. "Zen, quit! I think you're making him feel self-conscious about how he's dressed."

"Nah, that's not it. He's anxious about something else. I can feel it—"

"Shh! Your mom is just finishing up."

"We lay you to rest today, Poppa, next to our mother, your dear Ameara. We know that you are happy now that you are with her once more," Sam said.

As several men hoisted the casket onto their shoulders, those gathered stood to follow them into the courtyard, where they lowered Innis Moor into his final resting place. The funeral ended. People slowly began walking away from the gravesite, except Samantha. She took in a deep breath and turned her eyes toward the sky, where she saw the sun hiding behind some clouds. She felt less nervous and relieved that the funeral was nothing like she'd seen in television programs—filled with sadness and crying. *It was actually very peaceful,* she thought. "Goodbye, Grandpa. I'll miss you."

"Samantha," her mom said, coming up and wrapping her arms around her. "Are you doing okay?"

"Sure, Mom. I'm fine."

"It was a lovely ceremony for Dad. Just the way he would've liked it—short and simple," her mom said, pressing her cheek against Samantha's temple. "We're all heading over to the Maple House Bed and Breakfast for lunch just as soon as I thank some people for coming."

"Did Aunt Anna just mention something about food?" Zen asked Samantha, coming over just as his aunt walked off.

"You know, you were being really annoying during the ceremony," she replied.

"Don't blame me. It was that guy. He kept staring at us, so I started staring back at him. When he caught me staring at him, he gave me this crazy smile."

"What do you mean crazy smile?" Samantha asked as she tried to read the headstone in place over her grandpa's grave. Using her gloved hand, she rubbed away snow that was covering the name as she continued to quiz Zen. "I mean, were his teeth crooked or something? Not everyone has a perfect smile, you know."

"It wasn't a dental problem. It was just something about him that didn't sit well in my gut. You know what I mean?"

Samantha didn't know what he meant because she was only half listening to him now. She was more interested in reading the relatives' names that were engraved on the headstones. First was Ameara Muaura Fairland, August 28, 1951–March 20, 1987. Next to her name was Innis Moor, May 25, 1947–February 6, 2013. *And there's that same symbol of the crescent moon, cluster of stars, and sphere carved above their names. Just like on the mirror in my bedroom*, she thought.

"Did you hear what I said?" Zen's voice got her attention. "I said, 'There he is again.'"

The man with the backpack stood by himself a few feet away from the funeral guests gathered around Anna and Sam. "He's waiting to pay his condolences," Samantha answered, turning back to the headstones."

To the left of her grandparents' headstone were the graves of her great-grandmother and great-grandfather: Nanna Muaura Fairland, October 10, 1915–March 20, 1987, and Jack Williams, July 5, 1903–November 29, 1985.

What? Am I reading this right? She looked again at the

dates of death for her great-grandmother, Nanna Fairland, and that of her grandmother, Ameara Fairland.

"Well, why doesn't he just pay his condolences? He's just kinda standing there," Zen said.

Samantha realized she was reading the dates correctly. *How could that be? No one ever mentioned it before.*

"Samantha!" Zen said, jumping in front of her.

Shaking her head, she stared at her cousin. "Zen, look at the dates. Our Great-Grandma Nanna died on the exact same day as Grandma Ameara."

"So? What's the big deal?"

"Well, did you know that? What do you think could've happened to them?"

CHAPTER 8

IS THERE A MYSTERY THAT NEEDS SOLVING?

So, what do you think could've happened?" Samantha sat crisscrossed on her bed as she tried to pick Zen's brain about her discovery at the cemetery.

Sprawled out on her floor, Zen patted his stomach. "Right now, all I can think about is how full I am."

"Well, you scarfed your food down so fast that your poor mouth probably didn't have time to taste it," she scolded.

"I didn't eat breakfast this morning." Glancing at his watch, he looked shocked by the time. "It's after dinner! My poor growing body won't know what's happening to it since it's missing dinner too."

"Zen, you just said you were full. Can you focus on what I'm trying to ask you?" Taking a deep breath, she asked the question again. "Don't you think it's odd that Grandma Ameara and Great-Grandma Nanna died on the same day?"

"Why? People die all the time. Maybe after Grandma died, Great-Grandma was so upset that she died of a broken heart or something."

"People don't die from broken hearts. They die of heart attacks."

"You know what I mean. And if you want to know what happened so badly, why don't you just ask your mom how they died?"

"I thought of asking her during lunch, but then I thought maybe it's a little too soon. You know, we just buried Grandpa Innis and all. It's just that I can't help but wonder why no one ever mentioned it before. Why do you think your mom never said anything about it?"

"I don't know. It's not something you just go around telling anyone in normal conversation." Coming to his feet, Zen pretended to greet a new acquaintance. "Hello, how do you do? My name is Alexzender Arborden Fairland-Kita. I live in Hawaii, and I love to surf. And oh, by the way, my grandmother and great-grandmother died on the same day."

"Now that's just ridiculous," Samantha said. "Of course you wouldn't just say something like that to anyone. But we're not just anyone. We're family. Why didn't our parents ever mention it to us?" Narrowing her eyes, she leaned forward as she made her case to her cousin. "During lunch, I sorted in my head all the things that could've happened to them from things we already know. For instance, we know Grandma Ameara died young because Grandpa Innis raised our moms from little girls with Aunt Mayra's help. Now, I always assumed she died of an unexpected illness because she did die so young. But now that I've discovered that Great-Grandma Nanna died on the same day, Grandma Ameara couldn't have died from illness. I now think they must have died in a car accident together. Or something worse," Samantha concluded, pointing a single finger into the air.

"You think too much," Zen said. Kneeling in front of her open suitcase, he removed a book. "See what reading too many of these stories has done to your head? And where's the rest of your stuff?"

Groaning, Samantha plopped herself backward onto her bed before answering him. "All the rest of our boxes are coming by mail from Australia. I had to prioritize, so I grabbed what I thought was most important."

"Oh ... I can see where your priorities lie." One by one, he pulled more Nancy Drew books from her luggage: *The Secret of the Old Clock, The Hidden Staircase, The Clue in the Diary, and The Greek Symbol Mystery.* "I'm surprised you had any room to pack your clothes. You should've mailed the books with the rest of your stuff."

"Are you kidding? I had to bring this set. They're all first editions. I simply couldn't chance sending them by mail." Getting off her bed, she hovered over him with her hand held out. "Books, please."

"Ohhkaay." Rolling his eyes, he handed them over to her. "Well, Nancy Drew, if you were looking for a mystery, you should've been investigating that guy at the funeral."

"Are you still going on about him? Why would I investigate someone who was just paying their respects just like everyone else?"

"If he was just paying his respects, why did he leave before talking to anyone?"

"How do you know he didn't talk to anyone?" Samantha asked while arranging her books in her new bookshelves. "You said yourself that when you turned around, he was leaving. So, you don't know what he did before he left."

"Because I asked my mom, and she said she doesn't remember talking to him."

"That doesn't prove he didn't speak to her or anyone else. It only proves she doesn't remember him. Did you ask my mom or Aunt Mayra if they spoke to him? They could've."

"Well, I still think something was up with that guy. I felt it in my gut, and my gut is never wrong."

I'd better wait until the rest of my books arrive before deciding where to put these, Samantha thought, looking at the stack of Nancy Drews. Then she turned back to her cousin. "Why doesn't your gut ever tell you when it's full?"

"Ha ha! Because I'm never full for long. I burn it off in no time."

She had to agree with Zen on that point because he was as lean as a racehorse.

Before placing a hardback copy of a Nancy Drew book on her nightstand, she ran her hands along the book's spine. "I love old books," Samantha said, talking more to herself than to her cousin. "You know, if you're interested, the creator of Nancy Drew—Edward Stratemeyer—also created another mystery series called The Hardy Boys. You may really like—"

"No, thanks," Zen said, holding up his hand before she could go on. "I'll stick to my surfing and leave reading about mysteries to you. I have plenty of adventure in real life."

Thumbing through the pages of one of her books, Samantha thought that maybe Zen was right. Maybe because she read so many mysteries, her mind automatically looked for secrets and clues even where none were hiding. *People from the same family have died on the same day before and for perfectly normal reasons,* she told herself. Sighing, she held the book to her chest. Not having any close friends, she'd come to depend on her friendship with the fictional Nancy Drew. She thoroughly enjoyed going on the wonderful mystery adventures she found between the pages of her favorite series. Placing her copy of *The Hidden Staircase* back on top of the pile, Samantha made herself a promise: *Now that I'm putting down permanent roots, I will seek more adventures outside written literature, just as Zen does.* As she came to this decision, Zen yelled out in excitement from across the room.

"Now, this is so cool!" He was looking in the mirror mounted on her bedroom wall.

"Yeah, I thought that mirror was pretty interesting too," she said, coming to stand behind him.

"I don't think it's really a mirror," Zen said. "The glass is black like a TV screen, and it reacts like a computer monitor. Watch, I'll show you." He pressed the surface with his finger, and it shimmered, just as it had when Samantha touched it. "See that? See how it moves when I touch it? It reminds me of an app on my dad's iPad of a pond with fish. When I touch the screen, the water and the fish move, just like this surface."

"You know, when I was looking at it yesterday, I thought I saw light shooting across the surface," Samantha said.

"I saw that too. It looks more like a shooting star to me."

"Yeah, like a star."

Zen pressed his finger to the surface again. "See? There's the star," he said as the silvery-blue light streaked across the screen. "But then it fades to black again, like it's powering down. Maybe it has a short."

"Huh. So this is some sort of computer?"

"I think so. Did your dad see it? He's the computer engineer," Zen asked.

"He thought it was just light reflecting off the surface,

which made it appear to move." Samantha touched the wooden frame surrounding the glass. "Hey, Zen. See these carved symbols? I saw them on the headstones of our relatives today at the cemetery."

"Really? This frame does seem pretty old, doesn't it? And it's attached to the wall. I wonder if it was carved during the same time the house was built. But this glass inside the frame is new technology. I mean, computer monitors came out in the late 1940s or 1950s, I think. And touch screens were invented much later."

"Why would someone put a computer monitor into a wall frame?"

"No clue," Zen said, shoving his hands into his pockets. "But it is cool. Hey, I'm going down to see what's cooking for dinner. Coming?"

"No, I better unpack."

With her cousin gone, Samantha started placing her clothes in her dresser. But not long after he'd left, Zen was back, standing in her doorway.

"What happened? Couldn't find anything to eat?" Samantha asked.

"Mom said I have to wait," he said, looking disappointed. "They sent me back up to get you. Apparently, Aunt Mayra wants to talk to all of us before she leaves."

CHAPTER 9

PASSING OF THE TORCH

There was an unfamiliar person sitting in the living room window seat. Samantha couldn't see the face concealed in the shadows cast by the drapes, but she assumed, based on the legs and the size of the feet, that the person was a male. As she glanced around the room, it appeared only she knew he was there.

Aunt Mayra was gazing down at a book while standing behind a wingback chair in front of the fireplace.

Uncle Junzo was showing her dad something he had drawn on a napkin while Kitchet appeared to be nodding off in the corner on one of the smaller sofas.

As she and Zen squeezed between her mom and Aunt Sam on the larger sofa, Samantha was just about to inquire about the stranger when Mayra looked up from her book.

"I made notes," she said, waving her purple-covered book for everyone to see. "I don't want to forget anything—Oh, I didn't see you come in. Everyone, this is Addiwan."

Bright, amber eyes emerged from the shadows, followed by a strong, angular face, as Addiwan stood to greet everyone with a simple "Hello."

"Addiwan lives in the forest that borders this property," Mayra shared. "So, for those of you interested in becoming familiar with the lay of the land, he would be the person to see."

After nodding in agreement, Addiwan returned to his seat without saying another word.

By far, Addiwan was the most unusual-looking person Samantha had ever met. White flecks speckled the waist-length, golden-brown hair that framed his dark-olive complexion. He wore a black cable-knit sweater that matched his black pants, and his black leather shoes appeared to be molded to his feet. Samantha thought he was at least a foot and a half taller than her dad. She scanned her memory banks to find a familiar character or person akin to him but came up with nothing. One thing was for sure: The longer she stared at Addiwan, the harder it became to look away. There was something very uncommon about him compared to other people she'd met —and not in a bad way. She just couldn't put her finger on what it was yet.

"Where's Bess? Wasn't she just here a minute ago?" Mayra asked.

"She'll be along. She's making food for the young hungry one," Kitchet said, pointing in Zen's direction. "You know my Bessie."

"Zen," Sam said, turning to her son. "Didn't I tell you to wait until later?"

Samantha stifled a giggle as she watched her cousin try and act surprised at being accused of wrongdoing.

"B-but ... I didn't ask Bess for anything. Truly, Mom. I just said I was kinda hungry."

"Did I miss anything?" Bess asked as she rushed in. She laid a tray of sandwiches on the table in front of them before removing several leather pouches from her coat pocket and handing them to Mayra. "I remembered these."

"Oh, thank you. I completely forgot," Mayra said. "And no, we haven't started. You're just in time."

Samantha didn't feel hungry until she got a whiff of Bess's sandwiches. As she took a bite into one, the sweet corn sauce that generously covered slices of turkey and a creamy mild cheese filled her mouth. *Mmm ... So good.*

"There are several matters I need to address before I leave," Mayra said, taking a seat and opening her little purple book. "The first order of business is this house and the land. Anna and Craig have decided to live on the property known as Fairland. They are now the new caretakers. I have arranged for all necessary records to be placed in their names. If, for any reason, they decide to vacate the home, Sam and her family will take over the property. Sam, this is what you and Anna have agreed to?"

"Yes."

"Also, have you given any thought to what I suggested earlier concerning Zen staying here until the summer?" Mayra asked. "I really do feel it's important for him to get to know his ancestral home."

"Yes," Sam answered. "Me and Junzo discussed it, and we felt that since he's homeschooled, it wouldn't be too much of a fuss for him and Samantha to do their studies together. What do you think, Zen?"

"Trade in my sun and surf for cold and snow?" he asked. "Ahh ... I guess I'll make that sacrifice."

Samantha rolled her eyes at Zen's sarcasm.

"Good," Mayra said, glancing down at her notes. "Next, Anna and Craig. I want you both to understand that this land, all 178 acres and the homes on them, are never to be put up for sale or rented out to anyone. In addition, although the house the Kitchets reside in is listed on the title deed as Fairland owned, the Kitchets' home belongs solely to them."

"We understand, Aunt Mayra," Anna said.

"And what have you decided to do about your mother's flower shop, Essences?" Mayra asked, looking at Sam and Anna. "Would you like Rhiannon, Bess's niece, to continue to look after it?"

"I'd like to try my hand at running it with Rhiannon's help if she'd care to stay on," Anna said.

"If this is what Anna wants, I think that's a wonderful idea, since Junzo and I have our home and jobs back in Hawaii," Sam said.

"I'll talk with Rhiannon," Bess replied. "I'm sure she'd be happy to help you for as long as you need her."

"Craig, I understand you're planning to continue your business from home," Kitchet said.

"If all goes well with my meeting with the head honchos in California, yeah," Craig told him.

"There's a workspace behind the flower shop that I think would do nicely for an office. I'll take you to see it in the morning."

"Sounds like a plan," Craig said.

"Now, I'm going to share something that I hope will not be too upsetting," Mayra said in a more quiet tone. "The truth is, when Innis told everyone that he simply had the flu, he left out the part about also having had a heart attack—"

Samantha strained to hear over her mom's and Aunt Sam's shocked responses the reason her grandpa hadn't shared this information.

"Innis felt he would be just fine after the surgery, which he was ..." Lowering her head, Mayra added, "He couldn't have known pneumonia would take his life just a few short weeks later. After his death, Bess and I found a letter among his things dated the night before his operation that revealed he actually wasn't sure he'd make it. You see, the letter is a goodbye letter addressed to Samantha."

A letter for me? Samantha's mind began to race, thinking about what her grandpa's last words to her could be.

"We think he intended to leave one for each of you because we also found a letter addressed to Zen. But it was never finished. Why? We can only guess. But I feel that this one he did finish contains words meant for all of you." Handing Samantha the envelope, Mayra said, "So, Samantha, if you could please read your grandfather's words aloud."

Goosebumps rose on Samantha's arms as she took the envelope. She held it for a bit. Then, opening it, she wet her lips and began to read.

My little Samantha,

I will truly miss the nights we sat up reading your favorite girl detective novels. I enjoyed listening to you as you tried to work out the case before Nancy revealed the culprit.

Well, Samantha, I am offering you an opportunity to prove you have the stuff to be a detective. Here on Fairland land, there are Marvelous, Miraculous, and Magical mysteries waiting to be rediscovered. I hope you are up for the challenge and the adventure!

I will give you several hints about these "Mar-

vels," as I like to call them, to help you find them. The Marvels were hidden longer than the Fairland home has stood. (So, they are quite old.) And some are hidden in plain view.

Now, here are the steps you must take to locate them. If you don't take these steps, you will never find them.

Step 1: Have an open heart and open mind. With this first step, the hidden Marvels will find you.

Step 2: Be daring. Dare to see things differently and hear things differently.

Step 3: You will need the help of others to discover them. Remember, Nancy had the help of her friends—Bess, George, and Ned. So, drag Zen along for the adventure and anyone else who wants to be daring.

Lastly, some Marvels will be happenchance or happenstance. This means being flexible in your day-to-day life.

If you have been paying attention to my words, you will have noticed that I have not told you what these Marvels are. Are they vegetable, animal, or mineral? Are they treasures you can hold or only look at? Sights, sounds, or people? Well, these Marvels are all of these and more. That's why they are Marvelous, Miraculous, and Magical. And they are waiting to meet you!

Good luck. And, above all else, have fun,

Grandpa

After folding the letter, Samantha handed it to Zen. "What does it all mean?" she asked.

"Your grandpa meant for you to discover that for yourself. This is an adventure, like he said, Samantha," Mayra answered.

"Well, cherub, it sounds like you have something of a scavenger hunt to go on," her dad said.

"I would say it's more of a marvelous, miraculous, and magical expedition," Mayra said.

As their parents speculated about the meaning of Grandpa Innis's words, Samantha turned to Zen. "So, what do you think? she asked.

"What do I think? I think even Grandpa knew you needed some adventure in your life."

"All right, all right. Don't rub it in. I get it." Initially upset to learn just how sick her grandfather had been, she now felt happy knowing he'd thought of her before going into the hospital. And she couldn't help but be excited about what his letter promised to be an adventure of her dreams. *I'm actually going to solve a real mystery!* "Let's start first thing in the morning," she said.

"In the morning? Why?" Zen asked. "Why not tonight?"

"It's dark outside, for one thing," she said, pointing toward the window to show him that the sun had long gone down. That's when she noticed that Addiwan was no longer sitting in the window seat. *He didn't even say goodbye,* she thought.

"Ah, don't be a wimp," Zen said. "We'll get a couple of flashlights, and we'll be good to go."

She was about to yell something back at Zen for calling her a wimp when Mayra spoke up again.

"I have one more thing to do before I leave," she announced. "So, if I can just beg everyone's attention for just a little longer." Picking up the leather pouches that Bess gave her earlier, she said, "Several years after Samantha and Zen were born, Innis and I discussed that if either one of us died, the other one would make sure to pass on these family heirlooms. As I hand each one out, I ask that you all please wait to open them. Each pouch contains the same item, and it would be nice for you all to see them at the same time."

A thin strap bound the leather pouches together in sets of two. Tucked underneath the straps were slips of white paper with names written across them. Mayra picked up the first set and handed it to Samantha's parents. "These belonged to Muaura and Arborden Fairland, your ancestors and the first Fairlands to occupy this home."

Picking up two more pouches, she handed them to Sam and Junzo. "Sam, this was worn by your grandmother, Nanna, and your grandfather, Jack."

Handing over the last of the pouches, Mayra warmly said. "This one is for you, Samantha. It belonged to my sister, your Grandmother Ameara. And Zen, yours belonged to Grandpa Innis."

Lifting the flap of the soft tan leather pouch, Samantha found inside a pendant. It was made of half a rock that she recognized as an open geode—a rock structure that always held a crystal surprise inside its core. Her geode's core held a mixture of dark-blue and pale-blue crystals, which she noticed were the same as Zen's. The pendant fit nicely in her palm and was about three inches round. The rocky exterior was smooth from sanding or from time. Interlocking triangles made of a pink metal were attached to the geode's crystals and held something small in the center. Peering through the metal triangles, Samantha saw it was a seed. The seed was the size of a pine nut and had a translucent outer coating. Within the seed were veins that emanated light sparks, like the plasma lamps she remembered seeing in shopping malls. *How did someone put electrical wires in something as tiny as this seed?* she wondered. The pendant was suspended from a chain that was made of the same pink metal as the interlocking triangles.

"As you can see, these pendants have been specially made," Mayra said. "They all have different-colored crystal formations, but the same interlocking triangles are at the center of each one."

As her dad held up his pendant, Samantha saw that the crystals inside were dark purple and pink. "How is this seed giving off electrical charges? Or is it really a seed?" Craig asked.

"It's actually a seed. As to how it's giving off an electrical charge, well, that's a mystery I'll let you all work out on your own," Mayra answered. "But I must warn you against trying to remove the seed from inside the triangles."

Holding his pendant at arm's length, Zen asked, "Will it blow us up or something if we take it out?"

Mayra shook her head while giving Zen a half smile. "No, Zen. I wouldn't give you anything as dangerous as that. The seed is inside the metal casing for its protection, not yours."

"It's a beautiful piece of artwork," Junzo said, holding up his green and clear quartz pendant. "Thank you, Mayra, for the gift."

"Yes, thank you," the rest of the family chimed in.

"You're welcome. I must get going. But before I do, I'm going to steal a hug from these two," Mayra said, coming to sit between Samantha and Zen. "Zen, I understand from

Bess that she has made up a room for you across the hall from Samantha—"

"Really? I wanna see it," he said, jumping to his feet before being pulled back by his shirttail.

"Hold on. I'm not finished talking to you," Mayra said. "Goodness, you're like a runner at a starting line, bolting before the gun goes off. Samantha, next time I see you both, I hope some of your patience will have rubbed off on him."

"I'll try."

"I want you both to promise me that you'll take your Grandpa Innis's words to heart and search out the wonders of your new home. Also, there are records of our family's history and old photos in the attic. I'm sure you'll get a kick out of looking at those."

Samantha made a mental note. *Check out the attic.*

Planting a kiss on each of their foreheads, Mayra pulled them close, saying, "Ameara would be so proud to know she had two such lovely grandchildren."

Wiggling free of his great-aunt, Zen jumped to his feet again and ran for the stairs. "Okay. Bye, Aunt Mayra."

Shrugging, Samantha gave Mayra another kiss before following Zen up to his new room.

CHAPTER 10

WHISPERS OVERHEARD

Nice and soft," Zen reported of his new mattress. "Just like I like it."

Walking into Zen's new bedroom, Samantha felt their rooms were similar in size and appearance. The only difference was that his windows faced the back of the house, and hers faced the front.

"Hey, Zen. How long do you think the Kitchets have lived here?" she asked, taking a seat at the bottom of his bed to test out the softness of the mattress. "Do you think they have any grandkids our age? We know Bess has a niece, Rhiannon. Maybe she has kids."

"I don't know. I'm more interested in that stuff Grandpa Innis talked about in his letter. He mentioned something about treasures. Do you think it's some kind of rare gems or money hidden here on the property?"

"I don't think it has anything to do with money. I feel it has something to do with the trees."

"Or the treasure is buried under one of the trees! We should get a shovel and start digging."

"Zen!" Samantha gasped, shooting an astonished look

in his direction. "You heard how Aunt Mayra talked about these trees earlier. If you know what's good for you, you better not go digging under one!"

"Calm down. Even I know when not to push my luck," he said, opening his bedroom window. "Sooo, marvelous ... miraculous ... magical. What could that be?"

Leaning her cheek against her fist, Samantha searched for the meaning behind her grandfather's words. "Let's look closer at what Grandpa actually said. He said, 'the *Marvels.*'"

"Hey. Maybe he meant superheroes. You know, like the ones in comic books."

"Well, *marvel* can be short for *marvelous*, and *marvelous* means 'wonderful, amazing, glorious, something really spectacular.'"

"All of those words spell out *superhero* to me," Zen said. "I mean, trees are beautiful and all, but they just don't spell out *marvelous, miraculous,* and *magical.* Those words are meant for something truly amazing."

"I agree." Rubbing her eyes and yawning, Samantha all of a sudden felt very tired. "We can figure it all out tomorrow. I'm going to bed."

"Bed? Ah, come on. It's too early for bed. Tell you what. You stay up, and we can go check out the attic tonight."

"Sorry, Zen. I'm too tired, and our parents will be up in a bit to say good night."

"They won't come up. They'll get to gabbing and forget all about us."

"See you in the morning. And hey. Close your window. It's cold in here," Samantha said before leaving his room.

SAMANTHA GENTLY PLACED her new pendant in its leather pouch and set it on her nightstand as she got ready for bed. After taking a shower, she shut off her lights and climbed into bed. Yanking the covers up tightly under her chin, she warmed herself against the chill in her room while thinking, *I hope someone comes and lights the fire soon.* The white-faced clock on her dresser glowed in the dark, reading 10:45 p.m. Zen was right. It was way past the time her parents would normally come say good night. As she listened to the tree branch gently tapping at her window, she closed her eyes and began to dream. She dreamed of seeing her grandfather's face in the trunk of the large tree outside her window. In the dream, he parted his tree bark lips and repeatedly said, "Marvelous, miraculous, and magical things."

"Samantha, Samantha, wake up!"

She wasn't sure how long she'd been sleeping before being jostled awake. Opening her eyes, she saw Zen standing next to her bed.

"What ... what ... what's going on?" she asked.

"Come on. Hurry up. You gotta hear this" was all he said as he dragged Samantha from her bedroom.

She followed him into his room, which was illuminated only by the light coming from the fireplace. "Zen, what are we doing in here? Turn on the lights."

"Shh, be quiet," he whispered, pressing a finger to his lips. He signaled for her to stand with him in the shadows beside his open window, where Samantha heard Aunt Mayra's voice coming from below.

"I feel we should have said something about the call," their great-aunt said.

"What good would come of it? It would just upset Anna and Sam to bring back those memories so soon after their father's passing. No ... no, they have enough to deal with. Let's just stick to the plan." It was Kitchet's voice.

"I knew we should've told them the truth when they were older. I warned Innis that this day would come." Samantha could tell from Mayra's voice that she was very worried about something.

"I know, Mayra. We've been over this. But remember, this is how Innis wanted us to handle it."

Mayra sighed heavily. "Tell me again what happened."

"His car must've broken down because he was on foot when a truck driver spotted him about a mile out of Hearthshire, collapsed on the side of the road. By the time Bess and I arrived at the hospital, the medication had taken over his mind. He wasn't making any sense. We couldn't get out of him where he had gone or who he'd met up with. I can tell you this, Mayra. Innis seemed at peace in the end."

"Yes, but tell me exactly what he said, Kitchet."

"He said he finally knew who killed Ameara and—"

"Samantha, Zen. What are you two looking at?"

They both flinched and spun toward Anna's voice, which was coming from the doorway.

"This window won't stay shut," Zen said, fiddling with the latch. "Samantha came in to help me fix it."

Too stunned by the conversation she'd just overheard, Samantha said nothing. *Who killed Ameara?* she wondered as she stared blankly past her mother.

"How can you do anything in the dark? Here, I'll help you," Anna said, switching on the lights.

"Got it," Zen said, pretending to fix the bolt. "Thanks, Samantha. Now I can get some sleep without it blowing open." He pulled the curtains closed and jumped into bed.

"Do you need anything else?" Anna asked. "Should I ask your mom to come up or—"

"No, no. I'm good now, Aunt Anna. Good night."

As she headed out the door behind her mom, Samantha exchanged a puzzled look with Zen.

Back in her own bed, she watched as her mom threw a log on her fire.

"Good night, Samantha," Anna said as she walked toward the door.

"Yeah ... good night, Mom."

Her body may have been in her bed, but Samantha's mind was back in the cemetery. *I knew it. I knew something was odd about them dying on the same day.* Whispering into the darkness, she said, "But I would've never guessed it was murder!"

CHAPTER II

FACES AND MEMORIES FROM THE PAST

I heard Kitchet say that after Grandpa received a phone call, he left the house to meet with someone," Zen said, retelling Samantha what he'd heard outside his window. "Then he told Aunt Mayra that when he spoke to Grandpa in the hospital is when he found out the call had something to do with the day Ameara and Nanna died. That's when I ran to wake you up."

Piecing together Zen's account of the conversation and what they'd both heard, Samantha knew there was no mistaking it: Their grandmother and great-grandmother were murdered.

"But why, why would anyone want to kill them?" Samantha asked. She and Zen were standing outside, below his window and in the same spot where Aunt Mayra and Kitchet had stood when they overheard them talking. "Not sure, but it must've been something really bad to keep it hidden so long," Zen replied.

"Yeah, Aunt Mayra sure seemed pretty upset about not having told our moms the truth." Samantha peeked around the side of the house and toward the kitchen door, making sure her mom and Aunt Sam weren't coming out. "I knew something was off when I saw the dates in the cemetery. I just wish I knew what happened on the day Grandma Ameara and Great-Grandma Nanna died. And what do you suppose Grandpa actually told our moms about their deaths?"

"I don't know, Nancy Drew, but I know how we can find out. We can just go inside and ask them." Zen started toward the kitchen door, but Samantha stopped him.

"Zen, no," she squealed. "We can't tell them Grandpa lied to them. Besides, then we'd have to admit we were eavesdropping on Kitchet and Aunt Mayra." Samantha didn't want to be known as being a little snoop, especially by her own family, even though she knew that to be a detective, she had to be nosy. Or, a better word she liked to call herself, *curious*.

"I wasn't going to tell them anybody lied to them," Zen said. "I was just going to find out what they know about their mother's death."

"Well, let's wait for the right time. It would seem strange to just ask them out of the blue like that."

"You know, Samantha, our moms have a right to know that their mother and grandmother were murdered. And I'm getting the feeling Aunt Mayra is not going to tell them. So, it's up to us."

Samantha heard seriousness in Zen's voice—seriousness she'd never heard in an always nonserious Zen. And she knew he was right. *Of course, he's right*, she thought. *If anything happened to my mom, I'd want the truth. And hey— it's my grandmother and great-grandmother we're talking about. I want to know what happened to them!*

"I agree," Samantha said. "But first, we need to find out what actually happened before we say anything to them."

"How we gonna find that out?"

"There are many ways we can find stuff out."

"Okay. I'll follow your lead, Miss Drew," Zen said. "Where do we begin to look? It's been over twenty years since their deaths."

"It was a murder, so it would've been in the papers. We start by looking in old newspapers."

"I'll search on the internet for news. But wait a minute … Don't you think our moms would've at some point checked the newspapers about their mother's death?"

"Why would they if they didn't expect foul play?" *Foul play*. Samantha repeated the words to herself in her head. *What an odd set of words.* Foul, *meaning 'stinking, rank, rotten.'* This word, put with a word meaning "to have fun," just seemed off. Then again, murdering someone was also off.

"Oh yeah, that's right," Zen said, nodding in agreement. "Hey, I bet we can get the name of the detective who handled the case from the newspaper articles. Maybe he was the one who called Grandpa Innis to tell him he'd finally solved the murder."

"How do you know it was a male detective? It could've been a female."

"All right, don't get bent out of shape. My point is if we can find the detective, we can clear this all up quicker instead of just relying on newspapers and the internet."

"Now you're thinking like a detective, Zen."

"Yeah, see, and I didn't even have to read all those mystery books." Sighing, Zen looked down at his feet. He rubbed the tip of his sneaker over a rock that was peeking out through the snow-covered yard. "Here I thought I would be having an adventure searching for wonderful treasures."

"We can still do that. Grandpa said the marvels are right here on this property. What's stopping us from solving both mysteries?" Zen didn't look up as Samantha spoke. Then it dawned on her what was really bothering him. Aunt Sam had reminded Zen over breakfast that he had to return to Hawaii for his father's art show. Sam had arranged for Zen to connect with Craig at the Los Angeles airport while Craig was on his business trip to California. Together, they would travel back to Vermont.

"Sorry you have to leave today, Zen. But you'll be back before you know it, and we can compare notes on what we've found out."

"I know. I was just hoping I could stay. With all that's been going on, I forgot about Dad's art exhibit. But I promised I'd help him while Mom has her meetings with her editor." Shrugging, Zen gave Samantha a half-hearted smile. "Besides, the good thing about going back home is I'll be able to use a computer. It sounds like Uncle Craig won't have his up and running for a while."

"That's right, and you can get some surfing in before you come back," Samantha said, giving him a jab. "I'll do my part by digging through old newspapers at the library."

"Yeah, good luck with that."

"We should set a time before you return to check in by phone. You know—just in case something important comes up."

"Promise you'll let me know if you find any of those marvelous, miraculous, and magical things," Zen said.

"I promise."

Above their heads, a window opened. "Hey guys," Sam yelled down. "Come on up and see what we found."

Up in the attic, Anna and Sam were looking through old photos.

"Zen, take a look at this photo of your mom with her front teeth missing. Isn't she cute?" Anna said, passing around the photo.

"How old were you, Mom?" Zen asked.

"Six, I think. And oh, look. I'm wearing my favorite dress. I insisted on wearing it every single day."

"I remember that. Mom had to wrestle it away from you to wash it," Anna said.

The attic was one big open room that spanned the upper section of the house. The exposed beams were high in the ceiling. Several windows faced the front and back of the house, keeping the space well-ventilated. There were three old sofas and a couple of armchairs, along with several trunks and wooden crates stacked neatly in corners. Zen sat in a leather chair at a rolltop desk, happily rummaging in the compartments, while Samantha sat on a large rug with photos scattered in front of her.

"This is a nice photo. Where was it taken?" Samantha asked. She was holding a silver frame that contained a photo of a woman with wavy, light-brown hair who she recognized as her Grandma Ameara. She was holding a book and sitting in front of a willow tree, with Anna and Sam on either side of her. She wore a flowered dress, and around her neck hung the pendant that now belonged to Samantha.

"That picture was taken in front of my mom's 'special tree,' as she called it," Anna said, standing over Samantha. "Remember our picnics under the tree, Sam?"

"I do. She loved that tree, and so did I. Its branches hung down like long curtains. She would tell us the most wonderful stories that she imagined while sitting under her tree." Sam came to sit next to Samantha on the rug. "You know, most of the stories I write for children are from the tales my mother told us. Like my first book, *The Music of the Core People*."

"Really? I didn't know it was because of Grandma Ameara that you decided to write," said Samantha. "Tell me more about the story of the core people. Who are they?"

"The story my mother told was of a race of people who made their homes inside the Earth."

"Inside the womb of Mother. That's how she used to put it," Anna interjected.

"Yes, that's right," agreed Sam. "Inside Mother's womb, they played Mother's music, which keeps the harmony in nature. In my book, I used the backdrop of her story and added two little girls as my characters, who were hunting for the opening into the core people's world. Junzo sketched a drawing of two little girls trying to hear the music with their ears to the ground. The drawing reminded me of you and me, Anna. Remember how we used to do that?"

Anna threw her back her head, laughing. "I do remember. I also remember getting into trouble for telling you that the core people were going to take you away underground."

"That's funny, Aunt Anna," Zen said, joining in the laughter.

"I didn't think it was funny at the time," Sam said, making a face at her sister. "I was afraid to go outside, thinking hands would reach up and grab me."

"Aunt Mayra told me and Zen that we could hear music in nature. She said it was the trees', plants', and animals' way of talking to each other," Samantha shared.

"That's exactly what Mom told us," Anna said, kneeling by her sister and putting an arm around her shoulder. "I'll have to reread your book, Sam. Then I'll pass it along to Samantha—" Anna picked up the framed picture again.

"That's where I remember seeing those symbols, there on the book Mom's holding."

"What symbols?" Sam asked.

"The moon, sphere, and stars that are on the wooden frame in our old bedroom are also on that book."

Samantha brought the photo closer to her face, trying to see the symbols. All she could make out from the image was that her grandmother was holding a book.

"Mmm ... I don't recall a book with those shapes," Sam said.

"I remember because I used to trace my finger over them," Anna replied. "The cover felt so soft."

Yes! This is the opening I was waiting for, Samantha thought. "You know, these symbols are on our family's headstones in the cemetery," she said, handing the picture back to her mom. "I also noticed that the date Grandma Ameara died on was the same for Great-Grandma Nanna. What happened, Mom? I always thought Grandma died from getting sick. Were they both ill?"

A loud thump came from the corner of the attic, where Zen dropped the lid closed on a trunk he had gotten up to dig through. "Sorry, I didn't know the lid was so heavy," he said while boring a hole with his eyes into Samantha.

"No, they died in a car wreck while driving home together, Samantha," her mom softly said.

"Anna and I had helped Dad make lunch that day because we were going to have a picnic," said Sam. Looking at her sister, she then said, "Funny. I still remember first crying because it was getting too late to have a picnic and then crying because Daddy said Mom and Grandma were never coming home again."

Shuffling through the photos at her feet, Anna picked up one and handed it to Samantha. "This is your great-grandmother, Nanna Muaura Fairland." In the photo, Nanna was standing in front of a fireplace that Samantha recognized as the one in their living room downstairs. She'd seen many photos of her Grandma Ameara, but this was the first image she'd ever seen of her great-grandmother. Nanna appeared regal, wearing a fitted gold dress that highlighted her tall frame. Her skin was flawless dark ebony. She stared at the photographer through thin, almond-shaped eyes.

Coming to sit with them, Zen said exactly what Samantha was thinking. "She's beautiful and so tall. Maybe I inherited some of her tall genes. There's hope for me yet!"

"Nanna was very tall. When she walked, she glided like this." Sam came to her feet, demonstrating her grandmother's movements by moving across the floor in slow, sweeping motions. "Remember, Anna? We used to try and copy how she walked."

"Yes, I do. She had strange eyes too. They would change colors. No kidding. As you were looking at her, her eyes would change from brown to green and even blue. She told me it was her little trick. When she spoke, she turned her head to the side, and you saw how long her chin was from her profile," Anna recalled. "Mom said that most Fairland women were tall, but your Grandmother Ameara must have inherited her height from her father, Grandpa Jack, because she was pretty average height. I guess Sam and I did too."

"Oi, where is everyone?" Craig called out.

"We're up here," Sam called back.

Bounding up the stairs with Junzo and Kitchet behind him, Samantha's dad was all smiles as usual. "The space is perfect," he said. "It's right out the back of the flower shop."

Craig's voice faded out of earshot as Samantha and Zen stood off in a corner of the attic. "Hey, what gives?" Zen asked her. "First you tell me I can't ask them what they know about their mother's death. But then you go off and do it."

"I know ... but that was different," Samantha said.

"How so? How was it different?"

"Well, you were just going to march in the kitchen and ask out of the blue. When I asked, they were already on the subject of Grandma Ameara and stuff." Samantha could tell that Zen felt slighted. "Look, it just fell into place, okay? Come on, we should be happy we now know what Grandpa actually told them."

"I guess you're right."

"What are you two kidlings up to?" Kitchet asked, coming up behind them.

"Uh, um," Samantha muttered, unable to think of anything else to say.

"Oh, just digging around," Zen said, grabbing a handful of books from an open crate. "Ya know, Grandpa Innis said to look for marvelous, miraculous, and magical stuff."

Where does he come up with this stuff? Samantha wondered.

"Well, I think you should start outside," Kitchet said, eyeing them doubtfully before walking off.

"See how he looked at us?" Samantha whispered. "You think he heard what we were talking about?"

"Nay," Zen said, casually tossing a hand in the air. "He would've said something."

Shaking her head, Samantha couldn't get over her cousin's ability to lie so quickly and calmly under pressure. *I've got to learn that skill if I'm going to be a good detective,* she thought. Then, behind Zen's head, she noticed large flapping wings outside the attic window. The wings belonged to the black butterfly with red spots—the same butterfly she'd seen with the Kitchets. It leaned its head toward the glass, and if Samantha didn't know any better, she'd swear it was spying on them.

"Zen, look at that butterfly outside the window," she said.

"Butterflies aren't out—" he said, following her gaze. "That's the biggest butterfly I've ever seen."

Maybe sensing that it had been caught peeping, the butterfly slowly floated down and away.

"Come on," Zen said, bolting for the attic steps.

"Where are you guys going?" Sam asked.

"Outside," Samantha answered.

"Zen, we're leaving in an hour to catch our flight," warned his dad.

"Okay, Pop!" Zen called out. At the bottom of the attic steps, he shoved the books he was still holding into Samantha's arms. "Here, you can have these. I know how much you love them."

"Oh, you!" Running past her room, she tossed the books onto her bed and then caught up with Zen before he left out the front door.

CHAPTER 12

A GAME OF I HIDE AND YOU WON'T FIND ME

They caught sight of the butterfly as it headed for the forest opening just past the Kitchets' house.

"Let's stay back a bit. We don't want to scare it," Samantha said.

In the woods, small stones off to the sides marked a path leading through to a clearing. A thick layer of snow covered the ground, protected by the trees, which blocked out the sun. The smell of pine in the air reminded Samantha of the ponderosa pines that grew behind the home her family had rented in Flagstaff, Arizona. Directly in front of her, she kept her eye on the butterfly as it glided along. Every so often, it would stop and spin around to face them before flying off along the path.

"Get the feeling it's playing some sort of game with us?" Zen asked.

"Yeah, I do," Samantha said, halting in her tracks. The butterfly had stopped again. "What type of butterfly is out this time of the year?"

"I don't know. That's why I want to get a closer look at it."

As they inched nearer to it, the butterfly inched back toward them. Then suddenly, as if changing its mind, it flapped its large wings and made a sharp left turn down a row of spruce trees.

"It's trying to lose us!" Samantha yelled, running after it.

Zigzagging up one way, then down another, and between rows of trees, the butterfly led them deeper into the woods.

"Where's it going? I'm starting to get whiplash," Zen said, trying to keep up.

But keep up they did, darting through areas dense with snow-covered trees until finally ending up in another clearing and a dead end with no sign of the butterfly.

"Great. We've lost it," Zen said with a sigh. "That was a big waste of time."

Samantha took a deep breath. As she did, she noticed that the air in the clearing was different. It felt thinner. They were standing in a ring of trees that had hearty green leaves, smooth, reddish-brown trunks, and roots that grew above ground. To her, the roots resembled large, knobby feet. *These are different sorts of trees*, she realized. Then a funny thought popped into her head. *Maybe these trees go on walkabouts.* Her dad's friend, Mr. Jimmy, often talked about walkabouts. *Wouldn't it be funny if these trees just up and walked off in search of their true roots!*

"Oh well, Zen. We better go home."

But Zen had found the trickster butterfly bobbing between two of the trees. Zen stood like a mannequin, just watching it several feet in front of him.

Yes, there it is! Samantha thought. Feeling that maybe all their running around wasn't for nothing, she eased over to stand next to Zen. But just as she got close enough, whoosh! It flew through the tree branches. As it did, she thought she heard laughter. Not wanting to give up the chase, she was pushing back the branches to follow it when … She fell sideways into Zen and cried out, "Ahh!"

Heavy panting, warm breath, and a pink tongue washed her face. The tongue belonged to a large, hairy beast, who pinned her down with hairy, gray paws.

"That is enough, Gypsy girl. Let them up."

From her vantage point on the ground, Samantha spied soft black leather shoes snuggly molded to feet that were attached to long legs wearing black pants. Looking farther up, she saw Addiwan.

"What was that?" Zen asked, untangling himself from Samantha. Coming to their feet, they saw an Irish wolfhound by Addiwan's side.

"Hey, did you call that dog Gypsy?" Zen asked.

"Yes." Addiwan gently placed his hands on Samantha's and Zen's shoulders, then led them back through the way they'd come into the clearing.

"She has the same name my mom's dog had when she was growing up," Zen said, stepping out of the trees. He was followed closely by Gypsy, who nudged him onto the ground again.

"Imagine that," Addiwan said, helping Zen to his feet again. "Zen, do you have food in your pockets?"

"Yeah, a biscuit from breakfast. Can she have it?"

"Yes, but watch your fingers when you give it to her."

"Where'd you come from?" Samantha asked, dusting the snow from her clothing after her roll on the ground. *Strange. The butterfly disappears, and he just appears out of nowhere*, she thought.

"I live just through those trees, past the clearing where you and Zen were standing."

"Oh. Well, did you see a rather large black-and-red spotted butterfly?" she asked.

A mischievous look washed across Addiwan's face as his bright, amber eyes twinkled. This led Samantha to believe he wasn't going to give her a straight answer.

"No," he said.

Samantha tried asking her question another way. "Have you seen one like that before?"

"Yes."

Samantha's instincts were right. Addiwan was going to make her play twenty questions while he doled out his responses. "Is it normal for a butterfly to be out this time of the year?" she asked.

"Normal for most butterfly species? No."

"But then how does this butterfly survive in the cold?" Zen asked, tossing the last bit of his biscuit into Gypsy's mouth.

"He survives because he is rare unto himself," Addiwan said, walking off ahead of them. "I will direct you home from here. I was on my way to speak with your parents about Gypsy. She roams between my house and the Kitchets' house. We were hoping you two would give her a permanent home. She is a good girl," he said, stroking the dog on the head. From Addiwan's shift of subject matter, Samantha supposed he was done answering questions concerning the butterfly.

"She's huge, that's what she is!" Zen said. "I'd love to have her, but do you think she'll stay with us?"

"Gypsy would be happy to have children to play with again, and she would be a good guide dog. She knows the woods as well as I do. But we will have to ask your parents to make sure it is okay with them."

"I know my mom will be thrilled. She said we could get

a dog once we've settled," Samantha said. Then, thinking of the clearing they'd just come from, she asked, "Addiwan, is there something different about the air back there among those trees?"

"What do you mean?"

"Well, the air felt thin, like being in the mountains."

"Very observant," Addiwan said with a smile. "It is on a slightly different altitude, which makes the air a little … different."

"I didn't feel as if we climbed up any higher. That's odd," Samantha said.

Addiwan simply said, "Yes, it is."

They arrived back at the beginning of the forest, where Samantha could see her mom and Aunt Sam putting suitcases into their rental car.

"Hey, Mom! Look what Addiwan gave us. Can we keep her?" Samantha asked, running behind Gypsy, who was barking and wagging her tail like a propeller.

"Gypsy?" Anna looked to Addiwan.

Sam leaned down, running her hands through the dog's rough coat. "This can't be our Gypsy! Could it?"

"She is—" Addiwan started to explain.

"Of course it's not Gypsy after all these years," Anna said.

"I hope you do not mind, but I asked the children to care for her," Addiwan said.

"I think it would be great to have a dog around, and I know Craig won't mind," Anna said.

"Craig won't mind what?" Craig said, coming out of the house. "Oh boy, we have a horse."

"Dad, we can keep her, right?" Samantha said.

"Just as long you clean up whatever that horse puts out. She's your responsibility."

"Sweet! Come on, Gypsy. You gotta shake on that." Zen stuck out his hand, and the dog responded by licking it.

"I think that means she likes the idea of living with us," Samantha said with a laugh.

"Or she's looking for leftover crumbs from the biscuit," Zen said, wiping his hands on his pants.

"Ahem." They looked up to see Addiwan with his hands clasped behind his back. "If you two want to go exploring again, call upon me. I would be happy to show you around. It is never a good idea to wander into an area without knowing where you are going or how to find your way out." Turning, he walked off, coat flaring out like wings behind him, without so much as a goodbye.

"He's a little odd," Zen said.

"Yeah, he is odd, but in a good way. Hey, follow me upstairs. I need to talk to you before you leave," said Samantha.

Zen and Gypsy followed her into the house and up the stairs.

In her room, Samantha ran through everything again with Zen. "Now, don't forget our plan. I will check out the village library, and you will search your computer. You may want to write down the date Grandma and Great-Grandma died, like I have." She pulled a piece of paper out of her nightstand drawer. "It was March 20, 1987."

"I won't forget," Zen said, sitting on the floor and hugging Gypsy. "I like this dog. I wish I could take her with me."

"We can take turns with Gypsy sleeping in our rooms when you get back. Now, also check the dates after March 20, just in case there was a continuing write-up about the murder, which there should be. It was probably a big deal in a small place like Hearthshire. I'm sure they don't have many murders happening around here."

"You can never tell," Zen said. "Some small towns have just as many murders as big cities do. Take, for instance, the woods surrounding this place. There could be a murderer hiding out in there right now."

The hair at the base of Samantha's neck stood on end. "Don't even joke about something like that."

"Oh, come on! Do you really think someone could be lurking in the woods with Addiwan living back there? I was teasing."

"That's the thing. Until we find out what really happened to Ameara and Nanna and what Grandpa found out before he died, we don't know what's going on around here. So, I hope you're taking all of this seriously."

"I am taking this seriously."

"Zen, time to get going," his dad called from the bottom of the stairs.

"Coming!" Zen shouted. Then he turned back to Samantha. "Look, I wasn't trying to scare you. And anyway, you got this great new guard dog." He pointed over to Gypsy, who was fast asleep and snoring loudly. They both burst out laughing. "Well, she looks menacing."

After walking with Zen to the car, Samantha gave her aunt and uncle a hug and waved goodbye until their car was out of sight.

"How about I take you two out to eat tonight?" Craig offered.

"If I don't have to do dishes," her mom said, "it sounds great to me."

Waiting for her dad to pull Grandpa Innis's old green station wagon around to the front of the house, Samantha got a sense someone was watching her. She looked around toward the Kitchets' house to see if maybe they were standing in their front yard. No one was there. Shaking the feeling off, she climbed into the back seat and focused on what she wanted for dinner. "Can we have pizza?" she asked.

As the car carrying the Keen family disappeared down the hidden driveway, a woman with burnt-auburn hair stepped forth from a pine tree.

"You naughty boy, Crimsoner," the woman said, addressing the large black butterfly with red spots, which was perched on a limb above her head. "Did you truly lead those children into the sacrosanct area of the wood?"

Crimsoner floated down from the branch. "I was just having a bit of fun, Ashlynn."

CHAPTER 13

THERE'S THAT TAPPING AGAIN!

After getting into her pajamas, Samantha pulled her corkscrew curls up into a bun on top of her head. She stared at her reflection in the bathroom mirror as she meticulously brushed every tooth.

"So, what are you getting up to while I'm gone?" her dad asked when she entered her bedroom. He was stoking the fire while her mom picked her clothes up off the floor.

"I was hoping to check out the library in the village. You think I can, Mom?"

"Sure. I'll drop you off on my way to the flower shop. And, Samantha, the floor is not your clothes hamper."

"Sorry, Mom."

Outside her bedroom door, Samantha heard Gypsy galloping down the hall before bursting into her room. "Is it okay if she sleeps in here?" she asked.

"Yes, but not on the bed," her mom said, giving her a kiss on the cheek. "Don't stay up too late reading."

"I won't."

"Good night, cherub," her dad said. "Have fun at the library tomorrow."

"I always do."

Tuning off the overhead light, Samantha got into bed. "Good night, Gypsy," she said, patting the dog on the head. She switched on her reading lamp, then reached into her nightstand drawer for the piece of paper that held the date on which her grandma and great-grandma died. She carefully transferred the information from the slip of paper into her favorite oak-bound journal. The journal had been a birthday gift from Grandpa Innis when she turned six years old.

"I made it myself," she recalled him telling her. "From a fallen tree I found in the woods. It was the old oak's dying wish to become a book." Her grandpa had gone into the details of how he'd smoothed back the oak's bark and applied several layers of beeswax. The book was held together by a stitching of rope woven through a piece of leather he'd affixed to the book's spine.

There, Samantha thought as she closed up her journal. *Now any new information I find at the library will go directly into my book, along with any information Zen gathers.*

Feeling prepared for her detective work the next day, Samantha turned off her reading lamp, settled back against her pillows, and waited for sleep to overtake her. She counted down the time along with her clock. Seconds ticked into minutes, and minutes ticked into a half hour later. Sleep was not coming. Her mind kept going over her next day's task, and she thought, *I wonder how much information a newspaper article gives about a murder. I'm sure it'll say how they died. I wonder if it'll go into every gruesome detail. I hope not.*

Turning onto her side, she glanced down at Gypsy, who seemed to be sleeping quite peacefully. *Boy, I wish I could go to sleep that quickly.* Switching her lamp back on, she decided that maybe reading would help her fall asleep. She was about to grab her old standby, Nancy Drew, when she noticed the stack of books from the attic on the floor next to her bed. She picked a book from the top of the pile, then ran her hands over the faded, frayed pages. The text was a cross between pictorials and some form of another language. *Mmm, who could read this? Maybe it belonged to Aunt Mayra.* Placing the book aside, she picked up another.

Samantha could tell right away from the next book's flowered cover that it must've been someone's diary. That someone, she found out from the inside front page, was Ameara Fairland.

Oh, gosh. It's Grandma's diary! Excited, Samantha flipped through the pages, looking at her grandma's neat hand-written words. Then she shut the book quickly. *There may be things in here I shouldn't be reading. This is a diary, where people place their most private thoughts.* She was about to place the diary back on the pile when an idea came to her. *If I come across anything too personal, I won't read it.* With this rule in place, she gave herself permission to turn to the first page and read her grandmother's entry.

September 15, 1986
Sam did very well riding without her training wheels today. Now both she and Anna are racing up and down the driveway like pros. By the end of the day, we were all tired from running behind them.

It's only eight days until the harvest festival! Mayra will arrive in time for the equinox.

September 16, 1986
I took the girls for the first time to meet Ever. It was great to see them so excited to see her, and I was thrilled that Mom was here to witness the meeting with us.

Most of the entries were a paragraph or two long, in which Ameara wrote about her daughters' accomplishments, days in the flower shop, and continued trips to visit a person by the name of Ever. From what Samantha read about Ever, she appeared to be an elderly woman who told stories to her mom and Aunt Sam about her children and grandchildren, who made their homes around the world.

Though her eyelids were starting to get heavy, Samantha kept reading, telling herself she'd read only one more page, and then it became just two more pages. She was so engrossed in reading about her grandma's daily activities that she continued to read as she slid down in bed and lay back against the pillow. Then the writings stopped abruptly, with her grandma writing only two short sentences: *Mr. Lin, Maskhim. What does he know?*

Hmm. Samantha sat up to get a better look at the last entry. *It doesn't make any sense. These sentences don't flow with the last page, which talks about the coming spring equinox. Maybe there's a missing page.* She thumbed back through the previous pages and saw they were all in date order. *The date, of course,* she realized. *Look at the date!* Her grandmother had written this entry a day before she died. Samantha read the entry again.

March 19, 1987

Mr. Lin. Maskhim. What does he know?

The big, bold lettering suggested to Samantha that her grandma was leaving an important message to herself.

Samantha was reaching over to adjust the angle of her reading lamp when the sudden sound of tapping startled her, causing her to drop her grandma's diary between her bed and the nightstand. Her heart was already beating a little faster from her discovery when she remembered something. *It's only the tree's branches hitting the window.*

Giggling at herself for becoming frightened, she calmly picked up the diary as something fell from the back cover. It was a folded note addressed simply to Innis—her Grandpa Innis. Unfolding it, she read.

Innis,

I didn't want to wake you to say goodbye this morning. I felt you needed the extra rest after all my tossing and turning last night. Sorry. I couldn't stop thinking of Mr. Lin and the news he brings of the Maskhim. I will fill you in later this afternoon. Hopefully, it will all be good news. Kiss the girls for me.

Ameara

Samantha read the note over and over, piecing together what she felt must have occurred the day her grandmother died. *According to this note and her diary, Grandma was planning to meet or did meet with a Mr. Lin the day she died. But who is Mr. Lin, and who or what is the Maskhim? And where does Great-Grandma Nanna fit in with all of this?*

Jumping out of bed, she reached for her robe. *I need to talk to Zen!* Then she stopped. *Ah, Hawaii is five or six hours behind us. He's probably not even home yet. I'll have to call him tomorrow.*

If she hadn't been able to fall asleep before, Samantha definitely wasn't able to put her head to pillow now. She was too anxious. *I wish it was morning already.* Climbing back into bed, she opened her journal again and jotted down the name "Mr. Lin" and the word *Maskhim* from her grandma's diary. She had just finished writing when she again heard the tapping—this time much louder—which brought Gypsy to her feet.

"Hello."

It's that same male voice again! Samantha thought. She clutched her book and her grandma's diary to her chest.

"I saw a light on. I do not mean to disturb, but I would love to make your acquaintance."

That's not coming from the Kitchets' house. It sounds too close!

Climbing into the window seat, Gypsy touched her paw to the glass, looked back at Samantha, and whimpered.

"Do you see anyone out there, girl?" Samantha asked, pulling back the curtain.

"Ah yes, there you are. I have been told you are not Anna but Samantha," the voice gently said. "You are Anna's seedling."

"Who are you? And why can't I see you?" Samantha asked.

"You do not see me? Well, I am right here, right in front of you."

"All I see is this tree. Are you sitting in the tree?"

"I am the tree."

"You are the tree?"

"Yes, I am called Terrance."

That's what Aunt Mayra said! Samantha remembered.

"If you open the window, I will properly introduce myself."

Hesitating at first, Samantha decided to open the window less than halfway. To her amazement, a leafy limb reached inside.

"Hello, Samantha. My name is Terrance. I have been a friend to many a Fairland who have grown up in this home, and I am very pleased that a branch of the family has returned."

A tree is speaking to me! She was not hearing these words in her head or as whimsical music but as a real human voice. She turned to Gypsy for answers. "Am I actually talking to a tree?" she asked. "I don't get it." Then she laughed at the absurdity of the situation, "Well, now I'm talking to a dog."

"Why not talk to a tree? Trees communicate very well with humans, as do all organisms born of this planet."

"Why haven't I ever heard a tree speak before?"

"Have you tried speaking to a tree first and then really listened for us to respond?"

"No."

"Well, there you go," Terrance said. "Most will talk around us or about us but never really converse with us."

"That's a good point." She repeated her grandpa's words again to herself. *'Dare to see things differently and hear things differently.' Well, I have met my first marvel!*

"May I tell you a story, Samantha? My stories will help you better understand how we all came to live here together on this land."

"Sure, I'd like to hear your story."

"I will tell you the story of when the humans first came

to Veil Essence. Yes, that is a good place to start. You see, my kin and I, the first trees were—"

"Veil Essence. Is that the name of the enchanted tree kingdom you come from?"

"Enchanted tree kingdom? Oh, no. You are mistaken. Trees are not enchanted, and we have never been anywhere else but right here. Well, not here on this very spot. I was somewhere else before, then I moved. But I have been in this spot for … Oh, I have lost count of how long now since everything changed. I cannot remember. But I have digressed, and I have forgotten what I was going to say. Let me begin again. Samantha, I am the storyteller. I keep the stories that human children need to hear. So be patient and listen."

"Sorry, I won't interrupt again," Samantha said.

"As I was saying, Veil Essence was growing in human population. My kin gave shelter to those who stayed behind. Our home had been rattled to its core, and all needed to be resettled or sent back to their original homes …"

As Terrance spoke, Samantha stretched out in the window seat, pulling a blanket up around her as Gypsy lay next to her. The slumber she'd sought earlier was finally calling. *Don't fall asleep now*, she told herself. *I need to remember this so I can tell Zen.* Closing her eyes, she told herself she would just rest them as Terrance kept talking. He spoke of humans, who took refuge among the tree folk, and how some of the original trees agreed to hold onto the humans' story for safekeeping.

"I was called upon to be the young humans' story-teller," he continued. "When the parents felt it was time, they placed their children in the dreamtime seat, which is where you are lying now, Samantha. The dreamtime seat is carved from my branches, freely given by me ..."

This was all she remembered hearing before she entered the world of dreams. In her dream, she was being rocked in a large crib that was floating down on a sea of stars.

THE NEXT MORNING, Samantha woke to find she had slept all night in the window seat. Rubbing the sleep from her eyes, she flung her bedroom window open, stuck her head out, and looked up and down at the tree that called itself Terrance. *It just seems like a normal tree to me*, she thought.

Examining it more closely, she noticed the deep lines in the tree's reddish-gold trunk, which reminded her of the markings on an aged person's face. Leaning farther out the window, she touched the bark and found it to be smooth, like petrified wood. However, unlike petrified wood, this tree still grew leaves from its limbs. The leaves were similar to the hearty green ones she saw on the large, knobby, rooted trees in the clearing in the woods.

"Hello, ah ... Terrance." She listened, waiting for the familiar male voice to answer her. When it didn't, she decided to head outside to stand in front of Terrance's tree.

Standing in the front yard in a robe and pajamas, Samantha could see that Terrance's tree grew very close to her window. As Aunt Mayra had mentioned, his roots did extend right underneath their home. Gently taking hold of one of his branches, she called to him again. "Terrance, are you there?"

"Terrance sleeps during the day. He is more active at night," a soft female voice said.

Turning toward the voice, Samantha gasped more out of surprise than fright when she saw a woman emerging from the trunk of a pine tree. The woman wore a dress made of pine needles with strands of silvery thread intertwined within the fabric. Her hair was a burnt auburn with streaks of deep green, and she had the most beautiful chestnut-brown skin, which glistened with golden flecks. Taking several steps away from her tree, the woman greeted Samantha by name in her pleasant-sounding voice.

"Hello, Samantha."

"Did you just come out of that tree? How ... how did you do that?"

"I am the essence that resides within this tree. You may call me Ashlynn."

There's that word again, essence, Samantha thought. Then she looked at the woman with curiosity and asked, "What exactly is an essence? Is it like spirits that haunt trees?"

"No, that would be like me asking you if you haunt your body. I am the life force born with this tree. This tree is my physical body."

"And Terrance? I was talking to his essence?"

"Yes."

"But why couldn't I see him like I'm seeing you?"

"Terrance has not stepped out of his tree in a long time. I wonder if he still can. I must ask him."

"Samantha, are you out here?" Anna yelled from the kitchen door.

"Yeah, Mom. I'm with Ashlynn."

"I was looking all over the house for you." Then she turned toward the woman. "Hi, I'm Anna, Samantha's mom," Anna said, extending her hand in greeting.

She's solid, like a real person! Samantha thought as she

watched her mom grasp Ashlynn's hand. She fully expected her mom's hand to pass right through the tree essence.

"Are you a friend of the Kitchets'?" Anna asked.

"Mom, Ashlynn lives here. In this pine tree. She's a tree essence!"

"What?"

"You may not remember me, Anna," Ashlynn said. "Young children tend to be more attached to Terrance. It is all those lovely stories he tells them."

"Terrance," Anna said, glancing over at his tree. "Then he is real!"

"As real as I am standing here," said Ashlynn.

"I can't believe you grew up in this amazing world," Samantha said to her mother, "and never told us anything about it."

"Honestly, as I got older, I thought I'd made it all up. And that's why Dad left the letter," Anna said, snapping her fingers. "He hoped that Sam and I would remember once we came back home."

"Sounds like something Innis would do," Ashlynn said, stepping back in front of her tree. "Promise you will both visit with me now that you know I am here. Bess is lovely to talk with, but I have grown a bit weary of hearing about her meal plans." Then, as quietly as she'd appeared, Ashlynn disappeared.

Pushing at the center of the tree's trunk, Samantha thought she'd discover a concealed door. But she didn't. Her hand just lay against ordinary pine bark. "Extraordinary," she said under her breath. Then, much more loudly, she said to her mom, "I knew it! I told Zen that Grandpa's clues had something to do with the trees."

"Aunt Mayra never reminded me or Sam of any of this while we were growing up. I wonder why," Anna said. Then a grin spread across her face. "I can't wait to see your dad's reaction to all of this. But we have to cut your extraordinary discovery short. Rhiannon is expecting me at the flower shop. And if you still want me to drop you off at the library, you better get dressed."

In all the excitement, Samantha had almost forgotten that she was going to the library. Hurrying to her room, she quickly dressed and made sure she had her journal in her coat pocket before joining her mom for breakfast.

CHAPTER 14

IT'S ALL HERE IN BLACK AND WHITE

"Taking out any books today?" Anna asked, pulling up to the front of the Hearthshire Public Library.

"I'm not sure," said Samantha. "I really just want to have a look around."

"The flower shop is just across the square. Come over when you're done."

"Okay."

"If I don't hear from you within the hour, I'll come over and check on you."

With no time to waste, Samantha rushed up the wide stone steps, entered the white brick building, and headed straight for a woman standing behind a desk in the entrance area.

"May I help you?" the librarian asked as she transferred books from her desk to a book cart.

Stoic expression, graying hair, wire-rimmed glasses, knee-length navy skirt, matching cardigan, white shirt buttoned up to the neck, Samantha thought as she cataloged the librarian's appearance. *She reminds me of a smaller version of Mrs.*

Doubtfire. Then she said, "I was wondering if I could take a look through old newspapers."

Finally bothering to interrupt her task to peer at Samantha over her glasses, the librarian asked, "Which newspaper subscription are you interested in?"

"The local newspaper."

"That would be *The Hearthshire Ledger*," she said before turning her focus back to her book stacking. "What dates are you looking for?"

Opening her oak-bound journal, Samantha replied, "March 20, 21, and 22 of 1987, please."

"Those dates will need to be viewed on the microfilm machine." Stepping from behind her desk, the librarian directed Samantha to a cubicle near the reference area. "I will return in a moment with the microfilm."

Removing her jacket, Samantha took a seat in front of what looked to be a computer monitor. Off to the left of the monitor was a device equipped with a flat piece of magnifying glass, a spool-loading mechanism, and several buttons positioned toward the front. She had never used a microfilm machine, and she hoped she could use this one without too much difficulty.

While she waited for the librarian to return, she went over in her mind the events from that morning—meeting Ashlynn, the tree essence—and her talk with Terrance the previous evening. She particularly recalled the conversation with her mom over breakfast. She could still hear the excitement in her mom's voice as she said, "I feel like I've been sprinkled with fairy dust! I am seeing the world in magical ways after what happened this morning."

Samantha had to agree. She could never look at another tree in the same way again. However, the magic was starting to fade now that she was in the library. In its place was an anxiousness over what she might find in the pages of *The Hearthshire Ledger.*

The library door opened and closed, drawing Samantha's attention toward the front entrance. A woman carrying a small child placed a book and several DVDs on the counter.

"Thanks, Ms. Emily," the woman said as she waved to the librarian, who was just heading back toward Samantha.

"Did the boys enjoy the book I suggested?" Ms. Emily asked the young woman.

"I think they did. But of course they liked the movies even better."

"Of course. Nevertheless, we must keep trying to direct them more toward reading and away from the television. I will find a book yet that those boys of yours will enjoy, Casey. Have a good day."

Standing over Samantha, Ms. Emily removed a reel of microfilm from a small white box. "Are you doing research for a school project?" she asked.

Samantha hesitated. She hadn't expected the librarian to ask her why she wanted to view the old papers. "No. I'm looking up ... family history."

"I see. You're the genealogist of your family?" Ms. Emily attempted to give Samantha a smile, which came off looking more like a sneer.

"Yes, ma'am," Samantha answered, hoping that would put an end to the questions.

"Good. It is always nice to see young people taking an interest in their family history. Knowing where your bloodline started is very important."

Ms. Emily went on to explain how to use the device as she loaded the microfilm. By the end of her instructions,

Samantha felt confident that she'd have no problem navigating her way through the viewing machine.

"As I've mentioned, this microfilm has *The Hearthshire Ledger* for the months of March and April 1987. I have forwarded the film to the first date you requested," Ms. Emily said, standing back with her hands on her hips.

"Thank you. I appreciate your help."

"You are welcome. If you need any further assistance, come see me at the front counter."

Finally alone, Samantha pushed the little gray button on the front of the machine and began reading the articles in *The Hearthshire Ledger*. However, by the end of the March 20 newspaper, there was no news concerning the deaths of Ameara and Nanna Fairland. *Well, it had just happened,* Samantha thought. *It must be in the next day's paper.*

She advanced through page after page of the March 21 newspaper while occasionally checking the clock on the wall. At her last glance, it was 10:23 a.m. A scraping sound caused her to stand quickly and peek over the cubicle partition. It was just a teenage boy pulling out a chair at one of the nearby tables. Every noise made her think it was her mom coming to check on her. She resumed her search through *The Hearthshire Ledger*, but again, as she neared the end of the paper, she found no news.

Sitting back in her chair, she rubbed her eyes, which stung from squinting at the screen. *Where is it? It should've been big news.* Pressing her fingers to the sides of her temples, she had a thought. *Maybe we misunderstood. Maybe Aunt Mayra and Kitchet weren't talking about murder after all.* Covering her mouth, Samantha stifled a giggle. *Wouldn't it be funny if we were investigating a murder that didn't even happen?*

With this possibility in mind, she felt a little sense of

relief come over her. Nothing would thrill her more than learning it was just a misunderstanding. *But*, she recalled, *Kitchet did use the word* kill *in connection to the day Grandma died.* Samantha also couldn't dismiss her grandmother's last notation in her diary and the note she left for Grandpa Innis. It all pointed to murder.

I'll look through one more date, she decided. *If I don't find anything, well ... Then I'll just wait to hear what Zen finds on his computer.*

That's all it took. One more look—one more push of the little gray button—brought Samantha face-to-face with what she was seeking. There, on the front page of the Sunday, March 22, 1987, edition of *The Hearthshire Ledger*, her Great-Grandmother Nanna Fairland's narrow, almond-shaped eyes stared back at her. Samantha sucked in her breath as she braced herself to read the words underneath the photo.

Professor found dead in her office at Eastern Vermont University.

She must have read the caption at least three times before casting her eyes downward to read the rest of the article:

Dr. Nanna Fairland, a prominent professor of geography and longtime resident of Hearthshire, Vermont, was found dead in her office at Eastern Vermont University in the early morning hours of Friday, March 20.

Several hours later, Dr. Fairland's daughter, Ameara Fairland, also a resident of Hearthshire, Vermont, was found dead in her parked car one block from Darlington Airport in Clarkstown, Vermont.

Authorities are certain both crimes are linked because it was learned from Ameara Fairland's husband, Innis Moor, that his wife left the morning of the 20th to meet with her mother at her office at the university.

Kenneth Randall, a graduate student, found Dr. Fairland's body at 9:45 a.m. and immediately called 911. Mr. Randall told investigators on the scene that he saw a suspicious man wandering the university grounds shortly before he found Dr. Fairland's body.

When a couple on their way home from the airport discovered Ameara Fairland slumped behind the wheel of her parked car at 12:15 p.m., they alerted the Clarkstown local police, who pronounced her dead at the scene.

Authorities have stated that both women had been violently strangled, and they are treating this ongoing case as a murder investigation.

In 1972, Dr. Nanna Fairland was awarded the honor of department chair for her professional and academic achievements in the field of historical geography. She is survived by her daughter, Mayra Fairland, of New York City.

Ameara Fairland, the owner and operator of Essences, a local flower shop in Hearthshire, Vermont, leaves behind her husband, Innis Moor, and their two young daughters.

Violently strangled were the words that stood out on the screen and repeated loudly in Samantha's head, assaulting her brain. The rest of the article was just one long stream of nonsensical words trying to make sense of something that made no sense. It was too much to imagine, let alone comprehend, why someone would want to do this to her grandma and great-grandma. Especially after reading the loving, caring words Grandma Ameara had written in her diary about life and raising her daughters. *This is the reason,* Samantha concluded, *that Grandpa Innis didn't tell Mom and Aunt Sam the truth.* But now Samantha knew the truth. *How can I tell Mom and Aunt Sam that their mother was violently strangled?*

"How is your family history search going?"

Samantha leaped two feet above her seat when she heard Ms. Emily's voice from behind her. "Fine," she said a little too loudly, which made even the old librarian step back. Clearing her throat, Samantha tried again. "Sorry. I mean fine, thank you."

"Good. Do you need to look through any other newspaper articles?"

Samantha wished she had time to read the rest of *The Hearthshire Ledgers* on the microfilm, but she had to get over to the flower shop. "No. Oh, wait. Can I make a copy of this?" Samantha said, pointing to the article on the screen.

"Yes, I can help you with—" Ms. Emily stopped talking mid-sentence. Samantha felt her chair move slightly backward as the librarian grabbed ahold of it, trying to steady herself.

"Are you okay?" Samantha reached out, taking ahold of Ms. Emily's arm. She eased the flushed-faced woman into the chair next to hers.

"Yes. Give me a moment." Taking a handkerchief from her pocket, the visibly shaken Ms. Emily patted lightly around her lips before saying, "Why do you want a copy of this news story? Do you know these people?"

Confused by the librarian's reaction, Samantha wondered if maybe she knew her family or about the murder. "Yes. That was my grandma and great-grandma in the article, Nanna and Ameara Fairland. Did you know them?"

The stoic expression returned to Ms. Emily's face as she stared into Samantha's eyes. "I knew of Nanna Fairland, and I sometimes ran into her daughter, Ameara, at the flower shop. It was a shame those women had to die that way." Then, rising to her feet, Ms. Emily stated matter-of-factly, "I heard Innis recently died and that one of his daughters had moved back to the village."

"Yes, I'm—"

"Samantha," Anna called softly from the library's entrance area.

"Please don't tell my mom about the story in the paper," Samantha said.

"Why?" Ms. Emily asked, raising one eyebrow.

Samantha quickly explained as she saw her mom walking toward the back of the library, obviously looking around for her. "My grandpa never told my mom the truth about how they died. I just recently found out myself. I was curious as to what really happened to them. That's why I wanted to look it up. Please don't tell her."

"No, of course not. But why do you want a copy of the article if you have no intention of sharing it with your mother?"

"I thought ... well maybe somehow, if I found out what really happened, I could tell my mom the truth," Samantha confessed. "Can I please have a copy?"

"Oh, there you are," Anna called from near the reference desk.

"Hi, Mom. I'm coming."

"Meet me at the front counter. I will bring you your copy," Ms. Emily said.

Grabbing her coat, Samantha walked over to join her mom.

"Did you find any good books? Maybe a Nancy Drew you haven't read yet?"

"No, I was just looking around. You know how I love

just sitting among books. Anyway, I forgot that I need proof of identification to get a library card."

"Oh, that's right. Here, I can show my driver's license."

While Anna dug in her purse for her wallet, Ms. Emily returned and handed Samantha a copy of the newspaper article from *The Hearthshire Ledger*.

"Don't worry about it today, Mom," Samantha said, shoving the copy into her coat pocket. "We can do it another time."

"No, let's do it now. It shouldn't take too long." Anna handed Ms. Emily her license. "I hope you will accept my overseas license. I just moved back to Hearthshire a couple of days ago, and I haven't had the time to get a new one."

"It will be fine," Ms. Emily said, handing Anna a form. "I used to chat with your mother when I stopped into the flower shop. So, which one of Ameara's daughters are you?"

"Oh, really? Well, I'm Anna. My younger sister, Sam, lives in Hawaii now. I guess you've already met my daughter, Samantha," Anna said, proudly rubbing Samantha's back.

"Yes, we've met," said the librarian.

"You'll be seeing a lot of her, Mrs. ... Sorry, I didn't catch your name."

"Emily. Everyone calls me Ms. Emily."

Samantha held her breath. She was worried that while her mom made polite conversation with Ms. Emily, the old librarian would slip up and mention the newspaper article.

"Ms. Emily, Samantha loves Nancy Drew. She's been reading and collecting the series for about ... oh, maybe three ... four ... Yes, about four years now."

"We do have a nice collection of the Nancy Drew books here at the library," Ms. Emily said, handing Samantha her brand-new library card. "When you come back, I'll help you locate them."

"Thank you sooo much, Ms. Emily." Samantha hoped that if she emphasized her words, the librarian would catch that she was really thanking her for keeping her secret.

"I've taken over the flower shop," Anna said to the librarian. "Maybe we'll run into each other again sometime."

"I'm sure we will," Ms. Emily said. She grabbed ahold of her library cart and disappeared behind an aisle of books.

CHAPTER 15

REVISITING VEIL ESSENCE

Outside, the crisp February air whipped Samantha's unbound curls into a frenzy. *Why do I always forget my scrunchie on windy days?* she wondered. Stuffing her hair under her coat's hood, she buttoned up all the way to her neck.

"Hey, what do you say we head over to Embers Diner for some hot cocoa?" Anna said as they stood outside in front of the library.

What? No, Samantha thought. *I need to go home and figure out how to tell you about your mother's murder!* But she said, "Can't we have cocoa at home?"

"Home? Have you forgotten what we planned to do this morning?"

"Oh ... the flower shop."

"Yes. You do still want to go over and take a look around, right?"

"Sure, I just forgot."

"I think you'll find the shop is quite amazing. But first things first. Let's go get that hot cocoa. I'm freezing."

Following her mom across the village square, Samantha

stopped to get a better look at the centerpiece—the fireplace. *This must be the reason the village is called Hearthshire,* she thought. The fireplace's towering stones were at least six feet above her head. The opening that led into the inner hearth was wide enough for three adult-sized people to walk through, shoulder to shoulder.

Studying the clock at the center of the chimney, she noticed the two sets of numbers etched into the clock's glass-domed face. The outer set ran clockwise, as normal, from one to twelve. However, the inner, smaller set of numbers counted backward from zero to eleven, starting at the number twelve. Three gold hands indicated the hour, minute, and seconds, which now read 11:15 a.m. and six seconds.

Hmm, why so many numbers? she wondered. Behind the glass surface, there was a narrow ledge balancing two orbs—one black and one white—that rotated in opposite directions. Between these two orbs, a smaller clock rested with its hour, minute, and second hands mimicking the two opposing orbs by first rapidly spinning clockwise, then counterclockwise. Chiseled into the stone below the round face of the clock was this:

"Time is now the Heart of Matter. – Samu-EL."

"Samantha!" Anna called from the other side of the street.

"I'm coming." Turning away from the fireplace, she ran to catch up with her mom, who was just entering the diner.

Embers Diner resembled an old English tavern, with its wood beam ceilings, tables, and chairs set up close to a fire. Stairs led to another level. Samantha stood at what looked to have once been the bar, which now served as the ordering station. Every two seconds, she felt for the news article in her pocket, making sure it was still there. The sentence "Authorities have stated that both women had been violently strangled" kept popping into her head. She was so engrossed in going over the details from the newspaper that it surprised her when her mom's voice interrupted her thoughts.

"Huh? What?" Samantha asked.

"Sean asked if you wanted a mint sprig in your cocoa," Anna repeated.

"Are the pixies whispering foolishness in your ear, Samantha?" Sean asked. He swiped at the air around her head with a dishtowel as if swatting away a fly.

"Pixies? Are there pixies in here?" Samantha asked, searching the area for little winged fairies. After her morning, she wouldn't have been surprised.

"Not today," Sean said with a wink. "So, how about that mint sprig in your cocoa?"

"I'd like that, thank you."

"Another cocoa with a mint flower, Rhona!" Sean yelled into the kitchen. "Now, Anna, if you and Craig need any help around the house, just let me and Rhona know. We live very close by."

Samantha had met Sean Cullen and his wife, Rhona, after her grandpa's funeral. Sean was stout, with meaty arms and a bulbous nose. His thick, bushy, red hair fell to his shoulders and matched his red beard. Rhona was about the same height as Bess but with a larger body frame and dark-brown hair. Samantha remembered thinking when they met how much they reminded her of the cartoon characters Shrek and Fiona. Then she quickly felt terrible for comparing them to green ogres.

"I can hear those gears churning around in your noggin," Anna said, brushing a stray curl away from Samantha's forehead. "What are you thinking about?" she asked as they left the diner and headed down Maple Street.

Here's the thing, Mom. I thought I would play Nancy Drew and investigate the truth behind the deaths of Grandma Ameara and Great-Grandma Nanna. Guess what. I found out the truth. It's right here in my pocket. I just don't know how to tell you or if I should ever tell you. This was what Samantha really wanted to confess. Instead, she simply said, "I wasn't thinking about anything in particular."

"You're still okay with us moving to Hearthshire, right?"

"What kid wouldn't want to live in such a magical place? Really, Mom, I'm fine."

"I'm glad because it feels right, coming back home and running my mother's flower shop. Speaking of which, here we are." Positioning her arms out in front of her like a stage magician introducing a magic act, Anna announced with style, "Ta-da. Welcome to Essences Flower Shop."

Iron lettering spelled out "Essences" above the arched double wooden doors, which were flanked by multiple-paned windows. When Samantha stepped inside, an unexpected, warm, spring-like breeze blew past her ears. As it did, she heard faint whispers that sounded like the word *welcome.* Out of her peripheral vision, she saw shimmering specks of bright golden lights hovering close to her head before they darted off, disappearing into a leafy potted plant.

"Did I just see ... What did I just see?" she asked, pointing toward the potted plant.

"Flower and plant essences," Anna said with a giggle as she placed the "Out to Lunch" sign on the front door. "They do that every time someone enters the shop, but customers seem to not take notice of them. Come on. I'll give you the grand tour."

They started in the main foyer, where greenery grew everywhere. Samantha could hear but could not see birds singing. She assumed they were hiding among the lush vegetation, which gave her the impression of being in an indoor courtyard.

Off to the right of the entrance, there was a stone water well equipped with a hand crank and bucket tied to a rope. Wicker baskets and empty clay pots were arranged on the uneven cobblestone floors. Houseplants and more potted flowers decorated the window ledges.

On the left side of the shop were two rooms with half-glass door fronts. The first door had the words "Essences of Nature" painted on its glass. Inside was a medium-sized clay basin attached to the ground. Behind the basin was a rocky water feature with green leaves that smelled like mint growing between the stones. Again, Samantha noticed the tiny golden lights moving among the foliage.

"The essences are helping create oils, lotions, and liquid soaps in this room," Anna explained. "Bess's niece, Rhiannon, says the essences can change shape and color, depending on the type of flower or plant they are working with."

The sign on the second door's glass read, "Essences of Candlelight." Peeking in, Samantha saw a fire burning inside a small fireplace. The golden lights hung in the air around beeswax, wicks, and colorful candleholders of different sizes.

Farther back in the main entrance, a long butcher-block table displayed a beautiful array of potted roses, colorful rocks, and gemstones next to a cash register.

Next, her mom led her through an archway that connected to the back section of the shop. The large circular room held an indoor greenhouse with a glass ceiling. This back section also housed one more room, whose door was labeled "Flowering Teas." Inside, jars of different herbs and dried flowers lay near a mortar and pestle. Busy whizzing in and out of the greenhouse were those golden lights.

"What do you think of Essences?" Anna asked.

"Well, I never imagined it being this large on the inside," Samantha said, walking toward the front of the shop, then to the back again. "When you said, 'flower shop,' I pictured buckets of cut flowers, helium balloons, stuffed animals, and greeting cards."

"This used to be the village marketplace. That's why it's so big on the inside," said a very young-looking woman who emerged from the greenhouse. She was carrying a lavender plant.

"Samantha," Anna said. "This is Rhiannon. She's Bess's niece."

Rhiannon had short, black hair that framed her round face. Her eyes were bright blue, just like her Aunt Bess's eyes. She wore an ankle-length coat that was embroidered with flowers. It opened to show her wool tunic dress, which came to just below her knees and hit the top of her laced brown leather boots.

"The tall ones certainly made their impression on you," Rhiannon said, giving Samantha a hug. The top of her head barely reached under Samantha's chin.

"Yeah, my dad's pretty tall," Samantha said, shifting from one foot to the other. It embarrassed her when people mentioned her height. She was already three inches taller than her mom's mere five foot two inches. She only hoped she wouldn't grow to be as tall as her dad or Great-Grandma Nanna.

"You just missed Aunt Bess," Rhiannon said to Anna.

"She stopped by to invite you and Samantha over for dinner this evening."

"Your Aunt Bess has done too much cooking for us already," Anna said. "I'm starting to feel guilty."

"She loves to cook, so let her do it," said Rhiannon.

"To be honest, Bess has been a lifesaver. I haven't had time to stock the fridge," Anna confessed.

"See, it all works out," Rhiannon said, carrying the lavender plant into the Flowering Teas room. "What do you and Samantha have planned for the rest of the afternoon?"

"I was about to take Samantha over to see her dad's new office space. Then we're going home."

"I'd love to tag along. There's a piece of your family's history I'd like to show you."

Behind Essences were two buildings. Rhiannon called the first building "the new addition." Craig planned to set up his office there. It was a brick structure with one large open room and several windows facing the flower shop. The only furnishings inside were an impressive-looking executive desk and a leather chair.

The other building—a cottage with a thatched roof—was noticeably older. It reminded Samantha of some of the homes she'd seen in Donegal Town, Ireland. The only difference was that this cottage was quite taller than the cottages in Ireland.

"This is what I wanted to show you," Rhiannon said.

Cobblestones like the ones on the flower shop floor paved the way to the front door. Inside, the home smelled of fresh-cut grass after a rain. The clay walls felt warm, not cold as Samantha thought they would. In the front room, a low stool sat in front of the fireplace, where a large black cooking pot swung from a hook over a spit. Under the only window in the room, there was a dining table set with cups, plates, and eating utensils as if waiting for a meal to be served.

"This was the first home that our ancestors built in Veil Essence," Rhiannon proudly said.

Veil Essence? Samantha wondered. "The Veil Essence from Terrance's story?" she asked.

"Yes. If you take a look over the archway inside the flower shop, you'll see 'Veil Essence' carved in stone," Rhiannon explained. "That archway used to mark the entrance into the village. As time went on and the population grew, our ancestors built walls to enclose the marketplace. Essences Flower Shop is part of the original village of Veil Essence."

"Wow! Mom, did you know about any of this?" Samantha asked.

"I didn't. So, what you're telling us, Rhiannon, is that we own a piece of this village's history? Why isn't there a plaque or something on the building stating this is a historic site?"

"Mmm ... this is a question for Aunt Bess and Kitchet," Rhiannon said, hesitating a little.

"Is there a dispute of some sort going on?" asked Anna.

"No, it's more to do with the actual date when most people think the village was inhabited."

"Oh." Anna's face took on a look of concern. "I hope it has nothing to do with Indigenous land rights."

"Ask Kitchet at dinner tonight," Rhiannon said. "Hey, Samantha. Tell me. Did Terrance shock you when he spoke to you? You know, his being a tree and all."

Samantha wondered if Rhiannon really wanted to know how she felt about meeting Terrance or if she was simply trying to sidestep her mom's questions.

"I'll have to get used to him talking, ladies stepping out

of trees, and these little light essences flying around here in the shop," Samantha said.

"Rhiannon, which of our ancestors lived in this house after it was built?" Anna asked, returning the conversation to why they were there.

"Oh, yes." Rhiannon cleared her throat before taking up the story again. "The Kitchet clan, Muaura, and her parents all lived together in this house."

"Are you joking? All those people lived here?" Samantha just couldn't imagine it as she looked around at the room. Though the ceilings were lofty compared to most cottages, the home did not appear to have enough space to house too many people.

"They made do. Muaura's parents didn't stay too long. They decided to return to their original home. Soon after they left, Muaura began a family of her own. Then the Kitchets and the Fairlands moved up to the land where you live now."

"When was this place built? Late 1700s? Or was it around the early 1800s?" Anna inquired.

"I don't remember. I only remember the stories." Moving to stand behind one of the smaller chairs at the table, Rhiannon said, "Our families left the table set like this to remind us of the many meals, the joys, and the hardships our two families have shared. It's special to us. That's why I wanted to bring you both here."

"It is special. Thanks," Anna said.

"I want to show you one more thing." Rhiannon led them down a narrow hall toward the back of the cottage and into a room with a bed next to a writing desk. "This is the room where Muaura spent most of her time. Together with her parents, she wrote down your family's history and other very important information. They wanted their future generations to know all about their past. If I'm not mistaken, Innis packed away Muaura's book with Ameara's things after she died."

"Do you know where my mother's personal things were stored?" Anna asked.

"I would say in your attic. Look among the crates near the stairwell," Rhiannon said. "That's where most of Ameara's things would be."

"Rhiannon, I remember a small book my mother used to have," Anna said. "It had symbols of a crescent moon, sphere, and stars, just like on the frame in my old bedroom. Have you seen this book anywhere?"

"That's the book! That would be Muaura's book!" Rhiannon shouted. "Did Ameara ever read to you from it?"

"I mainly remember the stories she told about the core people and their music. Is this what Muaura wrote about?"

"She recorded a lot of information. But if you find the book, Anna, you'll discover more about your family's past."

"I knew that book was important! I've even dreamed about it since returning home."

I should tell Mom about Grandma Ameara's diary, Samantha thought. *She'll be pleased to have it. Oh, wait. No. I can't give her that diary. She'll notice the entry about Mr. Lin and the Maskhim and start asking all kinds of questions I'm sure Aunt Mayra and Kitchet won't answer truthfully. Then again, maybe she won't notice anything odd about the entry or even connect the date to the day before Grandma died.* Samantha shook her head. She realized that if Zen were there, he'd say she was thinking too much. *Okay, Samantha. Think! What would Nancy do in this situation?*

"I'm going home to look for it," Anna declared, swiftly turning. She headed out the front door of the cottage, back through the flower shop, and out to their car, leaving Samantha and Rhiannon trotting behind her.

"The book is pretty old and hard to understand!" Rhiannon yelled out as Samantha and her mom got into their car. "Take it to Addiwan when you find it. He'll be able to interpret its meaning."

"Addiwan? Why— Oh, never mind," Anna said, waving goodbye as she drove off.

On the ride home, half of Samantha's brain listened to her mom talking of finding Muaura's book while the other half wondered what she should do about the diary. The small village of Hearthshire disappeared behind them as their car veered onto the lane leading up to their home. She gazed up at the massive canopy of trees swaying their branches along with the rhythm of the wind.

"Hey, there's Bess," Anna said, tooting the car's horn to get her attention. "I'll tell her we'll be over for dinner tonight."

By the time Anna parked the car in the garage, Samantha had decided not to give Grandma Ameara's diary to her mom until she finished her investigation. She still needed to find out who committed the murders, why, and if they had ever been solved. After coming to this decision, she thought she would feel a sense of relief. But she didn't. She felt totally guilty, and she knew why. She'd never hidden anything from her mom before. But in the span of two days, keeping secrets and hiding stuff from her had developed into a habit—a habit she was not in the least bit proud of.

CHAPTER 16

NAMES OF ANCESTORS PAST

With her mom preoccupied with Bess, Samantha rushed up to her room with Gypsy close on her heels. She tucked the newspaper article into the back of Ameara's diary and slipped it beneath her bed pillows. But then she immediately reconsidered her hiding spot, thinking, *Mom may find it when she changes the sheets.* As she scanned the room, her eyes zoomed in on her Nancy Drew books. *Yes, perfect!* Grabbing the books, she fittingly sandwiched the diary between *The Clue in the Diary* and *The Greek Symbol Mystery* before placing them on the shelf opposite her bed.

"There, that should do it." A low groan came from Gypsy, who Samantha felt was staring at her judgmentally. "Don't look at me like that. I'll give it to Mom later, I promise. I just have to hide it for a little bit," she told the dog just as she heard Bess's voice in the hallway.

"I know we helped your father put everything up in storage. Your mother's things should be nearest to the stairs."

"That's where Rhiannon felt they would be. Oh, here

you are," Anna said, pausing in Samantha's doorway. "We're heading up to search for Muaura's book. Would you like to help?

"Sure." Glancing over her shoulder at her shelf, Samantha made sure the diary blended in naturally among the rest of her books before following Bess and her mom to the attic.

"Samantha, your mom tells me you found your first marvels," Bess said as she pulled back the attic window curtains.

"Yes, I did!" Samantha picked up a box and carried it to the area rug, where she made herself comfortable. "Bess, if trees have essences that can be seen, why don't other people report seeing them?"

"People do report seeing them."

"Really? When? I've never heard about it," Anna said.

"Sure you have. You know those stories of people getting lost in the woods and encountering helpful strangers who seem to appear out of nowhere?"

"It's just like the story that was all over the news when we were in Flagstaff," Samantha said. "When people searched all night for those lost girls?"

"Are you talking about the girls who got lost on their ski trip?" Anna asked.

"Yeah. Remember how, when they found them, one of the girls said a lady kept them warm all night? But she was gone by the time help arrived."

"This woman most likely was a tree's essence," Bess said. "Just like Ashlynn."

"Huh. I could have met a tree essence before and didn't even know it," Samantha said.

"Maybe. But it would've been in a heavily wooded area. And normally, as with those young girls in Flagstaff, a tree essence only appears when it is truly needed," said Bess.

"Why is that?" Samantha asked.

"Because trees have learned to keep to themselves, especially in places where there are so few of them, like in cities. Now, our home, Fairland, is very active with nature essences. But still, I've seen people come onto this land and not seem to see or hear them."

"Like I noticed in the shop today," Anna said, "with the plant and flower essences. I guess that's what's known as selective hearing and seeing?"

"Yes," answered Bess.

Samantha leaned against the box she was supposed to be looking through. She wasn't as enthusiastic as her mom was about finding her ancestor's old book. Her eyes were wandering around the room, looking for something more exciting to do, when she spied a door toward the back of the room that she hadn't seen the last time she was in the attic.

"What's behind that door?" she asked.

"I suspect more family stuff. There are generations of Fairland history up here," said Bess as she looked through a trunk. "Goodness, I thought Innis placed Muaura's book where you could easily put your hands on it."

"We'll find it," Anna said, grabbing another crate.

Ditching her box, Samantha headed for the door to see what was inside. It was a walk-in closet lined with shelves holding stacks of loose papers. On examining the papers, she found they were colorful drawings of planets and star clusters. *These are pretty*, she thought. Thumbing through the artwork, she noticed that the artist focused on two planets in particular. One was a small emerald planet labeled with the letters O-P-I-Y-U and the other a larger multicolored planet labeled E-L-P-H-I-A-M.

She returned the drawings to the shelf and reached for an orrery sitting on the very top shelf. A marbled yellow ball was at the center, surrounded by ten smaller gold balls attached to metal rods affixed to interlocking gears. Positioned farther away from the ten gold balls were three more gold balls, bigger than the other ten.

Blowing the dust away from the orrery's wooden base, she cranked a little metal lever on the side and watched the spherical planets revolve around each other.

"Hey, look at this," she said.

"Is it Muaura's book?" Bess asked, stepping into the closet. "Oh, you've gotten into Opiyu's stuff. She loved to draw and work with her hands."

"Op ... How did you say that name?" Anna's curiosity piqued, she put aside her search to join in on Bess and Samantha's conversation.

"O-PIE-you," Bess said slowly. "Opiyu was Muaura and Arborden's daughter."

"Wait. I saw that name on one of these drawings." Samantha picked up the drawing of the small emerald planet. "See right here."

"Yes," Bess said. "Opiyu and her brother, Elphiam, were named after planets their grandmother was very fond of.

"I'm not very savvy when it comes to astronomy," Anna said, "but I've never heard of those planets. And this orrery is holding five planets too many. Well, one of them is probably poor Pluto before it was demoted. Where is she getting these other planets? Or are they meant to be moons?"

"Maybe," Bess said, stepping out of the closet. "I do know that at least one Fairland from every generation has been interested in the stars, and Opiyu was no different."

"Is this the reason behind the symbol of the crescent

moon and stars carved into the gravestones and on the wooden frame in my bedroom?" Samantha asked.

"That's right."

"Were Opiyu and Elphiam the only children Muaura had?" Anna asked as she got back to searching through the crates.

"No, six. Arborden and Muaura had six children," Bess whispered. She seemed to drift off somewhere in the crevices of her mind. Samantha got the impression the older woman was seeing another time, another place. Then, clapping, Bess smiled and said, "Let me see if I can name them all in order. There was Samkin, Muluna, Elphiam, Aprena, Opiyu, and Muam. You are descended from their daughter Opiyu and her husband, Pan-AEL.

"I never thought to ask my father or my Aunt Mayra. However, now I'm curious," Anna remarked. "Bess, do you know my family's country of origin? Muaura's children's names are very unusual."

"I guess the names do sound a bit strange in today's world," Bess said with a chuckle. "I do know Muaura's parents, Oeans—pronounced O-EE-ANS—and her father, EL-Athu—L-AT-HUE—lived for a time in what is now considered the continent of Africa and in the Mesopotamia region. Muaura's parents traveled a great deal, just like you and Craig have.

"So, our ancestors are of African and Middle Eastern descent?" asked Anna.

"Yes and no. Your ancestors lived in that part of the world, but this is not where they came from originally. Remember what Innis always said. We are all children of the universe, born into this Earth. So don't get too hung up on this world's labels," Bess reminded Anna and Samantha.

"I liked when Grandpa used to say that. It made me feel,

I don't know, sort of connected to everybody else in the world," Samantha said.

"They're powerful words meant to unite people," Bess said.

"Bess, you really seem to know a great deal about my family's history," Anna said.

"Well, our families' histories are intertwined.

"Can you tell me more about Grandma Ameara? What was she like? Did she have a lot of friends?" Samantha asked. She thought that if she found out more about her grandmother, it would help her figure out who would've wanted to kill her.

"Your grandmother had an easygoing, sweet personality. She loved to spend time in the garden and her flower shop. But she spent most of her time with her family. Oh, Anna, she loved you girls and Innis so much," Bess said, beaming.

"But did she have any friends? Did she go out to dinner or to the movies with anyone besides her family?" Samantha pressed.

"She didn't have many friends outside her family, Samantha."

"You said not many. Does that mean she had at least one friend?"

"What's with all the questions all of a sudden about your grandmother?" Anna asked, looking up from her crate.

"I just wanted to get a better idea of what type of person she was. That's all."

"She rarely left Hearthshire, except for her trips to meet Nanna for breakfast at the university. Ameara was a good person who left us all too soon," Bess said solemnly.

No friends, Samantha thought. *Then who was Mr. Lin? Maybe he wasn't a friend after all and this was why Grandma was frightened to meet him. Or maybe he was a friend of Great-Grandma Nanna.*

Samantha was about to ask about Nanna when Bess sighed loudly and said, "I don't think Muaura's book is up here. Sorry, Anna. We can ask Kitchet during dinner. Dinner! I haven't even started it!" Then she hustled down the steps.

Even though Bess had said Muaura's book wasn't in the attic, Anna insisted on Samantha helping her look through the rest of the crates. It was at least another hour before they gave up and headed back downstairs.

"We should have a shower before going over to the Kitchets' place," Anna said, following Samantha into her room.

"Mom," Samantha said, stretching out on her bed, "do you mind if I don't go over for dinner with you? I'm all wiped out." She really was looking for time alone to call Zen.

"You're wiped out? You're too young to feel all wiped out," her mom teased, tickling her under her rib cage.

"Mom, stop ... please ... I can't breathe," gasped Samantha between giggles.

"That's fine. You don't have to come." Anna lay down next to her. "Do you want me to stay and keep you company?"

"No. Gypsy will keep me company, won't you girl?"

At hearing her name, the Irish wolfhound, who had been sleeping in front of the window, lifted her head and wagged her tail.

"If you two get hungry, I do have some leftovers in the fridge." Anna rolled off the bed and began her trek around Samantha's room, picking up clothes.

"Can I call Zen while you're gone? I wanna tell him about Terrance, Ashlynn, and everything else."

"Sure. Ooh, Samantha! Are you starting to throw books on the floor now too?"

"Uh ... no. What book?"

"This one," her mom said, picking up a book. Its cloth dust jacket slipped off, exposing a soft leather cover underneath. "Samantha! Where did you get this book? This is what we've been searching for. It's Muaura's book!"

"What?" Samantha leaped off the bed to get a look at the book her mom held.

"See the etching in the leather cover of the moon, stars, and sphere?" Anna asked.

Samantha could just make out the faint outlines of the symbols. Opening the book, she instantly recognized the random shapes and drawings on the faded pages from the book she had tossed aside the night she found her grandma's diary.

"Sorry, Mom. Zen and I picked up this book from the attic the other day. I didn't recognize it as the one you were looking for with that cover on it," Samantha said truthfully.

"I'm just thrilled to have found it," Anna said, skimming through the book. "Talk about old-world writing. Now I understand what Rhiannon meant. There is no way I can interpret this myself. Well, I better get ready."

Samantha listened as her mom's footsteps faded away down the hall, then she heard the shower come on in her parents' bedroom. Sitting on the floor next to Gypsy, she ran her hand over the dog's rough coat, waiting for her mom to leave. She didn't know how she'd managed to keep herself composed all day with all the new information brimming up inside her. She hoped that when she called

Zen, he would help her unravel all she had learned. Together, they would decide the next best course of action in their investigation.

CHAPTER 17

WHAT SHOULD WE DO NEXT?

With the telephone receiver pressed to her ear, Samantha sat on the living room sofa, impatiently drumming her fingers on the armrest. It was on the fifth ring when someone finally picked up.

"Hello?"

"Zen?"

"No, Junzo. Is that you, Samantha?"

"Yeah. Hi, Uncle Junzo. Is Zen home?"

"Yes, he's in his room. I'll get him for you. *Denwa*, Zen. It's Samantha."

A moment later, Zen came on the line.

"Hey, Samantha. What's up?"

"I have so much to tell you. Can you talk?" Without waiting to hear his response, she rushed on. "I know what really happened to Grandma Ameara and Great-Grandma Nanna. It's all here in an article I found at the library. And, Zen, get this. Grandma Ameara was worried about something the night before she was killed! I read in her—"

"Hold on," Zen said. Samantha heard a door close in the

background before he then asked, "So what does the paper say?"

Taking in a deep breath, Samantha read from the article in *The Hearthshire Ledger*, emphasizing certain sections. "Nanna was found in her office, but Grandma Ameara was found in her car at an airport." And, of course, the biggie. "It says both of them were violently strangled," she finished. "Now I totally understand why Grandpa lied. I mean, how do you tell your kids their mom and grandmother died like that?"

"Strangled ... Geez ... that's so terrible. Why do you suppose someone would want to do something like that to them?" Zen sounded just as shocked as she'd been when she'd first read the news. "The article doesn't even mention if they caught the person who did it."

"I know. It just said it's an 'ongoing case.' I wanted to search through more papers, but Mom came into the library."

"Listen, Dad's about to go out. As soon as he does, I'll jump on his computer and see what I can dig up."

"Can you call me back? I have some other stuff I need you to look up," Samantha said.

"Okay, sure." Then Zen hung up.

Samantha paced in front of the window, where she had a clear view of the Kitchets' home and its occupants. Bess hustled from the kitchen into the sitting area, carrying food like a jolly waiter, while her mom seemed to be in a deep conversation with Kitchet. Samantha became so fixated on the movements inside the Kitchet's cottage that it caught her by surprise when a tall, dark figure appeared on the Kitchets' doorstep. Bess opened her door, allowing the home's indoor light to cascade over the threshold, revealing Addiwan as the dark shadow. The phone rang, drawing

Samantha's attention away from the window and the little stone house, leaving the Kitchets and their guest to their dinner.

"Okay, I'm on the computer. Give me the name of a newspaper I can look up," Zen said when she answered.

"I don't know of any other newspapers in this area besides *The Hearthshire Ledger*."

"Okay, well, the article you read said Great-Grandma Nanna was a 'prominent professor.' So, let's do a search of her name and see what comes up."

Quietly, she listened to Zen tapping away at the computer. "Wow, did you know that Great-Grandma was also a writer?" he asked. "It looks like her last book was called *Only the Land Will Tell*."

"There's nothing about her death?" Samantha asked, not particularly interested at the moment in her great-grandma's books.

"Hold your horses. Oh, wait. Here's something in *The Darlington Press*. Okay, blah, blah, found in her office by a Mr. Randall, graduate student. Daughter Ameara Fairland, Darlington Airport," Zen relayed.

"Basically, the same stuff I read in *The Hearthshire Ledger*."

"Pretty much."

"When was that article dated?" Samantha asked.

"March 25, 1987."

"Nothing else came up in the search?"

"Nope. I just see the article you have from *The Hearthshire Ledger* and this one in *The Darlington Press*. Oh, wait. Here in *The Darlington Press*, it does give the name of a police officer. An 'Officer Bevin of the Hearthshire Police Department,' the article states, 'is working closely with the Clarkstown Police Department in this ongoing investigation,'" Zen read. "We should go talk to Officer Bevin. He'll be able to tell us what finally happened with the case."

"You think he's still in the village after all these years?"

"There's only one way to find out. Go to the police station and ask for him."

Samantha gasped. "I don't wanna go in there by myself."

Zen's laughter boomed in her ear. "What do you think they're gonna do? Arrest you for asking a question? Some detective you are!"

"I've just never been into a police station, and I prefer my first time not be by myself. Anyway, I'm sure there are other ways of finding out if Officer Bevin is still around."

"All right, do it your way. Just let me know if you find out any more important information," Zen said.

"I do have more very important information." Samantha opened her journal to where she'd written down the names from Ameara's diary. "Remember that stack of books you grabbed from the attic?"

"What about them?"

"One of them was Grandma Ameara's diary. I was reading through it when I—"

"You read Grandma's personal diary!"

"Zen, listen. In Grandma's diary, her last entry was the night before she was murdered. She wrote two short sentences. 'Mr. Lin, Maskhim. What does he know?'"

"Does she say who Mr. Lin is? And are you saying, 'mask him'?"

"No. Grandma wrote it as one word, like a name, with a capital *M*. Maskhim."

"Oh, okay. So it's a last name like 'Lin,' and she's asking what they know? But wait. She says what does *he* know, not what do *they* know. Maybe Maskhim is a place where Mr. Lin is from."

"I don't think so because I also found shoved in the back of the diary a note Grandma wrote to Grandpa. In the note, she tells Grandpa how worried she is about Mr. Lin and the news he brings of the Maskhim."

"Huh. So you think this Mr. Lin and Maskhim had something to do with the murders?"

"It sure seems that way to me. Or they at least know something about the murders," Samantha said. "Look at the evidence. She asks in her diary what Mr. Lin and Maskhim know. Then she leaves a note saying how worried she is. Zen, she turns up dead the next day! Why don't you try doing a search linking the names Mr. Lin or Maskhim with Ameara and Nanna Fairland."

"Good idea." Again, Samantha could hear Zen tapping away. "Nothing comes up by linking the names. I'll try the word *Maskhim* by itself. Maybe it will give us a clue if this is a name or a place." After a few seconds, Zen reported, "Nope. It's just giving me things like Halloween masks and stuff like that."

"Mmm. Do you think Grandpa gave this note and the information in the diary to the police? And if he did, I wonder if the police found out who Mr. Lin and Maskhim are and questioned them."

"I'm sure he did," said Zen. "Why wouldn't he?"

"I don't know. I'm just thinking out loud. I'll do some more investigating around here. If I find out anything else, I'll call you."

"I'll be here. Hey, have you seen that butterfly?"

"I haven't seen the butterfly, but I did meet a marvel! Actually, two marvels," Samantha said.

"You're kidding me. See, I knew I shouldn't have left!

Wait, what do you mean when you met a marvel? They're people?"

"Not exactly."

"Well, what then? Come on, give."

"They're trees!" Samantha said.

"Not with the trees again."

"Zen, the tree outside my bedroom window talked to me. I mean really talked to me like I'm talking to you."

"Are you sure you didn't hear it all in your own head?"

"No, it wasn't in my head. Not only that, Mom and I actually saw a tree essence. She introduced herself to us."

"Essence? Like what Aunt Mayra talked about?"

"Yeah, it's like the tree's spirit, its soul," Samantha said. "She said her name is Ashlynn, and—"

"I have to say, it all sounds unbelievable and a bit weird."

"Hey, I was there, and it took me a minute to believe it. But you know, after the initial shock of it, it all seemed normal and not weird at all."

Samantha filled Zen in about Essences Flower Shop, Rhiannon, and the search for Muaura's book.

"Man, I can't wait to meet up with Uncle Craig at the airport. Have you heard from him?" Zen asked.

"No. Not yet. He'll probably call sometime tonight or tomorrow."

Before hanging up, there was one more thing Samantha wanted to share with Zen. It was a nagging suspicion she'd had ever since she learned about the phone call Grandpa Innis received before he died.

"Zen, what if ... what if the person who called Grandpa was actually the person who murdered Ameara and Nanna? Maybe Grandpa found something out and the murderer lured him away from the house and killed him. We don't really know that Grandpa died of pneumonia. That's just what the Kitchets and Aunt Mayra have told us, and they've lied before about how our relatives died."

"I was wondering the same thing," Zen said. "That's why I told you to go to the police station. If Officer Bevin is still there, you can ask him if he was the one who called Grandpa to tell him they finally solved the case."

"And if he says he didn't call? What then?" Samantha heard no response on the other end of the line. "Zen, are you still there?"

"Let's think about that later," he finally answered. "Look, don't worry so much. I bet Officer Bevin did call Grandpa." Samantha could tell from Zen's voice that he was only trying to make her feel better.

"Yeah, you're probably right. You know me—too many of those mystery novels," she said, poking fun at herself. "Anyway, I have to go. I haven't had dinner, and my stomach is starting to hurt. You know how that goes." Samantha knew that the peculiar feeling in her stomach had nothing to do with hunger; it was the possibility that the killer was the caller and was somewhere still out there —maybe very close to their home. That was what caused the uncomfortable feeling in the pit of her stomach.

"Yeah, I know exactly what you mean," Zen said. "I need to eat before heading over to Dad's art show. I'll talk to you later."

"Okay."

"Hey, Samantha. We'll go to the police station together when I get there. Okay?"

"Okay."

Telling herself to put all thoughts of the murder case out of her mind, Samantha headed for the kitchen after she hung up. The sound of the refrigerator door drew Gypsy to her side to join in on the food hunt. "Hungry?" Samantha said to the big dog. "Me too. Let's see what we have in here." Finding several pieces of ham, she dumped them into the dog's dish.

"Here ya go, girl. It's all yours. I think I'll have some cookies."

Rummaging in the cupboards, she didn't find one box of cookies. "I forgot that Mom hasn't had time to stock up," she said, watching Gypsy lick her lips after finishing off the ham. "But I bet I know who will have nice homemade cookies. Come on. Let's go visit Bess."

Samantha held her coat closed as the wind tried to wrestle it open during her walk across the yard. Reaching the Kitchets' front door, she expected to hear people laughing and talking from inside, but it was quiet. She knocked softly and waited patiently for someone to answer. No one did. She knocked again, louder this time, with still no response from the Kitchets, her mom, or Addiwan. Walking over to the window, Samantha peeked in and was surprised to see that the small front room was empty.

"Where'd they all go?" she asked.

Going back to the front door, she twisted the door handle and found it to be unlocked. Hesitantly, she stepped inside the small, cozy home. A fire still burned in the fireplace, and dirty dishes were still on the table.

"Hello! It's just me, Samantha!" she called out, standing in the middle of the Kitchets' front room. The house was quiet. Obviously, no one was home. She was turning to leave when Gypsy took off into another room.

"Gypsy! Come here, girl," she whispered, chasing after the dog.

She found her in the kitchen, scratching at a rug inside Bess's pantry. "Don't do that. Let it alone, Gypsy," she said, trying to push the large dog off the rug. Gypsy barked and wagged her tail before grabbing a mouthful of the rug and dragging it across the small kitchen floor.

"This is no time for play," Samantha said as she tried to retrieve Bess's rug before it was destroyed. Walking across the kitchen floor, she noticed a difference in the sound of the floorboards where the rug had been. Looking closer at the wooden slats, she could see a small gold latch in one of the boards. Kneeling, she pulled on the latch, and it lifted up four floorboards at one time. She was now staring into a hole in Bess's pantry that had steps leading downward. But it was too dark to see where they led.

Could Mom and the others be down here? Why? she wondered.

"Mom ... Bess?" she yelled into the hole, but she heard only the echo of her own voice. "Let's go home, Gypsy." Lowering the floorboards, she put the rug back into place and left the Kitchets' warm home.

They could've gone to Addiwan's house, she was thinking when Gypsy stopped and turned back toward the Kitchets' house, barking. Ascending from behind the Kitchets' small stone home was a shadow. *What is that?* she wondered. Against the moonlit sky, the shadow grew wings and flew toward Samantha, sending her bolting for her house. She burst through the front door just as she heard the flapping of the wings above her head.

"Samantha?"

"Mom! Where'd you come from?" Samantha panted.

"The kitchen. I was just about to come up and check on you."

"But where have you been?"

"Don't you remember? I went to the Kitchets' house for

dinner," her mom said, walking into the living room and switching off lights. "Did you fall asleep?"

"No, I was talking to Zen." Going over to the window, Samantha pulled back the curtain and looked out toward the Kitchets' house. Like she had earlier that evening, she looked into their front room. Bess was shutting off lights, and Kitchet was drawing the curtains.

"How is Zen? Is he looking forward to his trip back here?"

"Yeah, he is. But, Mom, I was just at the Kitchets' house, and no one was there. And by the way, there's a large human-sized bird flying around this property. It tried to attack me!"

A look came across her mom's face that Samantha recognized as the look she gave when she was trying to hide something. First there was the look, then a simple explanation before her mom changed the subject altogether.

"Don't be silly. I was probably on my way home when you came over," Anna said. "I left by way of Bess's kitchen. And perhaps it was an eagle you saw or some other bird of prey. Did your dad call?"

"No, Dad didn't call. But—"

"Turn that light off near the front door," Anna said, already halfway up the steps. "I'm opening up the flower shop in the morning, so I have to get to bed. Good night, sweetheart."

"Good night, Mom."

Samantha knew something had happened over at the Kitchets' house, and it was apparent that her mom didn't want to share it with her. *That's fine*, Samantha told herself. As long as her mom was safe at home, she could have her secret. Samantha knew she herself sure did.

~

SAMANTHA ROLLED over in bed and saw her mom easing her bedroom door closed. *Is it morning already?* she wondered. Judging by the darkness of her room, she guessed it must be the middle of the night. Her clock read 11:45 p.m., confirming her suspicions. Awake now, she got up and headed to her door, figuring she'd go crawl into bed with her mom like she used to do when she was younger.

"No, it's okay," she heard her mom say. "Samantha was just talking in her sleep again."

I talk in my sleep? I never knew that. Samantha was standing in the hall, right outside her parents' bedroom door.

"Sam, it's amazing!" her mom continued.

Oh, she's on the phone with Aunt Sam.

"No, I'm telling you, it's all real. Just like when we were kids. But there is so much more. When do you think you and Junzo can get back here?"

She must be telling her all about Terrance and Ashlynn.

"They said it was time I saw it for myself, so the Kitchets and Addiwan took me there."

See it for herself? Where'd she go?

"Call me tomorrow and let me know your plans."

When she heard her mom end her call, Samantha ran back to her own room. Sitting in bed, she contemplated where her mom could have gone and seen something so amazing. *She couldn't have left the property.* Smiling, she thought of someone who might know the answer to her question. Tiptoeing over to her window, she whispered out into the cold night air. "Terrance, are you there?"

"Where else would I be?" Terrance asked. "Would you like to hear another story?"

"No, thank you. I wanted to ask you a question. Is there a secret place not too far from the Kitchets' house?"

"If it is a secret, how would I know? That is the whole point of a secret, right?"

"Yes, you're right." Samantha tried another way to ask her question. "Are there other places on this property that I haven't discovered yet?"

"I cannot answer that question since I am not aware of all the places you have discovered. Are you sure you don't want another story? It may help you go off to sleep."

"No, that's okay, Terrance. I think I can go back to sleep on my own. Good night."

"Sweet dreams, Samantha."

CHAPTER 18

GIRL DETECTIVE

D on't dawdle in there!" Anna yelled above the shower's running water. "I don't want to be late on my first day opening the flower shop. You sure you don't want to stay home and catch up on your sleep?"

"No, I'm coming!" Samantha yelled back.

"I'll feed Gypsy while you finish dressing. Meet me at the car when you're done."

Samantha had slept in again after staying up too late, trying to figure out her mom's whereabouts the previous evening. However, she had decided to put her mom's escapades aside and place her focus back on the murder investigation. This would involve going to the library this morning.

The clock in the village square had struck nine a.m. by the time Anna dropped Samantha off at Hearthshire Public Library on her way to Essences Flower Shop. Upon entering, Samantha found Ms. Emily powering up the library computer to begin her day.

"I didn't expect to see you again so soon," Ms. Emily

remarked when she spotted Samantha.

"I thought I'd look through your Nancy Drew section," Samantha said. Her ulterior motive was to ask Ms. Emily about Officer Bevin. She had a hunch the old librarian knew about everyone and everything in the village.

"As I mentioned to your mother, for a small library, we have quite a nice selection of Nancy Drew books," said the tight-lipped Ms. Emily, leading Samantha to the children's section. "Is there a particular title I can help you find?"

"No, I just figured I'd browse through the shelves," Samantha answered as she removed her coat and draped it over the back of one of the chairs.

"I'll leave you to it then. By the way," Ms. Emily said, turning back to Samantha. "How did your mother react when you showed her the article in *The Hearthshire Ledger*?"

"Actually, I haven't shown it to her yet."

"Oh, have you decided it was best not to share this information with her after all?"

"Not exactly. We decided to try and find out more information surrounding the murder. The newspaper article and the internet didn't tell us things, like if the murder was ever solved or who did it."

"We? Is someone else helping you with your search?" Ms. Emily asked.

"Oh yeah. My cousin, Zen, is helping me track down information."

"I see."

"Ms. Emily, do you know if there is an Officer Bevin who works at the local police station?"

"Why yes. He's the police chief here in Hearthshire. Police Chief Michael Bevin. Why do you ask?"

"We read, that is, me and my cousin Zen—"

"It is 'Zen and I,' dear. Not 'me and Zen.'"

"Right. Sorry. Zen and I read that Officer Bevin helped with the investigation."

"I vaguely remember Michael working closely with another officer." Rubbing her forehead, the elderly librarian said, "It was so long ago, you know, and my mind is not what it used to be."

"He was working with police officers from the Clarkstown Police Department," Samantha reminded her.

"That's right ... A detective from the Clarkstown area. You certainly have done your homework. What a clever girl you are."

Samantha smiled at the compliment. In the short time she'd known Ms. Emily, she'd gotten the impression that the librarian didn't hand out words of praise often. "Do you think I can go over and talk with Chief Bevin?"

"I don't see why you couldn't speak with him. He is a public servant."

Pulling on her coat, Samantha headed for the library doors. "Thanks so much for the information, Ms. Emily."

"You're not checking out a book?"

"I may come back later."

"Good luck," Ms. Emily called out. "I hope Michael can help you."

Samantha felt safe knowing that her mom wouldn't come looking for her at the library. They had already discussed that Samantha would make her way to the flower shop by lunchtime. Glancing at the clock on the old stone fireplace, she saw that she still had at least three hours to gather as much information as she could.

But will Chief Bevin even tell me anything? she wondered. This passing thought made Samantha slow her pace as she neared the police station. Her only goal had been to find out if he was still in the village. She hadn't thought about what she'd actually say to him. Now, standing on the bottom step of the Hearthshire Police Station, she hesitated about going inside. *What was I thinking? I can't go in there!*

"What do you think they're gonna do? Arrest you for asking a question? Some detective you are." Zen's teasing words came back to haunt her.

I'll show you what type of detective I am! she thought. Determined to prove to Zen and herself that she didn't just read about detectives and that she, Samantha, could be a detective too, she took a deep breath and pushed through the front doors of the Hearthshire Police Department.

Almost immediately, a lean young officer with wavy, jet-black hair approached her. "Can I help you, young lady?" he asked.

She was about to answer him but found that her mouth had gone dry, as if she had swallowed a cup of dirt. As the officer stared at her with raised eyebrows, she rolled her tongue around inside her mouth, managing to create enough moisture to say, "Officer ... I mean Chief Bevin, please."

"Okay, but let's see if maybe I can help you first. What is it you need to see Chief Bevin about?"

"I ... I wanted to talk to Chief Bevin about a murder case."

The officer's facial expression changed from curiosity to deep concern. "Why don't you take a seat at my desk, and let's start again," he said, flipping open his notepad. "Now, what is your name? And when did this murder take place?"

"My name is Samantha Keen. Ameara Fairland and—"

"Fairland?" Someone behind her asked. "Are you talking about the Fairlands who own that piece of land near the end of the village?"

"Yes," she answered, turning to address the voice coming from across the room.

An older man with receding, blond hair stood in a doorway. His navy-blue tie looked too tight around the thick neck supporting his square head. Tossing a file on the desk of the young officer who was helping Samantha, the man said, "I'll handle this, Roberts." Then he turned to Samantha. "I'm Chief Michael Bevin."

Chief Bevin directed Samantha into his office. After she walked in, he said, "Have a seat," while pulling out his own chair and sitting at an old, battered-looking desk. "Tell me, how do you know the Fairlands?"

Inside her coat, Samantha could feel herself beginning to sweat. "My mom is Anna Fairland. Innis Moor's daughter."

"That's right. Innis had two daughters who moved away when they were quite young." Chief Bevin picked up a baseball littered with signatures and rolled it between his palms. "How can I help you?"

"Well, I was wondering about the murders of my grandmother and great-grandmother, Ameara and Nanna Fairland."

Chief Bevin stopped playing with his baseball and tossed it into a tray of neatly stacked paperwork. "What about it?"

Okay, good. He's open to questions, Samantha thought. "I was hoping you could tell me what happened with the investigation." Trying to keep the sweat from running down from her armpits, she squeezed her arms close to her sides.

Leaning forward in his chair, he asked, "Is your mother looking to have this case reopened?"

"No. My grandpa never told my mom that her mother

was murdered. She doesn't even know I'm here." *Gosh, why did I say that? He's going to call my mom!*

"If you say your mother doesn't know the circumstances surrounding the deaths of her own mother and grandmother, how did you find out?"

Come on, you can do it, Samantha. Lie. Just do it. "I came across some notes in my grandpa's desk and read a newspaper article about the murder. This is how I found out you were part of the original investigation." *That was easy. Zen would be proud of me.*

"I see. Innis kept track of what had happened concerning the case?"

"Yes."

Chief Bevin got up and came to sit on the edge of his desk, facing Samantha. "I'm not sure what you found in Innis's notes, but I was only assisting Detective Davies of the Clarkstown Police Department. The murder happened in his district."

"Well, can you tell me why they were murdered and whether the person responsible was arrested?"

"If Innis kept good notes, it would have told you that the investigation went cold after a week for lack of leads, which means it was never solved." Throwing his hands in the air, Chief Bevin said, "That's it. There's nothing else I can tell you."

"Only one week?" Samantha couldn't believe what he was saying.

Walking behind his desk, Chief Bevin unlocked the right-hand bottom drawer and retrieved a folder. "It's not unusual for this to happen in some cases. But if you want to know exactly what we found out during this investigation, here it is." Sitting at his desk, he opened the folder and laid out the facts for Samantha. "Nothing was taken from either victim. Nothing was taken from Professor Fairland's office or from the university. Neither woman was ever involved with or connected to any past crimes or people with criminal backgrounds."

"What about the suspicious man the newspaper says the student said he saw on the morning of the murders? Did you ever find and question that guy?" Samantha asked.

"You're talking about what Kenny Randall reported to the police back then. It was speculated that this suspicious man drove to the airport in Ameara Fairland's car and boarded a plane. He was never questioned."

"There were no other suspects?"

"Like I said, this was Detective Davies's case," Chief Bevin said, returning the folder to his bottom drawer. "So, unless you or someone else has new evidence, this murder case remains cold."

Samantha got the impression that Chief Bevin was about to ask her to leave, so she rushed to ask another question. "I saw a man's name in Grandpa's paperwork. It was a Mr. Lin. Who is he?"

"Mr. Peter Lin's name was written on Professor Fairland's calendar. Your grandfather verified that Mr. Lin did have an appointment with Professor Fairland that morning. We couldn't locate Peter Lin to question him. It was suspected that Mr. Lin and the suspicious man were one and the same."

"So, Mr. Lin was the suspected murderer?"

"This was the theory."

So, Ameara was right to be worried, Samantha thought. "Have you ever heard of the name 'Maskhim'?"

"Maskhim?" Chief Bevin narrowed his eyes as he looked at Samantha. "Is that spelled *M-A-S-K-H-I-M*?"

"Yeah, this word was next to Mr. Lin's name."

"No, can't say that I have." Chief Bevin got up and walked over to the door, then held it open for Samantha. "I'm sorry I couldn't give you the answers you were looking for. If it helps, I can tell you that your grandfather seemed to have come to terms with his wife's and mother-in-law's deaths. He seemed at peace in the end."

At peace in the end. That's what Kitchet said after Grandpa Innis met up with whoever called him, Samantha thought. "Chief Bevin, did you call my grandfather before he died to discuss anything about the case?"

"No. Actually, I saw less and less of Innis over the years."

"How about Detective Davies? Do you think he would've contacted my grandpa with new information?"

"Detective Davies? No. He died eight years ago. Why do you ask?"

Lie number three coming right up, she thought. "A note that was stuck in with my grandpa's paperwork was dated recently. It said something about new information concerning the case."

"Interesting. As far as I know, the murder case of Ameara and Nanna Fairland is still unsolved." Chief Bevin handed Samantha a card. "If there is anything else I can clear up for you, or if your mother needs to speak with me, just let me know."

"Thank you."

Standing outside the police station, Samantha was now filled with more questions than when she went in. *I need to think,* she told herself as she headed back to the library.

Ms. Emily wasn't at her regular post behind the front desk. Instead, a younger woman with short, mousy-brown hair was stacking books onto a library cart. Samantha walked straight to the children's section and took a seat as far back in the corner as she could get.

Being around books gave her clarity. Not that she searched the books for answers to her concerns. It was that books created a wall that shielded out all unwanted noise and static. With her journal and pen in hand, she wrote down what she had learned from Chief Bevin.

1. *The police had only one suspect, a Mr. Peter Lin, who the police felt was the suspicious man Kenneth Randall reported to police.*

2. *The case went cold after one week. Police felt that Mr. Lin boarded a plane the same day he murdered them because Grandma Ameara's body was found at the airport.*

3. *Nothing was stolen from Nanna or Ameara. Nothing was stolen from the university. So why were they killed?*

4. *Chief Bevin said he didn't call Grandpa Innis, and Detective Davies has been dead for 8 years. So, who called Grandpa with news about the murders?*

Tapping her pen against her open book, Samantha studied her notes. *How did Great-Grandma Nanna know Mr. Lin? And this word* Maskhim. *What does it mean?* Samantha put her pen down and stared at the word *Maskhim.* As she did, something her grandpa wrote in the front of her oak-bound book popped into her head: *There is power in words, Samantha, and how people choose to use them. Always choose your words with care when you write in your journal. Someday, others will read your words and, from your words, decode who you are.*

She wrote the word *Maskhim* by itself on a clean page in

her book. *Okay, let's really see what this word is saying*, she said to herself. *It is a compound word of the two words* mask *and* him. Mask, *meaning "a disguise—to literally put on a mask, to hide one's face." The word* him, *well, that's simple: a man, a person. Hmm, a man hiding his face. Does Mr. Lin wear a mask of some sort? That can't be right. The student, Kenneth Randall, would have said that Mr. Lin was wearing a mask. I'm sure he would have noticed something like that.* Samantha looked at the word again, trying to figure out if it had any other meaning.

If I take off the M, *I find two other words.* Ask *and* him. *Maybe Grandma Ameara put the word* Maskhim *next to Mr. Lin's name because she wanted to ask him something. That can't be it either! Forget it.* She looked at the clock on the wall and saw it was after 11:17 a.m. *I better head over to the flower shop.*

On her way out of the library, she found that Ms. Emily had returned to her post behind the front desk.

"So, you have come back. Did you get a chance to talk to Chief Bevin?" the librarian asked.

"Yeah."

"The word is *yes*, dear. It sounds so much nicer than *yeah*." Ms. Emily smiled as she corrected Samantha. "Was he able to give you any new information?"

"No. He said the case went cold for lack of leads to follow."

"Oh, I'm sorry, Samantha. By the way, has your mother enrolled you in our local school?"

"No, I'm homeschooled."

"Oh, I see. To each his own, as the old saying goes."

Samantha thought she heard a hint of disapproval in the librarian's voice. Since Ms. Emily was a stickler for words, Samantha thought she'd ask her about the word

Maskhim. "Ms. Emily, have you heard of the word *Maskhim* before?"

"Maskhim," Ms. Emily said, adjusting her glasses against her face. "Now, where would you get a word like that? Did Chief Bevin mention it to you?"

"No, I just saw it somewhere, and I'm trying to figure out if it's a last name or a place."

"It sounds like a word children make up in those silly computer games. If the word is not in the dictionary, then it means nothing."

"Yeah—I mean yes—you're probably right," said Samantha, even though she knew that wasn't the case. The word *Maskhim* had meant something important to her Grandma Ameara, and she was determined to find out what it was. "Thanks again for your help."

"Weren't there any Nancy Drew books in our little library that interest you?" Ms. Emily asked, raising a single eyebrow at Samantha.

"Oh yes, there are many. But I better come back with my book list. I like to read them in order by release date."

As she made her way across the village square, Samantha noticed her mom standing in the flower shop window, smiling and waving to her. What Samantha didn't notice was the black SUV parked not too far from the library and the man sitting in the driver's seat, intently watching her.

CHAPTER 19

SENTINELS OF KNOWLEDGE

Charles Genelis arrived at his estate in the Austrian mountains in the early morning hours. An icy breeze followed him through his front door, causing flames inside a marbled fireplace to flicker.

He paused in front of a gold-framed mirror. "Good," he said under his breath after inspecting his image. He removed his wool fedora, exposing a crop of neatly trimmed, white hair. A young man stepped into the foyer to relieve Genelis of his full-length, double-breasted wool coat and leather gloves.

"Thank you, Otto," Genelis said, fixing his mint-green eyes on his assistant. He noted Otto's tweed gray suit and dark-brown bow tie, which matched his brown oxford shoes. "I see you visited my tailor."

"Yes, sir."

"Very good. When are the others arriving?"

"Two p.m., sir. Sir, I placed your correspondence on your desk, and your antiques from China have arrived. I secured them with the others." Otto patted each side of his slick, brown hair to make sure the part down the center of his head was straight. "Will you be having a nap, sir, before your guests arrive?" he asked, following Genelis into his office.

Otto Adelmann, whose father had worked for Genelis for twenty years until his death, still had a lot to learn about his employer. One of the things young Otto would discover is that though in his mid-seventies, Genelis was an avid mountain climber and cross-country skier who never napped.

"I never take naps, Otto. Please close the door on your way out."

Charles Genelis—known to his business associates as a generous philanthropist, collector of rare antiquities, and a world traveler—came from old money. What many did not know about this sophisticated, worldly man was that he was a member of an exclusive organization called the Sentinels of Knowledge. Very few people in the world knew of the Sentinels of Knowledge and its members. One learned of them by invitation only, and membership in this elite group of both men and women came only by being born into it. The Sentinels had maintained the same purpose since the group's conception: conceal all knowledge of humanity's origins. By decree of the members' ancestors, this knowledge had to always stay guarded, and the members were the only ones worthy of guarding it.

An urgent knock at his office door interrupted Genelis as he went over points for his afternoon meeting.

"Yes?" he called out.

"Sir, there is a call from the United States," said a flushed-faced Otto from the doorway. "The caller says it is very urgent. Shall I put it through?"

"Yes, Otto."

Unbuttoning his waistcoat, Genelis leaned back in his tufted leather chair and answered his call on the second ring. "Yes."

"Genelis, I've received a call from Hearthshire, Vermont," the male on the other end of the line said. "There is a member of the Fairland family, a Samantha Keen, searching into the deaths of the professor and her daughter. The interested party states that this young girl is getting too close to the truth. How would you and the members like to handle this?"

A deep shade of gold appeared around the pupils of Genelis's mint-green eyes when he asked, "Is it the same interested party we've spoken of in the past?"

"Yes, it is."

"Leave it with me," Genelis responded tightly before ending the conversation. Picking up the telephone receiver again, he placed a call.

"Simms, I need your assistance."

CHAPTER 20

THE WARNING

Standing inside the Essences of Nature workshop, Samantha watched the specks of golden essences of light merge with a potted lavender plant. They moved along its green stems and into the head of the purple blossoms. When they emerged from the plant, the once bright golden essences were now a rich mixture of green and pale violet.

"Watch what happens next." Rhiannon directed Samantha's attention to the essences as they dispensed a liquid substance into the clay basin attached to the floor, filling the room with the fresh scent of lavender. "In these small quantities, this potent liquid can be added to oils, lotions, and soaps. Later this week, I'll show you how teas are made."

Samantha couldn't take her eyes off the little essences of light as they repeated the steps of moving among the lavender plants and depositing their precious liquid into the basin. At the end of each task, the essences always returned to their original gold color. "Fascinating. Are they fairies?" she asked.

"No. What people call fairies have definite form. What you're seeing are pure elemental essences that can morph into any form they choose just by merging with another energy pattern, as they are doing with these lavender plants."

"I see," said Samantha.

"That was your dad on the phone," Anna said, coming into the workshop. "He and Zen are on their way back to Vermont."

"If you want, I'll close up, and you two can head home," Rhiannon said.

"Thanks, but Craig said they won't arrive until very late this evening. You go home, Rhiannon. Samantha and I can close up."

Oh good! Samantha thought. *Now I can tell Zen all about meeting Chief Bevin yesterday when he gets here.*

Samantha spent the rest of the afternoon putting together specialty baskets of scented bath products, tea assortments, and candle sets. She even got a chance to work at the cash register when her mom was busy helping customers.

"We did a nice day's work," Anna said, flipping the sign on the door from Open to Closed. "Can you take care of the front area while I sweep up in the back?"

"Sure, I can do that." As Samantha strolled around, switching off lights and straightening up shelves, she could hear the water bubbling over the rocks from inside the Essences of Nature workshop. The sound gave the shop a tranquil feeling that matched the quiet that settled along Maple Street.

Then the sudden ringing of the phone disturbed the peacefulness. Samantha picked it up. "Hello, Essences. This is Samantha. How can I help you?"

"Stop digging into the past," a deep, whispery voice said.

An explosion of wind pushed at the flower shop's door, rattling its hinges.

"Can I ... Can I help you?" she said again.

"You're drawing too much attention to your family—something Professor Fairland and her daughter wouldn't have wanted."

Stunned by the words, Samantha tried to quickly think of what to say. Deciding that maybe denial was the best way to handle it, she said, "I'm sorry. I don't think I know what you're talking about."

"Yes, you do!" the caller retorted. "Now, stop your line of questioning. This is not a game."

After a few seconds, Samantha heard dead air on the line and knew the caller had disconnected. But she stood rooted in her spot, gripping the phone with both hands and holding it tightly to her ear.

"Who was on the phone?" Anna asked.

"What?"

"The phone, Samantha. Who called?"

"Oh, I didn't catch who it was. We got cut off."

"I hate when that happens. Well, if it's someone we know, they'll call us at home. Come on. Let's go."

Samantha hoped that whoever it was would not try to reach them at home.

As they stood outside on the sidewalk and her mom searched through her keys for the one that would lock up the shop, Samantha examined every male who passed them. None of them made eye contact with her. But if one had, she wondered if she would know just by looking at him that he was the one who'd called.

"I need to stop by the grocery store on the way home," Anna said, finally finding the correct key. "I have to pick up goof food. You know what goof food is?"

How did he know to call me here, and what did he mean? Samantha pondered while shaking her head at her mom's question. *Maybe it's the guy who called Grandpa Innis!* This thought frightened her more than a bit.

"It's snack food that you and Zen can eat while you're up all night goofing off," Anna said with a laugh. "Your Aunt Sam and I had a goof food stash when we stayed with Aunt Mayra. Boy, did we eat."

As they walked to their car, Samantha remembered that she still had Chief Bevin's business card in her coat pocket. *He'll want to know all about this*, she thought.

"I was thinking of making spaghetti with garlic bread," Anna rattled on. "Yeah, that's a good choice. I can stick it in the fridge if your dad and Zen arrive after dinner. Spaghetti always tastes good the next day. So, are you getting in, or did you forget something?"

Wheels pounded the concrete pavement, startling Samantha from behind as a group of skateboarders whizzed by. She realized she had her hand on the car door but was looking off in the direction of the police station.

"No—I mean, yeah, I'm getting in," she said. Sneaking a quick glance at Chief Bevin's business card, she saw he had a cell phone number and thought, *I'll find a way to call him as soon as I get home.* The car pulled away from the curb, putting distance between her and the phone call. *Obviously, the person who the police decided boarded a plane twenty-five years ago has returned to the village. Or never left.*

Beside Essences Flower Shop, a powerfully built man stepped forth and stood beneath a lamppost, where light shined down upon his salt-and-pepper hair. After pressing one button on his cell phone, he said, "Message delivered," to the person on the other end. Returning his phone to his breast pocket, he walked back through the alley.

CHAPTER 21

ALL SAFE ON THE HOME FRONT

Sitting at the kitchen table, Samantha peeled garlic for her mom's spaghetti sauce. In her own home, she felt safe—safe enough to decide that she wouldn't call Chief Bevin this evening. She would wait to drag Zen with her to the police department in the morning. Together, they would tell Chief Bevin about the phone call.

"Are you sure I can't convince you to stay for dinner?" Anna asked Bess, who had just finished rolling minced meat into meatballs.

"Oh, no. This is Craig and Zen's first night home. I'm sure there are things you want to ... you know, discuss with Craig." Samantha caught the sly little wink Bess gave her mom and wondered if it had something to do with them all going missing the other night.

Dinner was quiet. Samantha was happy for that because inside her head were noisy voices. There was the voice of Chief Bevin detailing the facts of Ameara and Nanna's murder case. Then there was the voice of the caller, warning her to "Stop digging into the past." Glancing across the table at her mom, Samantha could see she was mulling things over in her head too. Occasionally, her mom would look in her direction, smile, and then stare off into the empty space between them. *Yep, Mom has something on her mind.*

"Samantha?" Anna said.

"Hmm?"

"Are you done with your dinner?"

"Uh-huh."

"Me too. Let's go in the living room. I have something I need to share with you."

This sounds serious, Samantha thought. Then she said, "Okay."

As they sat across from each other on the sofa, Anna reached for Samantha's hands and gave them a gentle squeeze before softly saying, "We've seen and learned a lot these last couple of days, haven't we?"

"Yeah." *You have no idea, Mom, the things I've learned.*

"Yes, a lot of things," Anna repeated, her voice drifting off to just above a whisper. She gazed around the room as if she were taking in her surroundings for the first time. Then she made eye contact with Samantha again and apologized. "Sorry. I'm acting a little strange, aren't I? I'm just trying to figure out the best way to tell you. You see, my family has been keeping a secret … a secret I've just been made aware of."

Kitchet must've told her! Oh, thank God. Now I can confess what I've been up to. But wait. She doesn't seem all that upset about it. Maybe she's just relieved to know the truth of her mom's and grandma's deaths.

"I'm sorry I didn't tell you about it earlier, but I needed to discuss it with your Aunt Sam, and she spoke with Zen about it before he left.

Here it comes. "Okay, I understand."

"Samantha, you know Muaura's book? The one we found the other day? Well, it turns out there's something hidden in our family's ancestry."

Whaaat? I wasn't expecting that! Samantha thought. Then she said, "There is a secret in our family tree? What?"

"We can trace our roots back further than most families can."

"Further than Confucius's family tree?"

"Let's just say we go so far back that if Immigration and Nationalization knew where our family originated, they would have to rethink their definition of *illegal alien*." Then, as fast as she could, Anna blurted out, "Samantha, our family's origins trace back to another planet before our ancestors came to live on this Earth."

"Our ancestors are from another planet?"

"It's not only our family. The entire human race came to Earth from other planets. I know it all must sound crazy, but there are other records besides Muaura's book that detail Earth's history. And it's not the information that's in our history books."

Talking trees, light essences ... Samantha wasn't completely shocked by this revelation. "How can stuff like this be kept hidden ... and for so long?" she asked. "And why keep it hidden? Isn't this the missing link that everyone's been looking for?"

"I don't know. What I do know is why our family has not shared this information. They're protecting the place the Kitchets took me to the other night. This place is where those other records are being kept."

"Does this place have anything to do with the hole in Bess's pantry floor?"

"How did you know?" Anna asked.

"Remember? I went looking for you over at the Kitchets' house, and that's when I found it. Where does it lead to?"

"It's a passageway that links to different areas. We have one here in our house. That's how I ended up in our kitchen the other night. I came through the passageway," Anna confessed. "Now, here's what's amazing. This passageway leads into the world of the core people—the very core people that Sam writes about in her children's stories!"

"You're kidding! Right here on our property?" Samantha exclaimed.

"It's just like from my mother's stories—a whole civilization living right beneath our feet!"

"What are they like? Are they human?"

"If you met them above ground, you wouldn't be able to tell them apart from anyone else," Anna said.

"What are they doing down there? Wait a minute. How can there be people living in the Earth? From all I've read, the inner core is as hot as the sun's surface."

"For the short time I visited, from what I could tell, they are just ... living as we are living up here. Kitchet told me that at one time, everyone on Earth had access to the inner core. But not anymore. Only a very few are able to gain entrance into their world. Oh, and it's not hot down there. It's quite pleasant, like springtime."

"Is the entrance only on our property?" Samantha asked.

"No. I asked the same question. Addiwan said there are entry points at certain locations across the Earth that lead into other communities. But they're kept secret."

"Well, that's it! All fairy tales and science fiction books should be placed in the history sections at our public libraries and taught in schools as facts because, clearly, that's where our real history can be found."

"Bess told me the other night that my mother had just begun sharing this information with Sam and me before she died," Anna said. "Now it seems that we're all going to get a crash course in Human/Earth History 101."

As if someone had thrown a switch in her brain, Samantha thought of something. "Mom, are you sure no one else knows this information besides our family?

"Yeah. Well, of course the Kitchets, Addiwan, and Rhiannon already know,"

"Um, would you say this information is something that someone would want to hurt or even kill for? I mean, this may be another reason behind all this secrecy, right?"

"I don't even want to entertain that thought. Why do you ask?"

Then a voice came from the front door.

"Oi, where are my lovely ladies!"

"Dad!" Getting up and hurrying to the front door, Samantha threw her arms around him. Her face buried in his chest, she hid from those around her what she knew was unmistakable. *Grandma Ameara and Great-Grandma Nanna were murdered because of our family's secret!*

"Hey, isn't anyone gonna help me with all this stuff?" asked Zen. Holding his surfboard, he had become stuck in the doorway.

"Zen, why on earth would you bring a surfboard? Where are you going to find a place to surf?" Anna asked, unwedging him from the doorframe.

"I'm sure the East Coast dudes are surfing somewhere," Craig said. "Don't worry. I will find a place for him this summer."

"Hey, bookworm." Zen waved in front of Samantha's face, but she was a million miles away in her own thoughts.

"I have new stuff to tell you," she whispered.

"I already know. Mom filled me in before making me sign a blood oath of secrecy."

"No, something else—"

"Are you guys hungry? I still have spaghetti out," Anna said.

"I'm starving," answered Zen. "I haven't eaten since leaving home."

"I guess that sandwich I brought you on the layover doesn't count!" Craig yelled after Zen, who raced for the kitchen. Removing his coat, Craig then looked at Anna with raised eyebrows. "So, I understand from your sister and Zen that there are some big developments you need to discuss with me."

"To say the least. Come on into the kitchen. I'll tell you all about it over a big bowl of spaghetti." Anna gave Samantha the same sly wink Bess had given her earlier.

Standing alone in the foyer, Samantha pounded her fist into her hand, speaking to herself in a hushed tone. "That's it. That's got to be it. *It's unmistakable!* I now know the *why* behind Ameara's and Nanna's deaths."

"This has to be the reason because, according to Chief Bevin, the police have ruled out robbery and all other logical explanations. Our grandma and great-grandma were murdered because of what they knew and what they had access to."

They were both in Samantha's room, sitting on her bed, stuffing their faces with goof food, and discussing the new details surrounding their murder investigation.

"I get what you're saying," Zen said. "But who'd know our family had access to this stuff?"

"There are at least two people who'd know—Mr. Lin and Maskhim, whoever Maskhim is. I haven't figured that one out. But remember, Grandma Ameara asked this very question in her diary. Read it again for yourself." Samantha tapped the open diary on Zen's lap. "'Mr. Lin, Maskhim. What does he know?' It all adds up."

Opening his mouth wide, Zen shoved in more potato chips. "Let me see … if I have … this straight," he said, talking with his mouth full. "Grandma and Great-Grandma were murdered for the information concerning the passageway into the world of the core people."

"And the library of records of Earth's history," Samantha added. "Remember that it's important."

"Of course," Zen continued. "So, Mr. Lin and maybe this Maskhim knew they had this information. Mr. Lin and Maskhim didn't get the information they wanted, so they killed them. Do I have that right?"

"Yeah."

"Okay. So, who is this guy who called you tonight at the flower shop?"

"Who do you think? It has to be the killer. Mr. Lin, of course."

"Ya think? After all these years, he's calling to tell you to stop digging into the past? That you're drawing too much attention to your family?"

"Yeah. Why not? Who do you think it is?" Samantha asked.

"I don't know. I just think if it were the killer, he would've said something more threatening. This guy just sounds like he was giving you a warning to be careful."

Samantha had to agree. It did sound more like a warning. "Who would know that I was searching around about the murder? It would have to be someone familiar with the case and our family."

"How about this librarian, Ms. Emily?" he asked. "She could've said something to the wrong person. Or Chief Bevin. You did say the man's voice was too low to identify. Maybe he's just trying to scare you into leaving the case alone. Perhaps he's bitter. He never got a chance to solve the big murder case, and here you come along, dragging it back out into the open again."

"Or maybe it's the person who called Grandpa Innis before he died," Samantha said, tossing another possibility into the pile.

"True. Whoever it is knows you've been digging around for the past few days—someone here in the village," Zen reminded her.

Samantha gathered up the copy of *The Hearthshire Ledger*, her grandma's diary, and her book of notes, then placed them all back into her nightstand. "Look, Zen. We've accomplished what we set out to do, which was discover the truth of how our grandma and great-grandma died. We've done this. That's enough. Now is the time to share this information with our moms, as we agreed."

The truth was that Samantha's head was reeling, and she was starting to agree with what the man told her on the phone that evening. She should stop digging. She'd obviously drawn attention to her family, and this was not good —especially knowing what she now knew concerning her family's history and the secret of what was hidden on their property. Ameara and Nanna Fairland would not want this information getting out. Samantha had a feeling they'd given their lives to protect it.

"I agree. It's not our job to solve the murder. Hey, the police couldn't even solve it, and they've had twenty-five years," Zen said. "My parents will be here in two days. Let's tell them then."

"You think we should tell Kitchet first since it was his conversation we overheard that started this all?"

"I do. He needs to know that there's someone out there who may have killed for the Fairlands' well-kept secret," answered Zen, flopping down on the floor next to Gypsy. He curled up with the sleeping dog, rubbing his nose in her wiry fur. "Well, Nancy Drew, you've solved your first case, and all in less than a week. How does it feel?"

"Strangely, not as good as I thought. I don't know. I guess it feels unfinished because we don't have all the answers."

"Look, life isn't a storybook, where all is known and solved neatly in the end. That's why I don't read those things. It gives people a false hope of how their life should be."

"I know. I just can't help but feel a little let down," Samantha admitted. "But hey, look at the exciting news we did find out. Hidden passageways into another world right on our property. And we found out that humans came from out there, in space! Come on, you have to admit that our life would make one heck of a great fantasy novel."

"I would trade all that information to discover hidden treasures on this property. Or at least learn that the marvelous, miraculous, and magical adventure Grandpa promised us meant learning we had some sort of magical powers."

"Well, how about the talking trees? That's magical. Wait till you see the essences in the flower shop. They do the most magical things with the plants."

"Yeah, yeah. Speaking of the talking tree, where's that one that talks to you at night?"

"It's Terrance, and he usually knocks at the window. But I'm sure we can call out to him. Pushing open her window, Samantha asked, "Terrance, are you awake?"

"Well, of course I am awake. Are you ready for a story?"

"Yes, please, Terrance. Terrance, I'd like you to meet my cousin Zen. He's going to be staying with us for a while."

Zen sat in the window seat with his legs tucked behind him, staring directly out the window and not saying a word.

Samantha reached over and shook him by the shoulder. "Zen, can you hear Terrance?"

"How's it doing that?" Zen jumped up on his knees and shoved his head out the window.

"Careful, young man. You almost snapped one of my limbs off," Terrance said. "It's still rather cold out here, and my branches are brittle."

Zen sat quickly back on his knees, "Sorry."

"It's so nice to meet you, Zen," Terrance said, sticking a limb inside the window.

Zen reached out and touched Terrance's branch gently this time, then quickly pulled back. "That's the same spark I got when I touched one of those large trees in our driveway."

"Oh, I am sorry. Sometimes, we forget to lower the intensity of our vibrations," Terrance explained. "Did I harm you?"

"No. It's just so unbelievable, so strange, so—"

"So marvelous, miraculous, or maybe just plain magical," Samantha said, finishing Zen's sentence.

"I feel a story is in order. It will help soothe everyone's energies," Terrance said. "I was telling Samantha the story of Veil Essence the other night, Zen. Let me catch you up on it. It will help you understand your new home. Make yourself comfortable. If you fall asleep, I will finish the story the next night."

Zen stretched out in the window seat with Gypsy by his side while Samantha lay in her own bed. Terrance began his story of how the trees gave shelter to the humans who wandered into Veil Essence—the Fairland family being among some of the first. How he, Terrance, was appointed the storyteller to the human children.

As she watched Zen drift off, Samantha recalled reading that people absorbed more knowledge while they slept. She felt this had to be true because she remembered the details of Terrance's story even though she had fallen asleep. Closing her eyes, she told herself the story in her head while Terrance continued to talk.

The humans were few in number at first when they arrived in Veil Essence. They had been wandering for days. Most were in shock and, like many of Terrance's tree kin, had lost their families to the fire and floods. The tree folk guided the humans to descend underground, where they would be able to find food and shelter. The Fairlands were some of the few humans who stayed in Veil Essence, and this was how a strong bond was created between the Fairland family and the tree folk of this land.

Terrance stopped talking. Looking over at the window, Samantha saw him reach a limb inside and close the window. This was when Samantha turned over in bed to join Zen in slumber.

CHAPTER 22

A STRANGER COMES KNOCKING

Through sleep-laden eyes, Samantha checked for the time and found a note propped up against her clock:

Dad and I are at Essences, but he'll be home later to check on you. I've left food on the stove. If you need anything before he gets back, go over to the Kitchets' house.

Mom

Zen uncurled himself in the window seat. "What time is it?"

"It's 9:45." Samantha pulled the covers back up over her head. She intended to sleep in. She needed it. After coming to the decision the night before to tell her mom all she'd been up to, her mind and body had completely let go. Gone was the anxiety of having to sneak around and hide things. Samantha vowed to herself that she'd never keep another

162

secret from her mom, ever again. *Detective work is exhausting*, she thought.

"Did I really hear that tree talking last night, or was I just dreaming?" Zen asked.

She peeked out with one eye to observe her cousin. He looked bright, eager, and ready to go this morning. Just the opposite of what she was feeling. "His name is Terrance, and yeah, he told you a story."

"Oh yeah, Veil Essence. Is that stuff true?"

"Yeah. Remember? I told you over the phone. The village of Hearthshire used to be called Veil Essence."

Zen opened the window and did exactly what she had done the morning after Terrance spoke to her. "Hellooo," he called out, too chipper for Samantha's taste. "Can you hear me … uh, Terrance?"

"He sleeps during the day." Samantha's voice sounded muffled from under her blanket cocoon.

"Open heart …" Zen yawned loudly, stretching his hands above his head. "Open mind."

"What's that?"

"Grandpa's clues. He said that first, you must have an open heart and an open mind. Having these two things will help us find the marvelous, miraculous, and magical people, places, and things. Or something like that. I heard Terrance last night, so my heart and mind must be open."

"Oh."

Zen continued quoting from Grandpa Innis's letter. "Second, be daring. Well, I'm always daring. That second clue, though. Grandpa definitely wrote that one for you."

"Yeah, right. You're the brave and daring one."

"Third, some marvels we'll need help in finding. I would say Grandpa was talking about the core people and their hidden world. Without the Kitchets and Addiwan, none of us would be able to find them."

"True," she said. *Geesh, he's just a beacon of knowledge this morning.*

"What are you doing? Get up!" Zen surprised Samantha by leaping onto her bed. "Let's go see what your mom's cooking for breakfast." He pulled the covers off her head.

"Stop!" Samantha was not in the mood for his high jinks. "Anyway, Mom and Dad aren't home. They went into the village. There's food on the stove."

"Perfect. After we eat, we can go talk to Kitchet. Now get up!" He dragged the blanket off the bed_and almost Samantha, too, as she tried to hold onto it.

"Hey!" She tossed her pillow at his head. "Leave me—"

Thump, thump, thump. It was the sound of the front door's brass knocker.

Standing poised to hurl her pillow back at her, Zen asked, "Who can that be?"

"Probably Bess or Kitchet. You were making too much noise. But wait. They never knock."

Thump, thump, thump.

"I'll go see who it is." Zen flung the pillow at Samantha's head, which she dodged, then ran into the hall.

Slipping on a robe, she was about to join him downstairs when he came thundering back in.

"It's him!" he exclaimed.

"Him who?"

"The guy from the funeral!"

"I told you he didn't get a chance to talk to our moms!"

"Oh yeah, right. Two weeks later, he thinks to himself, 'Oh, I never paid my respects. Let me pop around now,'" Zen said.

Thump, thump, thump. The persistent knock came again.

"It hasn't been two weeks. Let's just ask him ˅
wants," Samantha said as she brushed past him and
down the stairs.

"Wait" said Zen, following close behind her. "˅
Gypsy?"

"Mom lets her out in the morning."

"Well, we're not opening the door!" Zen whisp
he hurried down ahead of her.

"Gotcha, Mr. Brave and Daring."

From behind the heavy wooden front door, Zen a
his best deep man's voice, "How can I help you?"

"I am looking for Anna."

Samantha noted the stranger's pronounced
accent. And while Zen conversed with him, she tipto
to the living room window to sneak a quick glance at

He was dressed just as she remembered fro
funeral: jeans and a pair of well-worn shoes. He h
coat together with ungloved hands that, to her,
appear warm enough for Vermont's cold February m
A wool earflap hat covered his head, and he still carr
backpack slung over one shoulder.

"She's not available," answered Zen. "What'
name, and what do you want with her? I'll tell h
stopped by."

"I am family ... friend. Is Anna at the flower shop?

Samantha looked over at Zen and shook her
feeling they shouldn't give out too much information.

"I'm not sure," her cousin told the man. "But, like
if you leave your name, I'll tell her you're looking for h

The man was quiet and didn't answer Zen's que
So, he asked again. "I said, who are you, and what ˅
want with my Aunt Anna?"

"Don't worry. I will go see Anna at the shop."

"Wait!" Zen yelled. "Who should I say came by?"

"Lin. Peter Lin."

Samantha pressed her hands over her mouth to keep from screaming. She jumped back from the window just as Mr. Lin turned and walked away.

"Zen! That's him. That's Mr. Lin." She could hardly contain herself. She swiftly walked from the living room to the front door and back to the living room again, shaking her hands and trying to think of what to do next.

"Something's wrong. It doesn't seem right," Zen calmly said. Then, to Samantha's horror, he swung the door open wide and called out, "Mr. Li—"

She shoved him to the side and quickly shut the door. "What, are you crazy?" She ran back to the window to see if Mr. Lin heard him. He was nowhere in sight. *Thank goodness*, she thought.

"Samantha, we need to think for a moment."

"We need to call the police!" she yelled, racing upstairs to look for Chief Bevin's card, with Zen following her. "What's wrong with you? First, you tell me I think too much. Now you wanna waste time thinking?"

"Just ask yourself this. Why would a known killer come knocking at our door and tell us his real name?"

"Because he's a murderer. He strangles people. He's crazy in the head!" she answered while pulling open drawers. "You're the one who said he looked suspicious. Remember the day of the funeral?"

"Yeah, but now I feel something's off."

"Yeah, he's off." Then she exclaimed, "It's in my coat pocket!" and raced back downstairs, Zen still keeping up with her.

"What's in your coat pocket? What are you looking for?" he asked.

"Chief Bevin gave me his business card with both his cell and the station's number," Samantha said, digging inside her pocket and showing the card to Zen. "He said to call him if I needed anything. Well, I need him now!" She reached for the phone.

"Wait." Zen placed his hand over the receiver. "What are you going to say to him?"

"I'm going to inform him that Peter Lin just came knocking at our door. I'm going to tell Chief Bevin that the person who murdered our grandma and great-grandma is now looking for my mom!"

"I'm getting dressed," Zen said. "Don't go anywhere without me."

As Samantha stood there with the phone to her ear, it felt like an eternity passed between each ring. "Please pick up," she muttered.

"This is Police Chief Michael Bevin. Leave a message. Or, if this is an emergency situation, call 911."

With a huff, she hung up and dialed the number on the card for the police station.

"Hearthshire Police Department. How can we help you?" a woman's voice answered.

"Can I speak with Chief Bevin?"

"Hold, please."

As she waited, Zen came back carrying his sneakers. "What's happening? What did Chief Bevin say?"

"I'm waiting. He didn't answer his cell, so I— Yes, I'm here," Samantha said to the woman on the other end of the phone line.

"Chief Bevin has stepped away from his desk," the woman informed her. "Would you like his voicemail? Or can someone else assist you?

"No." Samantha hung up and started dialing again.

"Who are you calling now?" Zen asked.

"I'm trying his cell phone again."

"While you waste your time with that, I'm going over to get Kitchet. He'll know what to do."

"Wait! Don't go out there— Darn! His voicemail again." She slammed down the receiver. "Mr. Lin may still be out there."

Paying her no heed, Zen flung the door open. "Look, he's gone. I'll be back."

Locking the door behind him, she stood with her back pressed up against it. The house fell silent—too silent. She raced to the window, checking to see if Zen made it safely inside the Kitchets' home. She didn't see him. *He must be inside already.* She sat on the edge of the window seat and waited for him to return. Somewhere in the house, a clock ticked loudly, but it was not as loud as the voice in her head.

Mr. Lin is going to the flower shop. He's going to kill Mom. He's going to strangle her with his bare hands, and it will be all my fault! All my digging around, playing girl detective. I brought that killer right to our doorstep! She clenched her eyes shut. She couldn't stand to hear her own thoughts in her head.

Glancing out the window, she searched for Zen. *Why is he taking so long?* Her body was buzzing, and she felt like she was going to jump out of her skin. *Why am I just sitting here? I've got to do something. I've got to save Mom!*

She ran up to her room, threw on a pair of jeans and a sweater, grabbed her sneakers, then raced down the hall. When she was halfway down the steps, someone knocked at the door. She held her breath.

"It's us, Samantha. Open the door."

Recognizing Kitchet's voice, she allowed herself to

breathe again. As she unbolted the door, the small man stormed in, followed by Bess, Zen, and Gypsy.

"I told them everything," Zen said.

"Have you called your mom at the shop?" Kitchet asked, rushing toward the phone.

"No, I didn't think of that." Samantha's voice cracked. Tears ran down her cheeks. "I don't even know the shop's number!"

Bess grabbed Samantha into her arms. "Hush, child. Your mom is with your father. He won't let any harm come to her."

Kitchet was already on the phone. "Anna, has a Mr. Lin come by this morning?" He stood with one hand balled into a fist planted firmly on his hip. "Is Craig still with you? Close up shop and don't let anyone in. I will explain when I get there."

"What happened? Did Mr. Peter Lin come in?" Samantha and Zen asked at the same time.

"Calm down. Your mom said no one by that name came in, and your dad is there with her."

"Right. Let's go," Zen said as he and Samantha headed for the door.

"You two will do no such thing," Kitchet said, stopping both of them in their tracks. "You will stay right here with Bess. I'll go with Addiwan."

"Take the passageway," Bess said. "It'll be quicker."

"But—" Samantha started to protest.

"Gypsy, guard," Kitchet said. The dog stood up straight at his command.

After Kitchet left, Bess turned to Samantha and Zen and wagged her finger. Samantha knew she was about to deliver a scolding when the phone rang. Both she and Zen dived for the phone, with Samantha reaching it first.

"Hello," she said, breathless.

"This is Police Chief Bevin. I received two missed calls from this number."

"Chief Bevin! It's Samantha! Mr. Lin came by the house this morning. He's looking for my mom," she explained as Zen and Bess hovered close to her, hanging on her every word.

"Are you sure it was Peter Lin?" Chief Bevin sounded shocked by the news.

"Yes. And he said he was going to Essences Flower Shop to find her."

"I'm heading over."

"Yes, I understand. Stay away from the shop." Samantha continued talking into the receiver, even though she knew Chief Bevin was no longer on the line. "Got it." Hanging up the phone, she turned to Bess. "Chief Bevin said he's taking a police team over to the flower shop. You may want to warn Kitchet before he leaves."

"Oh, you're right. If he pops up from underneath the floor, they may shoot at him! Lock this door until I get back."

The minute Bess was gone, Samantha turned to Zen. "Get your coat. We can go out the kitchen door."

"What? Chief Bevin said to stay away from the shop."

"You do what you want. I'm going into the village," she replied.

But Gypsy ran past her, placing her large body between Samantha and the kitchen door.

"Now what?" Zen asked.

Samantha ran back into the living room, hoping the dog would follow her. But Gypsy didn't move. The dog stood her ground, eyeing Zen, who was still in the kitchen.

"Zen, run out the front door, then shut it behind you. I will meet you on the path. Hurry."

Zen broke into a run across the living room with Gypsy chasing after him. Samantha darted back into the kitchen, confusing the large dog, which allowed them to make their escape. Samantha ran as fast as she could down the driveway, with Zen coming up behind her.

"Wait!" he called out. "Listen. Don't you hear it?"

"What?"

He pointed to the massive trees that lined the drive. "Can't you hear them? They're trying to warn us about something."

It was hard to hear at first over her heart beating in her ears, but he was right. A collection of voices, both male and female, reverberated along the path. "Stay away from the barrier," the voices said as one.

"You hear it now?" he asked.

"Yes."

But it didn't matter what the voices were trying to tell them because Samantha kept on running. When she reached the end of the driveway, she encountered a haze of swirling green and white light particles. The particles were like a wall, clearly marking the division where the Fairland property ended and the road leading into the village began. There was no way around it. But, without hesitation, she ran right into the haze, immediately feeling pressure pushing against her body like hundreds of hands trying to force her out. Determined, she thrust herself forward, emerging on the other side. Looking back, she didn't see Zen, and the haze of swirling particles was gone. *What happened to him?* she wondered. Just as this thought crossed her mind, he plunged out as if coming through a hidden door.

"I don't think we should've done that," he said.

"Don't worry about it. Come on," she urged, quickly turning to see a familiar face off to the side of the road near a parked car. "Look! It's Ms. Emily. Maybe she'll give us a ride."

Smiling happily, Ms. Emily beckoned, and Samantha ran toward her. "Ms. Emily, can you give us a ride to my mom's shop?"

"Hey, get off me!" It was the voice of a distraught Zen. Spinning, Samantha caught a glimpse of him tussling with a man before a hard, cold surface collided with the side of her face and sent her spiraling into darkness.

CHAPTER 23

WHAT WAS AT THE ROOT IS NOW EXPOSED

Thump, thump.

The dull sound of knocking roused Samantha from her unplanned slumber. *Who's at the door now?* she wondered.

She was trying to slip back into the peaceful darkness of sleep when she realized she was not at home. Instead, she was in the back seat of a moving car, propped up on her side with her face tilted toward the window.

Where am I going? She leaned slightly forward. *Ouch, my face!* The left side of her face hurt terribly. Then she remembered being hit, hard, after seeing Zen— *Zen, where's Zen?* Looking to her right, she found her cousin slumped over in the corner on the seat next to her.

Zen's head bobbed lightly against the car's leather upholstery. A purplish bruise marred his left eye, and his lower lip was busted with traces of blood on the open wound.

Fighting back the urge to cry, Samantha turned her attention toward the front seat, looking for those responsible for her cousin's pitiful condition. To her dismay, she saw Ms. Emily sitting in the passenger seat.

They've taken her too!

Then, to add more confusion to her already confused state, Samantha saw the librarian glance over at the driver and smile adoringly. *What's going on?* Samantha wondered. Dark-brown hair and broad shoulders were all she could make out as she looked at the driver. *Who is he?*

It was time to wake Zen and alert him to their predicament. Taking hold of his knee, she gently shook him. He didn't respond. His eyes didn't even flutter. After a second attempt to rouse him with no response, she became worried. Placing two fingers to the side of Zen's neck, as her dad had once taught her to do, Samantha checked for a pulse. He had one. *He must be unconscious*, she thought.

Thump, thump.

Now that she was fully aware of her surroundings, Samantha could tell that the knocking was coming from inside the car's trunk.

"Kenneth, sweetheart. I thought you said you tied him up."

She barely recognized the sickly-sweet tone in Ms. Emily's voice.

"I did, but it won't keep him from kicking around back there. What else could I do?" The male driver sounded like a young boy pleading with his mother not to be upset with him.

Ms. Emily and this man stuffed someone in the trunk!

"Do you think this is a good idea, Mother? I mean, bringing them back here. This may force the police to reexamine the other cases."

"It's called poetic justice, dear," Ms. Emily callously replied. "The little snoop wanted to find out what happened to her self-righteous family members, right? We're simply obliging her and giving her just what she asked for."

"Are you sure *they* approve of what we're doing? You know that the Sentinels dislike headlines and scandal."

"Positive. I've already warned them of her meddling. We simply need to take care of this last little mess."

"Haven't I done enough for them?" the driver asked. "You would think after all this time, they would see fit to—"

"Kenneth, did I ever tell you that I attended the ceremony the day the Sentinels made your father a part of their inner circle?"

"Yes, Mother, you have."

"When I contacted the Sentinels earlier this week, I could tell they were ready to offer you your father's old post. You will soon be known as Kenneth Randall, director of historical genealogy for the powerful Sentinels organization. We are so close to returning our family to their rightful place among society. And you know the Sentinels are the only ones who can make this happen."

Could this be graduate student Kenneth Randall, who found Great-Grandma Nanna in her office? Samantha wondered. *He's Ms. Emily's son!*

"Let me go!" Zen said, thrashing his arms wildly.

"Good. You're both up," Ms. Emily said, glaring into the back seat. "It will save my son from having to carry you."

"What's going on?" Zen asked, rubbing the back of his neck and touching his lip. "Who are these people?" His speech sounded odd through his swollen lips.

"Zen, it's Kenneth Randall," Samantha said, leaning in closer to him. "You know, the man we read about in the paper? He's Ms. Emily's son."

"What? Who's Ms. Emily?" Zen asked.

Samantha could see he was still confused, so she tried again. "Zen, they have someone in their trunk. I heard them kicking around in there. I think Ms. Emily and her son had something to do with Ameara's and Nanna's deaths!"

"I knew you were a clever girl, Samantha, from the day I met you. Then again, you are the high-and-mighty Nanna Fairland's great-granddaughter," Ms. Emily said.

Samantha tried fitting the pieces together. *What's she talking about? Why would Ms. Emily be involved with something as awful as ... murder? Who are these Sentinels?* "I don't understand," she said. "What did my great-grandma ever do that would make you hate her and want to ... hurt her?"

Ms. Emily turned completely around to face the back seat. She looked Samantha directly in the eyes. "What did my great-grandma do?" she said in a little girl's voice, mocking Samantha. "No, you have it all wrong. It's what she refused to do. So, get that straight in your head. Nanna Fairland did nothing for Kenneth."

"What ... But I still don't understand. What was she supposed to do for Kenneth?" Samantha asked.

"Tell the truth! Morally, self-righteous Professor Nanna Fairland was supposed to tell the truth!" Ms. Emily screamed at the top of her lungs.

Then, just as quickly as the old librarian had lost all self-control, she composed herself. Touching her hand to her chest, she took in deep, long gulps of air. Ms. Emily's eyes took on an unexpected tenderness as she reached a finger out to touch Samantha's cheek, causing Samantha to recoil.

"I've met your mother, Samantha. She seems like the sort to teach you that when someone asks you a direct question, you must answer honestly. Is that correct,

Samantha? Your mother teaches you to be truthful?" Ms. Emily asked in her now calm voice.

"Yes ..." Samantha hesitantly answered. She wasn't sure where this was leading.

"Well, thank goodness Kenneth saw fit to kill Nanna and Ameara before they could pass their lying ways on to your mother because they were both LIARS!"

Samantha flinched at hearing Ms. Emily's demented words and grabbed hold of Zen's hand.

"Your great-grandmother was in possession of crucial data important to the Sentinels, and Kenneth knew it. Data that my dear late husband spent a lifetime researching. I personally feel Nanna stole my husband's research records from the university. If she had done the right thing and handed that data over to the Sentinels, it would have solidified my son's position with them and maybe saved her own life." By the time Ms. Emily was done talking, her face was as red as a beetroot.

"Well, if your son already knew this stuff, why didn't he just give it to these Sentinels himself?" Zen piped up, now fully with the program.

"I didn't have the precise coordinates for the location the Sentinels were searching for. My father never discovered it. However, your great-grandmother did," Kenneth said, his dark eyes peering at them through the rearview mirror.

"But how do you know she did?" Samantha asked.

"I did several research projects under Professor Fairland, so I had access to her field notes. That's how I came across her data for an area in West Africa that looked very similar to my father's findings, with one exception. Professor Fairland had mapped out an area very close to the place where my father suggested that the Sentinels begin their search. I tried to get more information from her about this area. She brushed me off, telling me it wasn't research for the university. That it was data for her next book. Essentially, she told me nothing, and she was careful that I never saw that data again. This was when I knew I needed to tell the Sentinels about her and let them handle the situation."

Kenneth made a hard left turn, causing Samantha and Zen to roll into each other and jostling around whoever was in the trunk. Righting herself, Samantha saw a sign that read, "Eastern Vermont University."

"I stood outside Professor Fairland's office that morning and listened as she discredited me to the Sentinels representative!" Kenneth spoke his words through gritted teeth. Samantha could tell that the more he spoke, the angrier he became and the more erratically he drove. He seemed to be reliving what had happened that day twenty-five years earlier. She held onto the seat as he steered the car away from the campus buildings and down a back road near the university grounds. She thought that maybe she and Zen could jump out and make a run for it. But looking over at Zen, she wasn't sure he was in any shape to take that leap.

From the front seat, Kenneth went on with his frenzied recounting of events. "At first, I didn't understand why she would lie about even being in West Africa," Kenneth said, pounding his fist on the steering wheel. "I soon had my opportunity to find out why she was lying when the Sentinels representative suddenly left her office and ran down a back stairwell. That's when I entered her office and confronted her."

Kenneth pulled into a secluded area at the edge of the university that led into a heavily wooded area. Samantha looked over at Zen. She could tell by the look in his eyes that they were thinking the same thing—that they were in serious trouble.

Kenneth turned off the car and faced the back seat. His dark-brown eyes were set close together in his soft, doughy face and under a protruding forehead.

"I demanded to know why she wouldn't simply tell the representative what he wanted to know. She looked at me with pity and started lecturing me on the people I was associating with," Kenneth said, laughing now. "She had the audacity to tell me how horrible these people were. She called them 'these people.' Then she called them 'Maskhim.' By her daring to mention this name, I knew she was their enemy and now mine. I dealt with Nanna Fairland and then with Ameara as she tried to escape through the woods as I knew the Sentinels would've wanted them dealt with."

Staring at Kenneth's hand gripping the headrest, Samantha couldn't help but imagine what he'd done to her grandma and great-grandma with that hand. Hearing the click of the glove box, she looked over at Ms. Emily, who was pulling out a gun. The librarian handed it to her son, then they both exited the car.

"Zen, they're going to kill us." Samantha's voice quivered from anger at what Kenneth had confessed to doing. But mostly, her voice was shaking out of fear.

"Not if I can help it," Zen said bravely through swollen lips. His left eye was already sealed shut. "Samantha, look!" he said, pointing out the car's back window.

Kenneth was dragging Mr. Peter Lin from the car's trunk. His hands were tied with a cord behind his back, his coat was torn, and his face was bruised. Samantha knew he must have been exposed to Kenneth's fist.

"You were right, Zen. Mr. Lin had nothing to do with

Grandma's and Great-Grandma's deaths," Samantha said. She watched as Kenneth pushed Mr. Lin onto the car's hood. Ms. Emily, now holding the gun, stepped forward and pressed it against Mr. Lin's back.

"Get out of the car," Kenneth said, opening the door.

"If you let us go now, I'm sure you'll be able to get far enough away before the police find you," Zen said, climbing out of the back seat. "If you kill us, the police will never stop hunting for you. You don't want that for your mother, do you?"

For his answer, Kenneth kicked Zen in his backside, causing him to fall face-first onto the snowy ground. Hurrying to his side, Samantha helped her cousin up. Zen now had dirt mixed in with the blood clinging to his bottom lip.

"I can see you have inherited that nasty Fairland trait of lecturing on things you know nothing about," Kenneth said. "What your family and others have failed to understand is the far-reaching power and influence the Sentinels have. Even if my mother and I are apprehended, we will never see the inside of a jail or courthouse. The Sentinels will cover for me, as they did twenty-five years ago and as they did when I killed Detective Davies with his own gun. See, Detective Davies wouldn't stop snooping either. I had to kill him when he found Professor Fairland's car in our barn."

So, Detective Davies didn't give up on the case as everyone thought he did, Samantha thought sadly. She felt a hard shove to the back as Kenneth indicated that she and Zen had to get moving.

"So do not try and lecture me on what I should do," Kenneth said.

"Kenneth," Ms. Emily said, directing Mr. Lin to stand

between Samantha and Zen. "You walk in front of us. I will guard them from behind."

As they followed Kenneth deeper into the woods, Samantha could sense the trees around her holding their collective breath. There wasn't a breeze, a rustle of leaves, sounds of birds, or any form of nature moving within these woods. Everything was queerly still. In Samantha's mind, there was no doubt that she, Zen, and Mr. Lin were being led to their deaths. And the trees knew it.

Her unbound curls fell into her eyes, briefly shielding her from the nightmare of where she was and what was about to happen. Silently, Mr. Lin and Zen walked beside her. The only sound they made was their feet crunching in the snow. As they marched on, Samantha told herself that if she was going to die, she had to know why. Why, exactly, after twenty-five years. Why, as Kenneth said, he and Ms. Emily were being protected by the Sentinels. And why the three of them were being marched to their deaths now.

"Ms. Emily, if this Sentinel group covered everything up twenty-five years ago, why are you doing this now? According to Chief Bevin, everyone still believes Peter Lin is the murderer. Why did you come out to our house this morning?" Samantha asked.

"Blame yourself, Samantha, for what is about to happen. You kept coming back, digging around for more, asking all sorts of questions about the Maskhim. I had to contact Kenneth," Ms. Emily said in a matter-of-fact manner. "We came to your house this morning to find out exactly what you knew. That's when Kenneth spotted someone leaving your property—someone the Sentinels assured us would never surface again. That was Mr. Lin. And that's when we knew we had to handle this situation ourselves. Again."

A funny little smile crossed Ms. Emily's face as she shared more information with Samantha. "This morning was kismet as everything lined up perfectly for us. After Kenneth took care of Mr. Peter Lin, we started up to your house." She paused, and a frown creased her brow when she added, "But our car engine started acting strange. The engine kept shutting off, and the car would slowly roll back down your driveway. That was odd. No matter. Not too long after, I spotted you and your cousin running out to us. Everything worked out perfectly. It was fate."

Samantha put her head down, not daring to look at Zen's battered face. She had gotten him into this mess. She just wouldn't listen. Thinking this would be the last opportunity to tell him she was sorry, she leaned forward to get his attention. The sun momentarily blinded her as a ray reflected off something glittery bouncing at the center of Mr. Lin's chest. Shading her eyes, Samantha saw hanging from a black leather cord a geode rock pendant that looked curiously like the one she herself wore! Puzzled, she searched Mr. Lin's face for an answer.

"We are family," Mr. Lin said when he saw that Samantha had recognized his pendant.

Understanding dawned on her. This was what Mr. Lin was trying to tell her and Zen earlier. Samantha nodded, indicating that she understood. Tears filled her eyes for the missed opportunities. Great-Grandma Nanna and Grandma Ameara had died not knowing this was what Peter Lin was coming to tell them twenty-five years before—that he was part of their family. Instead, he would forever be blamed as the one who'd killed them, and Samantha had the feeling Peter Lin was being set up once again—this time for the murders of her and Zen. Glancing back at Mr. Lin, she found him oddly smiling at her. He then winked before shouting one word.

"RUN!"

To her surprise, she saw Mr. Lin swiftly whirl and head-butt the old librarian, knocking her to the ground. Then she and Zen took off in different directions, leaving the shouting Ms. Emily swearing to her son.

"You idiot! I'm fine! Go after them."

Samantha was scared. She didn't know which way to go. She just kept running, running deeper into the woods. As she ran, she began to hear voices calling out to her and telling her, "This way! Run this way. Run toward us!" It was the trees giving her directions. She listened to them this time, very carefully.

"He is coming. I hear him. He is coming your way. Crouch down next to me," the whispery female voice of a maple tree told her.

Doing as the maple said, Samantha knelt down, her knee sinking into a patch of snow. She threw her arms around the tall maple's trunk. She closed her eyes and began to tremble.

"Who is it, sister?" Samantha heard the tree next to them ask.

"It is him," the tall maple answered. "The one who brought violence to our wood many springs ago."

A shot was fired, a man groaned, and a woman screamed. The woods screamed, and birds flew out overhead. Samantha panicked. *Zen, it must be Zen. He's shot!* She let go of the tree and started running again.

"No, stay put!" the maple tree cried out to her.

She couldn't stay put. She had to help Zen. So, she started running in the direction of the gunshot. She glanced over her shoulder, checking for Ms. Emily or her son. Then she tripped over what she thought was a tree root but turned out to be a leg attached to a body that she fell flat on top of. She stopped breathing, fearful of seeing Zen dead beneath her. As she rolled over, she saw dark-brown eyes gazing blankly at her out of a soft, doughy face. It was Kenneth Randall!

Samantha heard herself screaming, but her voice felt detached from her. She scrambled to move away from Kenneth's lifeless body. Still screaming, she crawled to her knees and tried to stand up but couldn't.

Hands grabbed her by her coat, pulling her up. It was Zen! As he pulled her along, she heard the sound of a gun being discharged. Time slowed. When Samantha turned, she saw a single bullet fired by Ms. Emily, who was standing several feet behind them. A body flew horizontally across Samantha and Zen's path, taking the bullet full on. It was Peter Lin.

Samantha tried to reach for Mr. Lin, but Zen pushed her in front of him, yelling, "Move! Keep running!" From behind them, she heard the angry, vicious cries of Ms. Emily as she chased the two cousins. Taking aim, she let fly another bullet, but it sailed over their heads.

Samantha could see a bridge ahead of them. But as they got closer, she saw that only a few planks remained, hanging down by a single rope over a cliff. Grabbing onto Zen, she swiftly changed direction so they wouldn't fall into the hole. With nowhere else to go, they ran back and into Ms. Emily, who was running straight at them, gun pointed.

Samantha was starting to close her eyes, not wanting to face the inevitable, when a large, dark shadow descended fast behind Ms. Emily. As it got closer, the wind picked up, caused by the flapping of enormous wings that were attached to the body of a man with a hawk's face. As the being swooped down toward them, Samantha felt herself being lifted by her coat, along with Zen, off the ground. Below, she heard Ms. Emily's cries, her voice trailing off as she fell over the side of the cliff. Samantha thought that the sight of the large man-bird must have caused the woman to lose her footing.

Coming back down to Earth, the man-bird tilted his head, blinking his bright, amber eyes at Samantha and Zen. His large, pale wings disappeared into his black wool coat, which swept out behind him.

"Addiwan," Samantha whispered.

Right in front of them, the man-bird's face morphed back into that of the tall, thin man.

"Now, that's cool," Zen said before passing out.

Rushing to his side, Samantha placed her cousin's head into her lap.

"He will be fine," Addiwan said, leaning over Zen as sirens blared in the distance. "Stay right here. They are coming for you." Expanding his wings, he took flight.

Samantha didn't have to wait long. Several police officers, followed closely by her dad, came running toward them.

Zen was carried out on a stretcher, as was Mr. Lin, who was badly injured from the gunshot wound. But he was still alive. Kenneth Randall's covered body was also taken away, but helicopters remained. They were busy lowering men over the cliff to recover Ms. Emily Randall's body.

CHAPTER 24

TIME DOES HEAL WOUNDS

Dr. Julius Raymond, a recent addition to Clarkstown's Elm General Hospital, stood by Zen's bedside in the emergency room. The strikingly handsome doctor with ebony skin and black eyes read over the chart before explaining Zen's condition to Samantha's parents.

"He has a slight concussion and bruised ribs, and I put three stitches in his bottom lip. The bone socket around his left eye is intact, but he will have one heck of a shiner for a while."

"Yes, Doctor ... but ... will I ever surf again?" Zen asked hoarsely, half in a daze from the pain medication. His question drew chuckles from those standing around him, which included the Kitchets, who'd joined Anna and Craig to listen to Zen's prognosis.

"I can safely say you will surf again, young man," Dr. Raymond said with a laugh. Then he turned to Anna and Craig. "Other than that, I am recommending he stay overnight. I understand he was unconscious for a while. I want to keep him under close observation."

"I wazzz ... just takin' a nap," Zen said, slurring his words.

"I think that would be wise, Doctor," Anna said as she tenderly rubbed Zen's arm.

"I will stay with him tonight," Craig offered.

"No, dear. You go home with Anna and Samantha. I will stay," said Bess.

Pulling back the privacy curtains around Zen's bed, a nurse entered, wheeling Samantha in to join the rest of her family. "Here she is," the nurse said, handing Dr. Raymond a folder. "The radiologist's notes are inside."

While Dr. Raymond looked over her chart, Samantha glanced around the room, noticing the worried looks cast in her direction. Zen lay with his eyes closed, obviously sleeping, with his mouth open. *Aunt Sam is gonna kill me when she hears about what happened and sees her son's face!* she thought. She focused on her mom, and her heart immediately sank. Anna had learned all the horrible details of Ameara's and Nanna's deaths when Samantha relayed Ms. Emily's and Kenneth's confessions to Chief Bevin. Her mom hasn't spoken a word about it yet.

"You sustained a pretty good hit to the side of your face, young lady," Dr. Raymond said.

"But I feel fine." Samantha got up out of the wheelchair. "Really, I do." Actually, she felt sick to her stomach from the whole experience. All she wanted to do was go home, soak up to her neck in a hot tub of water, and cry until she couldn't cry anymore.

Gently placing his hands on Samantha's shoulders, Craig said, "Why don't we let the doctor tell us how you're doing."

"I think it's safe for her to go home this evening," the doctor said. "Just make sure to keep an eye on her tonight.

Does your family have a local doctor who can do a follow-up examination of Samantha and Alexzender?"

"No, we don't," Anna answered.

Removing a card from his pocket, Dr. Raymond handed it to Craig. "I have an office in Hearthshire. Call and make an appointment. I'd like to see them in the next couple of days."

As soon as Dr. Raymond left, Chief Bevin stuck his head in, gesturing to Anna and Craig. "Can I speak with you both?"

They walked out, and Samantha peeked through the curtain to see her parents huddled with Chief Bevin. She heard Peter Lin's name.

"Young miss, you were told not to leave the house."

Turning, she found Kitchet staring at her. "I'm so sorry," she said as tears welled up. "I was worried about Mom."

"You have got to understand that precautions are put in place for everyone's safety," Kitchet said firmly.

"You both could have died!" Bess said, removing her handkerchief from her pocket and dabbing away Samantha's tears, which now flowed freely. "Luckily, the tree folk tracked your movements. That's how your parents were able to alert Chief Bevin. Of course, we had to lie, telling the police that we were the ones who witnessed the two of you being put into the car by those ... those people!"

Kitchet took Samantha by her hands, quietly telling her, "When we lost Ameara and Nanna, we were all devastated. Completely devastated. So, when you and Zen went missing, all ... all I could think of was how I had failed Innis and how we had lost more of our children."

Samantha laid her head against Kitchet's shoulder, promising him, "I'll never do that again. I swear that my detective days are over."

Kitchet patted her on the back. "That's all I wanted to hear."

"Mr. Lin is out of surgery," Anna said, walking in and carrying a backpack. "The bullet hit him in his left shoulder, causing no long-lasting damage. The doctors are amazed at how his body is rapidly recovering."

"That's good news," Bess said, giving her a hug. Then, taking a step back, she looked Anna in the eyes and asked, "How are you?"

Samantha watched her mom lower her eyes and shake her head, indicating she was fine.

"We never meant to hide the truth of Ameara's and Nanna's deaths," Kitchet said, staring down at his feet." It's just that your father—well, all of us—wanted to give both you and Sam time to heal after losing your mother at such a young age."

"I don't blame you and Bess one bit, Kitchet." Anna pulled Samantha to her, planting a kiss on her bruised cheek. "And I certainly don't blame Dad. He was correct in not telling Sam and me. Knowing exactly how Mom and Grandmother died wouldn't have changed the fact that they were gone."

Samantha squeezed her mom tightly as she sighed heavily. She was relieved to hear her mom's words, but it still didn't change the fact in her mind that she hadn't been honest with her from the beginning.

"I just can't believe it!" Craig said, stepping back through the curtain. He plopped himself in a chair and continued to rant. "I was just talking with Chief Bevin, and he told me this librarian and her son even killed a police detective. And all for what reason? Does anybody know? It's just crazy!" Standing up again, he announced, "I'll tell you this. I'm forever grateful to Mr. Lin for taking that bullet."

"Speaking of Peter Lin," Anna said. "He gave the nurse his backpack, telling them to make sure I looked inside. This is what I found." She handed Kitchet a book that closely resembled Muaura's book. It had the same crescent moon, stars, and sphere etched into the leather cover. "How can this be? I thought there was only one copy."

"Oh, I completely forgot!" Samantha said. "Mr. Lin is related to us somehow."

"Huh? Related to the Fairlands?" Kitchet inspected the book, and as he did, his eyes widened. "There were actually two copies of Muaura's book. One copy that stayed in the Fairland home. That's the one you have, Anna. The other belonged to Muaura's son Elphiam, who relocated with his wife to France long ago. We lost contact with a descendent of this line, and we all assumed this book was lost forever, like him." Kitchet looked over at Bess.

"Would that lost family member's name be Raoul Pépin? That is the name Mr. Lin gave the nurse when he gave her this." Anna dangled between her fingers the geode pendant that Samantha had seen Peter Lin wearing earlier that day.

CHAPTER 25

THE INVISIBLE MAN

It was 2:15 a.m. when a powerfully built man with salt-and-pepper hair strolled right past the nursing station in the intensive care unit at Elm General Hospital. He entered Room 258, where Peter Lin was resting comfortably. Only the sounds from the machines that monitored Mr. Lin could be heard above his steady breathing. The man stood cloaked in the shadow at the foot of the hospital bed, watching and knowing that he didn't need to say a word. His presence would announce him.

Mr. Lin stirred, drowsily opening his eyes. He scanned the darkness and saw no one. However, he felt someone was there. "Yes?" he asked.

"How are you feeling, Peter?" the deep, whispery voice asked.

It was only once the man spoke that Mr. Lin could see the dark outline standing in the shadows. Clearing his throat, Mr. Lin answered, "I feel ... fine."

"That's good to hear. I'll let you rest now. Goodbye, Peter."

"Wait. Do I know you?" Mr. Lin tried to rise but couldn't. The medications had left him weak.

"Please don't try and get up, Peter. That would be a foolish thing to do so soon after surgery."

Leaving Mr. Lin's room, the man took the stairs, descended one flight, and stepped into Dr. Julius Raymond's office. Dr. Raymond sat at his desk, studying the test tubes of blood he held in his hands. He was unaware the man had entered.

"Julius, are those the blood samples we asked for?" the man asked.

"Oh, Dennan," Dr. Raymond said, coming to his feet. "Yes. I'll notify you of the results for Alexzender Kita, Samantha Keen, and Mr. Peter Lin as soon as I have them."

"Good. Make it sooner than later. The group will want to know right away."

"Yes, I understand," answered Dr. Raymond.

Walking to the end of the corridor, Dennan took the elevator to the children's unit. Slipping into Zen's room, he parted the curtains surrounding the bed. Peering through a narrow slit, he viewed Zen sleeping as Bess dozed in a chair by his bed.

Satisfied, Dennan turned and left, blending into the night.

CHAPTER 26

THE CASE FOR MR. PETER LIN

Chief Bevin and Officer Roberts stopped by the Fairland home the next afternoon. They were there to wrap up the details surrounding the case of Nanna and Ameara Fairland and to discuss Peter Lin.

"His story seems to all check out," Chief Bevin said, taking another sip of green tea. "Twenty-five years ago, a young Peter Lin came into this country, hoping to reconnect with distant relatives—your family, the Fairlands."

Chief Bevin didn't need to explain to Samantha's family that Mr. Lin was a relative. Kitchet had spoken to Mr. Lin earlier at the hospital, questioning how he'd come into possession of the book and the pendant. Mr. Lin told Kitchet he was a direct descendent of Raoul Arborden Fairland Pépin. When Mr. Lin's grandfather died, he left the book and pendant to him. According to Kitchet, Raoul Pépin was, in fact, the name of the relative the Fairlands had lost contact with long ago.

"When Mr. Lin arrived in America, he made arrangements to meet with Professor Fairland," Chief Bevin continued. "However, when Mr. Lin knocked at Professor Fairland's office door, he states that she shouted for him to run before he could enter. Mr. Lin then states a man pursued him, but he was able to get away when he ran into the woods adjacent to the university."

"Kenneth Randall did say whoever was questioning Great-Grandma Nanna ran out of the room," Samantha added.

"This sounds about right because according to your and Alexzender's statements, Samantha, this is when Kenneth confessed to entering Professor Fairland's office," Chief Bevin said.

"Yeah, Kenneth was really pissed off that Great-Grandma Nanna didn't tell this bigwig guy from some organization ... What did Kenneth call this group again, Samantha?" Zen asked. Propped against a mound of pillows on the sofa, he was switching his icepack from his eye to his lip.

"Sentinels. The Sentinels group," Samantha said.

"Yep, that's the name. I guess this group was interested in finding some tombs and junk. Kenny wanted this Sentinels group to give him some sort of high-powered position that his father once had. Since Great-Grandma was a respected geographer with the university, I guess he got it in his crazy head that she could help him," said Zen.

Boy, Zen handled that well, Samantha thought. Kitchet had already warned them to tell Chief Bevin the truth but to reveal nothing that could point to hidden locations or records that could endanger the family again.

"Well, I ran a check for any organization going by the name 'the Sentinels' and found none," Chief Bevin said. "I even had Interpol run a search in its database, and it came up with nothing."

"So why would Kenneth Randall and his mother give Samantha and Zen the name of a fictional organization?" Craig asked. "What was the purpose of that?"

Officer Roberts turned to his superior and asked, "May I offer an explanation?" Chief Bevin nodded, and Officer Roberts stood up to present his theory. "I discovered that Birchem Randall—Kenneth's father and Ms. Emily's husband—lived a very luxurious lifestyle as a genealogist with a background in geography. The Randalls traveled a great deal when Kenneth was a boy. But when Birchem passed away, Emily Randall had to sell many of her possessions to pay the bills. When we searched the Randalls' home yesterday, we discovered many rare antiques. My guess is Kenneth was involved in the black-market antiquities trade. He was trying to give his mother the lifestyle she had loved before Birchem died. Maybe there is a group he was working with, and the name 'Sentinel' is code for something else. A way to hide their illegal dealings."

Officer Roberts sat down, then added, "Most of this is guesswork, you understand, since we have no way to question the suspects. However, from the Randalls' own confessions, I'm pretty confident this was the reason behind the murders."

"I agree," said Chief Bevin. "I think Professor Fairland found out what Kenneth was doing and confronted him about it. Then, when Ameara arrived on the scene, Kenneth must've felt she also knew something about his illegal dealings and went after her too. Unfortunately, we all know what happened to her when Kenneth caught up with her in the woods." Opening his notepad, Chief Bevin said, "Mr. Lin was a witness to the whole incident. He states, and I quote, 'While I was in the woods, a woman walked past where I was hiding behind some trees. I was going to say something to her when a man approached her and grabbed her by the neck. I must have made a sound because he turned and looked at me. I recognize him now as the man who put me in the trunk. Kenneth Randall. He let her go, and I saw her fall to the ground. He started to walk in my direction, so I started to run. I was scared. I am not sure if I lost him or if he was even chasing me. But I got out of the woods and asked someone for a ride back to the airport. I stayed in New York for two days, and I tried to contact Professor Fairland at her home. There was no answer. After I learned in the papers she was murdered, I boarded a plane for China that same day.' End quote," Chief Bevin concluded. "I guess the police did get one piece of this case right back then. Mr. Peter Lin did leave the country, but he was not the murderer of Ameara and Nanna Fairland."

Samantha felt Chief Bevin and Officer Roberts had pleaded the case quite well for Mr. Lin, but she still had a question. "But what brought Mr. Lin back into the country after so many years?" she asked.

"Guilt, but not because of murder. Guilt had plagued him for all those years from not reporting what he had seen happen to Ameara all those years ago," Chief Bevin said, looking directly at Anna. "I know, Mrs. Keen, that Mr. Lin is anxious to tell you how sorry he is. However, he did say he was glad he had a chance to apologize to Innis before he died."

"It was Mr. Lin who called Grandpa Innis," Samantha and Zen said at the same time.

"Yes," Chief Bevin confirmed. "Mr. Lin called Innis, and they met at a diner halfway between here and Maynard County. Mr. Lin told me that Innis appeared happy to finally know the circumstances surrounding his wife's death. At the end of their meeting, Innis told Mr. Lin he would arrange for him to meet with me at the police station to clear his name. As we all know, Innis died before this could happen."

Samantha smiled to herself. *This is why Grandpa felt at peace before he died. He finally knew what happened because Peter Lin told him. But I wonder who this Maskhim is that Grandma Ameara was wondering about. And Kenneth seemed to know about them.* Samantha wiggled her eyebrows, but then she smiled again. *Well, now that I know who Peter Lin truly is, I'll just ask him what he knows about Maskhim. Case closed!*

"Case closed," said Chief Bevin as he stood to leave with Officer Roberts. "By the way, Samantha, Alexzender. Did either of you have a gun that you fired at Kenneth Randall?"

"No," they both answered.

"Why would you ask these kids if they had a gun?" Craig asked. "We don't own a gun, and neither of them would know how to use one. Anyway, I thought you said his own mother, Emily Randall, shot Kenneth by mistake."

"Sorry, Mr. Keen. I had to ask," said Chief Bevin. "Here's the thing. The bullet that killed Kenneth was not fired from the gun we recovered with Emily Randall. No matter. We're thinking Emily must have had another gun, and we just haven't been able to locate it yet." Chief Bevin smiled. "You folks enjoy the rest of your day."

CHAPTER 27

CORNELIUS SIMMS

A phone rang inside a home somewhere on the west coast of the United States. A tall, pale man in his late fifties with thinning, white hair hurried in to answer it.

"Simms," he said.

Simms stood in his living room, facing his window and watching his neighbor water their lawn. He leaned his long frame against the back of a chair while dropping his briefcase at his feet.

"I'm trusting everything worked out as planned," said Charles Genelis on the other end of the phone line.

"All taken care of, sir. You may inform the Sentinels that Kenneth and Emily Randall are no longer loose cannons," Simms reported. "I did try and reach you, sir, with this news."

"Otto did inform me of your call."

Genelis didn't sound quite like himself, Simms noticed. He sounded tired, which was unusual for Genelis. "Is there anything else, sir?"

"No, Simms. We appreciate your taking this case. We know you are ... semiretired."

"You can call upon me again anytime. Sir, now that the Randall case is settled, would you like for us to continue with that other matter?"

"No, I'll let you know when to pick that up again. We would like the Randall situation to cool down first," said Genelis. "By the way, how are your daughter Leeza and her family enjoying life in their new hometown?"

"Very good, sir. They are enjoying it very much. Thank you for asking after them."

"On a personal note, Simms, I will be away for an extended period of time and unreachable. If anything should come up, leave word with Otto, and I will get in contact with you."

"Yes, sir," Simms said. Then Genelis ended the call.

Picking up his briefcase, Simms made his way down a hallway lined with wallpaper of swirling floral patterns against a dark-brown background. He stopped at the end of the corridor, faced what appeared to be a dead end, and ran a finger along the floral pattern. Locating a button concealed within the fabric, he pressed it, causing the wall to slide open and reveal a hidden office.

Upon entering, Simms walked directly over to a wall safe, where he secured his handgun inside. At his desk, he opened his notepad to the page that held the names of Emily and Kenneth Randall and drew lines through them. He had labeled the next page "Fairlands." The names "Nanna and Ameara Fairland" were written at the top of the list with a thin black line through them. He then added the names of Mayra Fairland, Anna Fairland-Keen, Sam Fairland-Kita, Alexzender Fairland-Kita, and Samantha Fairland-Keen. Below Samantha's name, he placed Peter

Lin's name with a question mark next to it. Leaning back in his chair, Simms stared at Mr. Lin's name.

"Well, Mr. Peter Lin. Who are you really? And how were you able to conceal yourself for so long?"

Leaving his notepad on top of his desk, Simms stood up and straightened a framed photo of his daughter and granddaughter taken together. He switched off the lights before exiting his office.

CHAPTER 28

MAGIC MADE SIMPLE

O h no— No, pleeeease!" Samantha heard a girl's voice pleading. Her own lips were moving. It was her. She was the screamer!

Her eyes flew open—darting left, then right—and finally focusing straight up, staring at a ceiling. A second earlier, she'd been running for her life. Her heart was still racing, thundering in her ears and throat. Brushing back the curls clinging to her sweaty forehead, she told herself, *I'm safe. It's okay.*

Slowly, her heart rate returned to normal when she realized she was in her own bedroom. Tossing back the covers, she swung her legs over the side of the bed, firmly planting her feet on the floor and allowing her head to clear. Her clock read 8:13 p.m. She remembered heading to her bedroom soon after Chief Bevin and Officer Roberts left. She had climbed into bed, not even bothering to remove her outside clothes, and had immediately fallen off to sleep and into a nightmare.

In her dream, she was in the library, sitting in the children's section. Ms. Emily was walking toward her, pushing a library cart. On her cart, instead of books, there was a serving tray with a domed lid concealing its contents. Ms. Emily parked her cart next to Samantha. Smiling, the old librarian said to her, "Have you met my sweet boy?" Ms. Emily proceeded to lift the domed lid off the tray. There lay Kenneth Randall's soft, doughy head, his dark-brown eyes staring out vacantly. Samantha screamed, pushing the cart away from her. She ran through the library, toppling book-shelves while darting down the aisles. She saw a flashing red exit sign and ran for it, her hand outstretched as she tried to reach for the door to make her escape. Ms. Emily appeared again, blocking her way. Raising her arms, Ms. Emily pointed her gun and fired. The sound of the bullet whizzing past her ears woke Samantha up.

She rushed into her bathroom and splashed cool water over her face. Recalling her dream reminded her just how dangerous the situation had been for her and Zen. Ms. Emily and Kenneth had killed three people—at least three she was aware of—to gain the favor of a powerful group. And Samantha knew these murders had everything to do with the knowledge her family was concealing—not some illegal antiquities trade as Officer Roberts surmised.

Drying her face, she rubbed her forehead extra hard, trying to wipe away the thoughts running through her mind. "How many more people like Ms. Emily and Kenneth Randall will come searching for my family?" Samantha asked the reflection staring back at her from the mirror. "Do these Sentinels still think we know something? They must be convinced after twenty-five years that we know noth-ing," she reasoned with herself before returning to her bedroom.

The sight of her jumbled bed didn't suggest a peaceful slumber. It screamed more nightmares. *I wonder if Zen is still awake*, she thought. Heading across the hall, she found his door open and his room empty. Deciding that he must be downstairs, she found him sitting at the kitchen table with her parents, Addiwan, Aunt Sam, and Uncle Junzo. *They must have arrived while I was sleeping*, Samantha assumed.

"You look terrible," Zen said, frowning at the sight of her. He was sipping something from a teacup that he held with both hands.

"Thanks." Then, giving her aunt and uncle a hug, she said," Sorry for getting Zen into trouble."

"We're just happy you're both alive," Sam said.

"Besides, Zen would've found other ways to get into trouble," Junzo added.

"Oh, thanks, Pop," Zen said.

"Are you hungry?" Anna asked Samantha. "I saved you a dinner plate."

"No, thanks, Mom. I'm not hungry."

Sliding into a chair next to Zen, Samantha asked him, "What are you drinking?"

Extending his right pinky finger, Zen pointed his nose toward the ceiling and, in a snobbish tone, answered, "It's tea. Addiwan made it for me."

"The herbs will help reduce the swelling around his face and help him sleep," Addiwan explained.

"I can use some of that if it will help me sleep peacefully," Samantha said with a yawn.

"I will make you a cup." Removing a small cloth pouch from his pocket, Addiwan poured a tiny amount of powdered substance into a cup, added hot water, then handed the brew to Samantha.

"Are you having trouble sleeping, cherub?" Craig asked.

"A little." Looking down into her cup at the purplish-blue liquid, she raised the cup to her nose. It smelled a bit like the lavender liquid from Essences Flower Shop and something else she couldn't identify. Samantha really didn't like tea, but as she took a sip, she found the way it slid down her throat and warmed her belly very soothing. Smiling, she nodded and gave Addiwan the thumbs-up sign, then took another sip.

"Thanks for saving our lives— Hey, you turned yourself into a bird." Samantha recalled Addiwan's stunt. "How did you do that? Did you perform some type of magic?" Looking at Addiwan in his usual black dress attire, she hoped he wasn't some sort of dark sorcerer. She really couldn't handle any more secretly twisted people in her life, as Mrs. Emily turned out to be.

Addiwan's bright, amber eyes twinkled as he answered. "If you are asking me if I have the ability to shift my appearance, then yes, I can perform what some humans call magic. I do not call it magic. It is a normal way of being for me."

"But most people can't alter their faces to look like a hawk or sprout wings and fly. Are you ... human, Addiwan?" Samantha had to ask the question. From the moment she'd met him, she'd sensed there was something very different about him. And from the silence around her, she could tell that the rest of her family wanted to know the answer to the question too.

"I am a human. I am a human who has retained the capability to do what most humans have lost the ability to do, which is control their physical structures. Let me explain it this way. Rhiannon said you witnessed the pure essences working with plants."

"Yeah, they can take on the form of whatever plant life they work with," Samantha said.

"Exactly," Addiwan agreed. "Everything, even humans,

is made up of pure essence or energy frequencies that create form. People and things may appear fixed and unchangeable. However, they are not. They can be as fluid as water and as light as air. I will demonstrate the truth behind this idea."

Extending his arm out in front of him, Addiwan transformed the structure of his right hand into thousands of colorful light pixels. "This is my essence, my energy pattern."

Everyone gasped.

"What happened to your hand? Your flesh, your bones? All of it! It's all gone!" Samantha said, leaning in closer to get a better look at where Addiwan's hand used to be.

"It is still here. You cannot see it because I shifted the pattern of my hand's frequency."

"How?" Junzo asked.

"By saying a word in my head. Some would say that I cast a magical spell. Now watch. I am going to say another magic word out loud."

Samantha held her breath, waiting to hear that all-powerful word that would restore Addiwan's hand to normal.

"HAND" was all he said. And before their eyes, Addiwan's hand reappeared at the end of his wrist.

"Oh, wow! He's like David Blaine!" Zen said, nudging Samantha. "I'm gonna learn how to do that."

"*Hand?* The magic word is *hand?*" Samantha just couldn't accept that such an ordinary word could conjure such an extraordinary result. "How is that a magic word?"

"It created what I asked for. Yes?" Addiwan replied.

Not able to hide her disappointment, Samantha exclaimed, "Yeah, but ... *hand* is something everyone knows, like *chair* or *table*. I thought magical words were, you know, magical, like *abracadabra* or *bibbidi-bobbidi-boo!*"

"Hmm," was all Addiwan said. Then he asked, "What do you create when you say the words *abracadabra* or *bibbidi-bobbidi-boo*?"

"Whatever I wish for ... I guess."

"You guess? Why leave it to chance? It really is simple," said Addiwan, looking at everyone in the kitchen. "Abracadabra is a fine word. However, if you are going to use this word or any word, make sure you understand the vibrational pattern of what it is meant to create. Words are powerful, and they *will* create the energy pattern they are designed to create."

Taking another sip from her cup, Samantha thought about what Addiwan just said. Then it came to her. "So, that's what Grandpa Innis meant when he said there's power in words."

"Correct. And that, Samantha, is how I transform myself."

"Can you teach me to do that? Transform?" asked Zen.

"Son, first learn how to just be a boy," Junzo said.

"There is your answer," said Addiwan, standing at the kitchen door as he prepared to leave. "Good night."

The door had barely closed when Zen offered up his opinion of Addiwan. "I always thought Addiwan was a cool dude!"

"You did not. You said you thought he was odd," Samantha said, finishing her last drop of tea. "I always thought he was unusually interesting."

"It's like shape-shifting," Craig said, getting up from the table to place his teacup in the sink. "This is what Addiwan is talking about. Most Indigenous people talk of it, and we've all read about shape-shifters in our cultures' folklore.

Even in some cultures today, there are shamans who claim to do what Addiwan does."

"And on that note, you two should head off to bed," Anna said, pointing to Samantha and Zen. "Your Aunt Mayra is arriving tomorrow."

Back upstairs, Samantha lingered at the threshold of her bedroom door, uncertain if she really wanted to enter.

"What? You're not tired yet?" Zen asked.

"Zen, are you having trouble sleeping? You know, since the incident in the woods?"

"Nah. Why? Are you?"

"I had a nightmare about Ms. Emily and Kenneth," she shared. "You know that whole episode of being attacked and almost dying was pretty scary. It doesn't bother you?"

"Well, sure, it bothers me. I don't like being punched in the face. I certainly didn't like being chased through the woods by a madwoman and her son. It was like being in a scene from *Psycho*."

"So, how are you able to close your eyes and not relive it all again?"

"It's because I surf the waves."

"Surfing? I don't get it."

"It's like this," Zen said, leaning against her doorframe. "When my dad taught me to surf, it scared me. I couldn't balance myself on the board. I'd fall over, taking in a mouthful of salt water. Then, when I learned to balance, a wave would come out of nowhere and knock me for a loop. After it all came together for me, Dad told me his philosophy on surfing and why it was important to learn. He said life is like surfing. You have to find your balance. And even if you're cruising along, a big wave, like the Randalls, may knock you for a loop. Don't let it keep you down. If you do, the water will drown you. You have to get back up and find your balance. Get it?"

She did get it. As frightening as the incident was, she couldn't let it consume her or get in the way of a good night's rest. "Thanks, Zen," she said, giving him a hug.

"Good. That will be five bucks for my therapy session."

"I'll pay you when you actually have your therapist license."

"Fine. No more free consultations from me," he said, entering his room. Then poking his head back out, he asked, "Hey, can you take me to meet Ashlynn tomorrow?"

"Sure, that I can do."

SAMANTHA FELT RESTED the next morning. When she'd gone to sleep the night before, she'd dreamed of sprouting a pair of lavender wings, flying out her window, and traveling high above the Earth. It was such a peaceful feeling. Actually, it was the best sleep she'd had since learning of Grandpa Innis's death. *It must have been because of the tea Addiwan gave me*, she thought.

Moving casually around her room, she straightened her bed, picked up her clothes from the night before, and took an extra-long shower. Wiping the fog from the bathroom mirror, she studied her face. The bruise on her left cheek was still there but no longer painful. Turning away from her mirror, she dressed for her day by pulling on a pair of wool socks, donning an oversized white sweater over a pair of jeans, and grabbing her sneakers. Downstairs, she joined Zen for breakfast before heading over to Ashlynn's tree.

Watching Zen circle Ashlynn's tree for a second time, Samantha noticed that the swelling on his face had gone down considerably. *He's almost back to looking like his old Zen self*, she thought.

"So, do we knock on the tree trunk or what?" he asked.

"I don't know. The last time, she just stepped out."

Zen placed a hand to the side of his mouth and leaned over to whisper to Samantha. "Maybe she doesn't want to be seen talking with you. You know, because of that stunt you pulled, breaking through that barrier. All the trees are probably talking about it."

"Hey, you stepped through that barrier too!"

"Yeah, but I was just following you. I was the one who told you we shouldn't. They know who the troublemaker is. Did you notice that Gypsy slept in my room last night? She wants nothing to do with you."

"Gypsy slept in your room because you have food in there. She always follows the food." Secretly, she did wonder whether what Zen was saying might be true. *Terrance was rather quiet last night too. He normally says good night, even if he doesn't tell me a story.* Perhaps the trees were avoiding her.

"I just don't know about you, Samantha. You've gone completely rogue," Zen said.

"Hey, you're the one who told me to stop living my adventures through books. Besides, I was worried about Mom."

"Ah," Zen sighed. "Samantha, Samantha, Samantha. What am I going to do with you?" Holding his hands out in front of him as if he were on a diving board, he explained. "There's a time to dive in with both feet." Then, placing his hands in a prayer position, he concluded. "Then there are times when you must sit and contemplate the situation. That's another five bucks for my therapy services."

"Well, I felt the situation called for action, not contemplation," she retaliated, her hands planted on her hips as she leaned into her cousin's face. *Okay, my peaceful feeling is gone.*

With all their arguing, Samantha and Zen hadn't noticed that Ashlynn had appeared right in front of them until she spoke.

"I knew I heard voices. I apologize for not coming out to greet you sooner. I thought it was just the chatter of the two squirrels up in my tree. They are always arguing with each other as to how many nuts each should carry."

The lovely tree essence, with her burnt-auburn hair with streaks of deep green, glided toward them.

"Sorry, Ashlynn," Samantha said. "We didn't mean to make so much noise. I wanted you to meet my cousin, Zen."

"It is very nice to meet you, Cousin Zen," Ashlynn said with a smile.

"Wow!" Zen said, gazing at the tree essence. "Can I touch you? Will my hands go right through you, like a ghost?"

"Zen!" Samantha said, feeling embarrassed by his questions.

"It's fine, and yes, you may touch my hand, Zen."

Lightly touching Ashlynn's hand, he said, "Your hand is so soft."

"Why, thank you. It feels nothing like the bark of my tree, does it?" Ashlynn said, giving Zen a wink. "So, what are you two younglings up to besides coming to visit me?"

"We're supposed to take it easy. We both got into a bit of trouble. I'm not sure ... if you ... heard anything about it?" Samantha hesitantly asked.

"Mmm, yes, I know something about it. I sent out the message for the barrier," Ashlynn said.

"Just for the record," Zen said, casting Samantha a sideward glance. "It was not my idea to leave. I wanted to obey the warning."

"It was good, Zen, that you stayed by Samantha's side. If she had been alone, it might not have been a happy ending," Ashlynn said.

Zen puffed out his chest and said, "Well, I would've never let her go by herself. Oh, did you see my black eye and my lip? I put up a fight. I tried not to let them take us."

Samantha looked down. She felt stupid now, having run through the barrier as she did. "I didn't mean to cause so much trouble. Really, I didn't. I was just worried about my mom," she confessed.

"Oh, I understand you wanting to protect your mother, Samantha. Even we tree folk have the instinct to help those we care for. But I must caution you to please pay attention to the warning if it should happen again."

"Believe me, Ashlynn, I have learned my lesson," Samantha said.

"How does this barrier thing work?" Zen asked.

"It is created by the concentrated energy of most of the trees on this property. Through our roots, we can communicate with each other and sense humans' intentions from the energy flowing from their feet. We felt strong negative vibrations from the woman and the man, and we prevented them from coming onto the property."

"Then how did we get through?" Samantha asked.

"As hard as we tried to keep you in, somehow, you both forced our barrier to bend and let you through."

CHAPTER 29

AUNT MAYRA QUESTIONS PETER LIN

N one of us ever dreamed the kids would try to investigate the murders of Ameara and Nanna," Mayra said, taking another bite of her sticky bun."

"Police Chief Bevin believes that the Randalls killed Mom and Grandmother Nanna because they were dealing in the illegal antiques business," Anna told Mayra. "But I tend to agree with Samantha and Zen. It has to do more with our family's knowledge of hidden passageways into the inner Earth."

"See," said Zen. "Me and Samantha, we figured out the truth, and the police still have no clue."

"The police will never know the full truth, Zen," said Mayra. "This is how this group works—in the shadows, where no one really knows who they are or what they're doing." Tapping her temple, Mayra confessed, "However, I must admit that I don't recognize the name 'Sentinels.'"

"How about the name 'Maskhim'? Do you recognize it?" Samantha asked.

"Yes, but how do you know—"

"Kenneth said that Great-Grandma Nanna had the nerve to call the Sentinels by the name 'Maskhim,'" Zen said.

"And Grandma Ameara mentioned how concerned she was about the Maskhim," Samantha added. By the look of confusion on everyone's face except for Zen's, Samantha knew she had to go ahead and fess up about the diary. "I found Grandma Ameara's diary in the attic. She mentions the Maskhim in there."

"Samantha—" Anna started to scold her, but Mayra intervened.

"Can you please bring me Ameara's diary?" she calmly asked.

Hurrying to her room, Samantha grabbed the book and hurried back downstairs. She opened to Ameara's last diary entry, saying, "See, this is where she mentions the Maskhim. And here in this note to Grandpa Innis, she mentions it again."

"Mom's diary. I never knew she kept one," Sam said, rubbing her hand over the book as though it were a long-lost treasure.

"Is there anything else you two may be hiding from us that we should know about?" Anna asked, looking from Samantha to Zen.

"Hey, ask your daughter, Aunt Anna. It was her idea to hide stuff and snoop around Grandma Ameara's diary," said Zen, pointing the finger at Samantha.

Samantha narrowed her eyes at her cousin. *Rat!* she thought. Then she said, "No, Mom. And I swear I was going to give it to you when I finished the investigation."

"Samantha, this is not a game or a mystery from one of your Nancy Drew books you're trying to solve. It's our lives—"

"Well, it looks like I need to pay a visit to our newfound relative, Mr. Peter Lin," Mayra said. "It seems he was coming for more than just a family reunion. He knows something about the Maskhim too."

"Can I come? This is the last piece of the investigation I haven't worked out," Samantha said.

"Samantha Muaura Fairland-Keen!" Anna said, spilling the contents of her teacup as she firmly planted it on the kitchen table. "Haven't you heard anything I've just said?

"Yes, but—" Looking at the rise of her mom's eyebrows, Samantha knew not to continue trying to argue her point.

"Who are these Maskhim?" Sam asked as she flipped through the pages of Ameara's diary.

"They are people you never want knowing what we have access to here on this property," Mayra said. "They are the ones we actually thought were responsible for Ameara's and Nanna's deaths. The Maskhim are also the reason Innis felt it wasn't safe for you and Sam to stay here in your home when your mother died. He didn't want you two anywhere near here if they came asking questions." Mayra put on her coat. "Anna, I'd like Samantha to come with me, please. She's worked hard to solve this case, and she should have the opportunity to at least hear the answer Mr. Lin gives of what he knows about the Maskhim."

Yes! Thank you, Aunt Mayra, Samantha thought.

"Can I come too?" Zen jumped to his feet.

"No," Sam said. "Remember, you said you had nothing to do with Samantha's investigation."

"I ᴋɴᴏᴡ Anna and Craig thanked you, Mr. Lin, but I wanted

to express my thanks for saving Samantha here and Zen," Mayra said, sitting in a chair next to Mr. Lin's hospital bed.

"Peter ... please," Mr. Lin said with a grin. "Call me Peter."

"I don't want to take up too much of your time, Peter. I just wanted to meet you and welcome you to the family. And, oh yes. I almost forgot. Samantha has a question for you."

This caught Samantha off guard. She hadn't known that her Aunt Mayra wanted her to ask the question.

"Um," she said. "I found a note from my Grandma Ameara ... something about information you had about the Maskhim. What was it you wanted to tell them?"

"My grandfather told me the story of how my Great-Great-Great-Grandfather Raoul Pépin hid from the Maskhim in China to protect his family. After my grandfather died, I went to France to find Raoul's family, but they were all dead. I knew Raoul also had family by the name of Fairland in Vermont. I located Professor Fairland, and she agreed to meet with me," Peter shared.

"You only wanted to tell Nanna about Raoul? There was nothing else?" Mayra asked.

"Yes and return the book." Then, clutching the pendant around his neck, Peter said, "Anna said it would be okay if I kept this. It meant so much to my grandfather."

"Of course, Peter. It belongs to your family. Our family," Mayra said.

"Thank you."

"Was there anything else your grandfather told you about the Maskhim?" Mayra pressed.

Before answering, Peter's deep-set black eyes looked toward the door as though he was checking to make sure no one else was listening. "He said they are hiding the truth about people."

Sitting up straighter in her chair, Mayra leaned in close to him. "Do you know what the truth is that the Maskhim are hiding?"

Pointing toward the ceiling, he said, "That we all come from up there, in the stars."

Leaning back in her chair, Mayra appeared satisfied with his answer. "What are your plans, Peter? Are you going back to— Where are you from, and what type of work do you do?"

"From the village of Molin, in China. But I have nothing left there," he told her.

"Where are you staying in Hearthshire?"

"I am renting a small room in Maynard. I was wondering, is it possible for me to visit the Fairlands at the house when I leave the hospital?

"Of course. You're family. Our home is your home."

Samantha noticed how pleased he looked after Mayra said he could come out to the house. *Poor guy. No wonder he was so desperate to get close to us at the funeral*, she thought.

"One more question, if you don't mind," Mayra said. "Do you know if the Maskhim are connected to a group calling themselves the Sentinels?

"I know nothing about the Sentinels."

Outside Peter's hospital room, Samantha asked Mayra, "So, what do you think? Do you think the Sentinels are working with the Maskhim?"

"Mmm ... I don't know, Samantha. I know it's a little strange that the Randalls obviously knew the name 'Maskhim' but said they were working for the Sentinels."

"Do you think the Maskhim and the Sentinels are two different groups trying to find out the same information?"

"I'll have to get back to you on that after I do some research," Mayra said as she lowered her voice. She took Samantha by her elbow and led her farther down the hall. "But there's something about Peter that just doesn't fit."

What's that?" Samantha's ears perked up as she sensed that maybe there was another mystery brewing. "Do you think maybe he isn't really related to us?"

"No, that's not it. I'm wondering what exactly Peter meant when he said he has nothing left in China. I took it to mean he has no finances because he didn't say what type of work he does. But if Peter has no money, how is he able to fly all over the world?"

"Yeah ... that's true. Where is he getting his money? That's a good catch, Aunt Mayra!"

"I can think like a detective too, you know," she said, pushing the button for the elevator. "We'll figure it out, Samantha. But let's remove our detective hats for now. The rest of the family is probably waiting on us. Remember, we have an appointment to meet with our neighbors."

"THERE YOU ARE, DR. RAYMOND," a nurse said, spotting the doctor just as he stepped from a corridor next to Peter Lin's room. "Dr. Hail is expecting you in his office right about now," she said, glancing at her wristwatch.

"Vicki, can you please let Dr. Hail know I'll be a little late for our meeting? I need to make an important phone call," Dr. Raymond said as he watched Samantha and Mayra board the elevator at the end of the hall.

CHAPTER 30

INTO THE LAND OF THE CORE PEOPLE

Kitchet grabbed hold of one side of the hutch that lay against a back wall in the dining room. Swinging it toward him, he exposed a concealed door and pulled on a knotted rope that doubled as the door's handle. "Mind your step," he said, allowing Bess and Mayra to walk through first. Samantha would have never guessed that an unassuming blue cupboard that held dishes from past generations would somehow lead them into the hidden world of the core people.

"Oooh, so C. S. Lewis," Sam remarked to Anna as they walked through the door closely behind Bess and Mayra.

Trailing behind his mom, Zen asked, "Who's C. S. Lewis?"

"See, that's why you need to visit a library or at least a bookstore every once in a while," an exasperated Samantha said. "C. S. Lewis wrote *The Lion, the Witch and the Wardrobe*." She stepped through the doorway, down two short steps, and into almost complete darkness. With only a little light filtering through from behind her, she could barely see Zen standing right in front of her, but she could certainly hear him.

"Why would I need to do that when I have you to tell me or can just look it up on the internet?" Zen snidely remarked.

Several feet in front of them, Mayra and Bess lit candles inside glass lanterns mounted to the walls, filling the passageway with a soft, yellow light. With the help of the light, Samantha could now see that she stood in a bricked tunnel with a curved ceiling, which allowed for plenty of headroom. Behind her, she heard the sound of the hutch swinging back into place as Kitchet shut the door after Craig, who was the last to come through.

"I can't believe we have a hidden passage in our house!" Craig said, like a kid visiting his first candy shop. "I always wanted to find one of these when I was growing up."

"Me too," Junzo chimed in. "Hey, Kitchet. How far does this thing go?"

"Not too far. At the end of this tunnel, we'll turn left through another door and head downward."

The small group followed the swinging hand lantern lights that Bess and Mayra carried along the not-too-narrow passageway. They quietly walked single file. In the quiet, Samantha's mind ran rampant, wondering who and what she would encounter in this new world.

They'd walked for little less than half a mile by Samantha's estimation when they reached the end of the tunnel. As Kitchet had said, they turned left into an alcove, where he pushed open another door and began descending stone steps.

Samantha said, "Now this reminds me of one of my Nancy Drew books, *The Hidden Staircase*. In the book, Nancy finds—"

"All right, all right, we all know you can read," Zen said. "Give your brain and our ears a rest from your literary knowledge."

Ignoring her cousin's rude remark, Samantha began to count to herself each step that her high-top purple Converse sneakers landed upon. At around about the hundredth step, the surroundings changed from the plain brickwork to moss and vines growing along the walls. She felt a sense of peace as they moved downward, as though the Earth was welcoming them. After about 342 steps, they arrived at the bottom, and the ground gave way to dirt.

A section of a massive tree took up most of the space, with its large roots extending in all directions. It appeared that Kitchet had led them to a dead end. Then Samantha felt an instant connection to the tree when the same energy she'd felt the first night in her bedroom flowed into her feet.

"This is Terrance," she said.

"Terrance?" Craig asked.

"The tree that stands next to Samantha's bedroom window," Anna said.

"Its roots extend under the house?" asked Junzo in amazement.

"Yes. Terrance settled here to protect the entrance and those who live beyond the threshold," said Kitchet. "Let's go where expected."

"But the tree. How can we proceed?" Craig asked. Just then, two of Terrance's roots slid apart, creating a way wide enough for them to pass through. On the other side, Bess and Mayra extinguished their lamps as a glimmering of natural light streamed in from a circular opening.

"Are we in an underground cave?" Zen asked, noticing rock walls.

"This is the entranceway into the inner world," Kitchet

said, moving to the front of the group. Plump blue grapes hung down from a vine over the mouth of the entrance. Pulling back the vines, Kitchet let in a warm breeze, and on that breeze drifted in the elusive large black butterfly with red spots. It flew directly up to Samantha and Zen and introduced itself.

"Crimsoner Rowan," the butterfly said as it gave a bow from its red thorax. "Don't refer to me as a bug. It's Crimsoner or Rowan, just like that. Get it? I am an elder. I work with all types of small flying creatures and assist the plant elders." He hovered oddly in front of them without flapping his wings. It was as if the air around him froze, keeping him suspended. "So, if I hear about anyone pulling the wings off any creature, they'll have to answer to me!" Crimsoner's large black eyes looked directly at Zen when he stated his last word.

"What are you looking at me for?" Zen asked, obviously shocked at the implication. "I'd never even think of pulling the wings off anybody."

Nodding in satisfaction, the butterfly softened his tone a bit. "Good. Then we will get along just fine. Everyone, follow me," Crimsoner Rowan instructed, flitting off in front of them.

Craig stared off after the butterfly with a puzzled expression. "Scientifically, I can't even begin to explain what I just saw and heard."

"Don't worry about it, buddy," Junzo said, wrapping an arm around Craig's shoulders. "I don't think you'd find words in the scientific vocabulary that would help explain it anyway. Just tell yourself that anything you see and hear from this point on, you'll file away under tales of the unexplained."

"Rowan will lead you from here," Bess said. "We'll see you all back at the house."

"Lead them? I cannot lead bodies that are not moving!" the butterfly said, flying back to the group.

"All right, Rowan. Lead on," Mayra said.

Samantha found Crimsoner Rowan's "I don't take no nonsense" attitude humorous and surprising. "If I ever imagined a butterfly talking, I sure wouldn't have expected one to sound so, I don't know, gruff," she said to those around her, whispering so the gliding butterfly in front of them wouldn't hear her.

"Yeah," Zen agreed. "Nothing delicate about that one."

"Rowan can be a bit ill-tempered, but he's very knowledgeable about all things concerning the nature community," Mayra assured them. "And he keeps himself well-informed about the changes happening in the human world as well."

Vivid was the word that popped into Samantha's head when she got her first look at this new world. She imagined an artist soaking up concentrated paint from his palette and, without care, dripping it onto this scenery. A rainbow of wildflowers dotted fields upon fields of deep-green grass. She passed honey blossom trees, inhaling their sweet-smelling flowers of the most delicate of pinks, deepest of purples, crispest of whites, and juiciest of orange hues. Under her feet, loose turquoise pebbles marked clear walking paths. The sky was a brilliant blue, and there was a sun! It hung high overhead, warming the stone-and-timber homes that lay along the ridge of the landscape.

"Hello, neighbors!" called out Sean and Rhona Cullen from Embers Diner. "I told you we lived close by," Sean said.

Word must have gotten out that the newcomers from above had arrived because people began to cluster in small groups.

It's just like Mom said, Samantha thought. *They're just normal people down here in all shades, shapes, and sizes. And they're doing what most humans do—coming out to have a stickybeak.*

"What do you think of your new home now, Samantha?" Sean asked, shaking her hand with his large, meaty paws. "Here, let me show you around—"

"Get lost, Cullen," Crimsoner said, flying down between Samantha and Sean. "I'm leading this expedition."

"Oh, I beg your pardon, Elder Rowan." Sean chuckled. "I didn't mean to butt in."

Note to self: Never get on this butterfly's bad side, Samantha thought.

As they walked on, she took note of how the core people dressed in simple, loose-fitting cotton clothing of bright shades, just like their landscape. If anything, she felt that she and Zen stuck out the most in their sneakers and jeans. Another real difference she noticed was there weren't any shops of any kind. *I'm not big on shopping, anyway. If I had to, I could live very comfortably down here, just as long as I had my books.* And since Mayra had told her they were visiting a library today, she knew there must be plenty of those down here.

Crimsoner Rowan flew over a stone bridge that arched over a stream, then led them up to a door that was at least ten to fifteen feet high and built into the side of a grassy mountain.

"This is where I will leave you," the butterfly said in a more tapered-down tone than earlier. But then, in his normal, gruff voice, he said to Samantha and Zen, "Hey, I will see you two again above ground when the flowers bloom. I have things I need to teach you." He proceeded to fly away backward, never taking his almost human-like eyes off them.

"Oh ... okay," Samantha said.

"Don't say, 'okay'!" Zen said, nudging her. "I'm not sure I want to learn what he's offering to teach.

"I remember this place from the other night. This is the entrance to the library," Anna said.

Inside the structure, they walked upon red clay floors with small pieces of purple stone deposits. But what fascinated Samantha were the walls. They were made of clear quartz crystals. Unlike the caves in Chihuahua, Mexico, where the large quartz jutted at different angles, these crystals formed the walls and emanated light. Then there was the music. The same rhythmic tones that had filled her bedroom now filled these chambers.

"Do you hear that?" Samantha asked.

"Yeah," Zen said. "It sounds like the music those guys make in your country, Uncle Craig, when they blow through those poles."

"A didgeridoo. Yeah, it does a bit. But I hear voices."

"Throat singing, maybe?" said Junzo. "The type of singing the people of Mongolia do."

"Throat singing, huh? I've never heard of it," Samantha said.

"Actually, you're hearing the Earth singing," Mayra shared. "Come along. The library is just this way."

They passed several corridors before Mayra led them into a room about fifty feet from the entrance. "Here we are," she said. "This is the records library."

Samantha had never seen a library quite like this one. It

seemed more suited for a boardroom, with its oblong table made of a thin, reflective black surface and twelve metal straight-back chairs. Off to the left side of the entryway was a set of stairs leading to a loft decorated with cushioned wave-shaped lounge chairs. Most unusual about the room were the circular cubbyholes that ran from floor to ceiling and were perfectly carved into the crystalline walls. Each of the holes cradled an assortment of crystals, metals, and other gems.

"They have rooms filled with pretty colored rocks," Sam said, looking over at Anna. "Remember how Mom told us that story about the core people? And here we finally are."

"Yeah, here we are," Anna said with a smile.

"Wow! Who are these chairs made for? Look how high up I'm sitting," Craig said.

Glancing over her shoulder, Samantha saw her dad sitting in one of the chairs at the oblong table. His feet dangled clear away from the ground.

"Man, Uncle Craig, you look like a baby sitting in a high chair," Zen said, laughing.

"Listen, everyone," Mayra whispered. "I meant to tell you—"

Mayra's words became lost behind the collective gasp that rang out in the room when in walked the tallest woman—the tallest person—Samantha had ever seen.

"Welcome, everyone. Welcome to the Record Library," said the ginormous woman. She stood next to the oblong table and held the back of one of the metal chairs, which were obviously tailored for people of her size. Samantha guessed the woman to be at least ten feet tall. And she was quite light on her feet because there had been no indication she'd been approaching before she entered the room.

Her fair hair was pulled into a bun, and she wore a teal

sari dress that matched her beautiful, oval, deep-green eyes. Her eyes reminded Samantha of the depictions of ancient Egyptians, whose eyes seemed to extend back to their ears. Despite her height, she appeared normal in appearance.

"Fawna." Mayra spoke up when no one else did. "I'd like you to meet Anna and Sam. They're Ameara's daughters. And their husbands, Junzo and Craig. And these are their children, Samantha and Zen. Everyone, this is Fawna, who is the caretaker of this library."

"It is always wonderful to meet descendants of Muaura and Arborden," Fawna said as she rested one hand under her long chin and surveyed her guests. "I gather from the expressions on your faces that you assumed Addiwan to be quite tall. That is until you met me, of course." Her statement of the obvious made everyone laugh, breaking the tension. "Knowledge of your heritage is clearly missing. I think some study of the records in this library will correct this deficiency."

"How are we to study with no books?" Samantha pointed out, disappointed to find that her favorite pastime material was absent in what was supposed to be a library.

Gracefully, Fawna glided over to one of the cubbyholes and removed a crystal. "These are the books you will learn from," she said, handing the crystal to Samantha.

The smoky quartz crystal was no longer than Samantha's thumb. It had six flat surfaces at the tip and a jagged base. Samantha remembered a shop she and her mom visited in Sedona, Arizona, in the Tlaquepaque courtyard. She had picked up a crystal similar to the one she was holding. The shop's owner had asked her if she'd picked up the crystal because she felt a connection to it. She didn't understand what the woman was talking about; she had simply picked up the crystal because she liked examining the many shapes she saw inside it.

"This crystal holds volumes of information," Fawna said, crouching to talk to her.

"Really?" Trying to figure out if what Fawna told her was even possible, Samantha took a closer look into the crystal. Though it was beautiful in appearance and contained what looked like trapped clouds, she saw nothing even resembling written language outside or inside the crystal.

"No actual books? Sweet!" Zen said, looking over Samantha's shoulder at the crystal. "Uh, Mom, Dad? Can I have all my schoolwork put on a crystal?"

"Uh, no," Sam answered.

"How would you insert and extract data from a free-standing crystal?" Craig asked.

"Very simply. I will instruct you on the use of these recordkeepers on your next visit," Fawna said, returning the crystal to its position. She motioned for them to follow her as she exited the library and led them back to the entrance.

"Well, I'm very interested to learn. When can we come back?" Craig asked.

"Any time you like. The library is always open, even if I am not here. Just never remove the records."

"Fawna, did we actually travel into the inner core of the Earth? Or are we just several miles below the ground?" Sam asked as they crossed over the stone bridge.

"You are within one of this planet's inner core chambers." They stopped at the opening to the passageway that would take them home, as Fawna explained further. "There are many doorways located around this planet that connect to worlds just like this one. Some are inhabited, and others are abandoned."

"Yes. My mother mapped out a number of these doorways in her travels," Mayra said.

"More importantly," Fawna said, "Nanna was trying to connect to others, such as your family, who are appointed to shield these worlds and the wealth of knowledge stored within them."

CHAPTER 31

IMAGES IN THE DARK POOL OF THE LOOKING GLASS

All of your questions will be answered," Mayra said, throwing up her hands in defense. "I promise."

"I thought this was why we were brought to the records library—to become enlightened about this planet's past," Craig said. Samantha could clearly hear the frustration in her dad's voice. "Yet we're told we have to come back another time to learn more. What's that all about, Mayra?"

Samantha felt sorry for her great-aunt. Ever since they'd said goodbye to Fawna, the questions hadn't let up, and they were still coming as the group exited the passageway into the kitchen.

"Why does Kitchet want to talk with us in Samantha's bedroom?" Sam asked.

"Because he has something to show you, and you can only see it in her room," Mayra explained for the fifth time.

"Well, I've got dibs on Samantha's bed," said Zen. "Remember, I just got out of the hospital. I'm exhausted."

Lounging on Samantha's floor next to Gypsy, Rhiannon and her flowered Technicolor coat joined the group.

Addiwan stood looking out the window, paying little attention to the others in the room. Samantha dangled her feet over the side of her bed while Zen lay propped against her pillows.

"So, what do you think this is all about?" Zen asked.

"I know as much as you do." Samantha grabbed a pillow from behind him and sat back against her headboard. As he readjusted himself, Samantha saw his eyes open wider, and she knew he had come up with his own idea as to what he thought was about to occur at this gathering.

"Hey, maybe they're going to tell us we possess powers," he said. "Powers so special that we all have to be secreted off to an undisclosed location for our safety."

"Don't you think we'd know if we possessed special powers by now?" Samantha asked.

"Well, maybe we don't know we have them because they're dormant or something," Zen said with a shrug.

"Samantha and I paid a visit to Peter Lin today," Mayra announced. "He's expressed an interest in coming by when he's discharged from the hospital. I see no problem with this. But please don't share any information with him about the passageway, the core people, and all that you'll hear this afternoon in this room. We simply don't know enough about him. And until we do, I think it would be wise to keep this information to ourselves."

Then all eyes shifted to Kitchet, who was standing in the middle of them. He said, "I know you're all overwhelmed and full of questions. This is why I've asked you here—to attempt to answer them. At the same time, I'll fulfill Muaura's and her parents' wishes to make sure their future generations know the true story of the human race and, sadly, its downfall."

Taking Muaura's leather-bound journal from his pocket, Kitchet went on to say, "You all know this journal records your family's journey. And from your visit with Fawna, you now know that the history of the human race is stored in her records library. To help make sense of it all, I'm going to share a special message from your ancestors, which is stored on a device here in Samantha's room."

"Device? What type of device?" Craig inquired.

Samantha knew that the black-surfaced mirror hanging behind Kitchet was the device even before he pointed at it.

"Aha! I knew it!" Zen yelled. "It's some sort of computer, isn't it?"

"Yes," Addiwan replied.

"A computer?" Craig asked as he examined the mirror from all angles. "How is it powered? Where is its wiring or circuit board?"

"The materials in this computer are vastly different from what's in computers currently used," Addiwan explained. "There is no wiring. Its crystal circuitry is not tapered down or trapped within this planet's electromagnetic grid system. It is capable of receiving and sending signals well beyond this planet, which we will witness today. This surface," he said, coming to stand in front of it, "is sensitive to the touch of anyone born from the Fairland line. But only a Fairland of a certain age can retrieve the data."

"How old do you have to be?" Samantha asked. "The mirror ... I mean computer reacted when Zen and I touched it."

"As I said, the surface is sensitive to any Fairland's touch. However, it will not activate the message unless you are a Fairland who has lived on this planet for over forty years. This ensures that the elder Fairlands have the opportunity to pass Muaura's written information along to the younger Fairlands."

"This is where Mayra comes in," Kitchet said. "She will be able to activate the message sent by Oeans and EL-Athu."

"Muaura's parents. Aren't they long dead?" Samantha asked.

"They're dead to this world but very much alive back in their own world," Kitchet said with a smile. "Let's let them explain. Mayra, can you do us the honors?"

"Certainly." She placed her palm on the computer's screen as everyone in the room leaned forward to see what would happen next.

The dark surface shimmered just as it had when Samantha and Zen had touched it. Then everyone saw the shooting star. But this time, it did not fade back to black. Instead, into view came another scene that was as clear as a high-definition television. The image on the screen was of a woman and a man, both appearing to be as tall as or taller than Addiwan. They were standing in a room with graphs, and stellar objects floated in midair directly behind their heads.

The woman was wearing a lavender sari dress that covered her from her shoulders down to her unseen feet. Her skin was a rich bronze, and her wavy hair, which was jet black, flowed loosely to her waist.

The man's short, curly, dark hair framed his ebony skin. It was a striking contrast to his catlike amber eyes, which matched the gold tunic he wore over loose-fitting black pants. Samantha felt this man's eyes were very similar to Addiwan's.

Then the woman stepped forward and said, "We are hopeful this message is being received despite the fact that our last message was never retrieved. We will continue our transmissions as scheduled, though we have been advised that our daughter's children, our line, may have ended. Many of Ma-Mu's original human ancestors have stated that their descendants have failed to retrieve their transmissions. It is believed that they have succumbed to the energy pattern of forgetfulness and failed to pass the truth on to their children. Knowing the extra precautions that have been placed among our descendants, we will assume nothing has gone amiss and continue our transmissions, as we have done every thirty years in your time."

As she finished her last sentence, the woman turned and joined the man, who had taken a seat behind her in a high-backed metal chair similar to the ones in the records library.

Samantha glanced at Zen. He, like everyone else in her room, was staring, captivated by what they were watching. As the woman sat and began to address them again, Samantha turned back to the screen to listen.

"I am Oeans. EL-Athu and I," she said, indicating the man by her side, "are your ancestors." As she spoke, whatever recording device they were using zoomed in closer to their faces. Her elongated black onyx eyes were just like Fawna's. EL-Athu's golden eyes were similar in shape. Oeans's face was triangular and very delicate in appearance, whereas EL-Athu's jaw was square with pronounced cheekbones.

"Eighty thousand of your years ago, EL-Athu and I arrived on Ma-Mu. Ma-Mu was once the name of the planet you now call Earth. We were not the first to come. Prior to our arrival, another form of human made your planet their home. These humans lived closely alongside the plant and mineral essences. The plant and mineral essences were the original inhabitants of the planet. They welcomed many travelers to their beautiful blue land, and for a time, all beings Ma-Mu hosted lived in harmony."

Oeans stood once more. With a long, slender finger, she touched the open air in front of her, and a small green planet appeared.

"I originated here," she said, indicating the small planet. "This planet is called Opiyu. Opiyu is home to the restorers of the life force. I traveled here." As she pointed again, a larger multicolored planet came into view, with two darker planets on either side. "This planet is home to EL-Athu and other humans known as the EL. The EL are the alchemists of form, and they call their planet 'Elphiam.' The two darker planets beside Elphiam are its way stations. EL-Athu and I traveled together to Ma-Mu with our sons Ata and Tuam."

Extending her hand to EL-Athu in an invitation to join her by her side, Oeans said, "Ma-Mu's placement within its universe made it conducive to becoming the meeting planet of the minds. This young planet saw the establishment of major learning centers of diverse disciplines. For this reason, our family came, as did many others, to contribute and partake in the sharing of knowledge. Our fondest memory of our stay on Ma-Mu was the birth of our children Muaura and EL-Gene."

"Great advancements were achieved, which benefited the entire multiverse," EL-Athu said, taking up the story. "That is until an error was made." EL-Athu's voice was clear and sharp. "A research group studying tonal compositions recreated the tonal pattern of Ma-Mu and the tonal patterns of other planets. Ma-Mu's elders advised them to discontinue their research. A number of their tonal characters were at frequency levels greater than what the planet could handle. Regrettably, some of the researchers chose not to heed the warnings, and their experiments set into motion disastrous events that almost annihilated the planet."

Waving, EL-Athu brought up in front of him a holographic image of a blue planet. "An energy infraction occurred as a result of the tonal experiments. To hold Ma-Mu together, a counter electromagnetic force was created. This counterforce came with consequences."

As he continued to explain, the holographic image of the blue planet with its unified land mass changed. It now resembled the Earth today, with its separated continents spread across the surface. "Ma-Mu's upper layers were pulled apart. Weather conditions dramatically changed on the planet, forcing life forms that lived above ground to seek shelter within her core. The planet was in turmoil. No one expected the energy infraction to cause such devastation. Life on nearby planets was destroyed." EL-Athu paused, lowering his eyes from the screen.

"Is he talking about the stories of the great floods?" Samantha asked.

"Yes," Addiwan quietly said before EL-Athu began to speak again.

"Because of this energy infraction, another manifestation came about, which was not discovered until things settled above ground. Ma-Mu's tonal pattern was dramatically altered."

Drawing two circles with his finger moving in opposite directions, EL-Athu further explained. "A time pattern formed adjacent to Ma-Mu's original tonal pattern. These two opposing patterns, moving side by side, created a cyclical deterioration that caused most humans and other life forms to lose their ability to control their regeneration process. Meaning humans lost control over their physical forms and began to age. Aging was not the worst thing to happen. Some humans regressed to an early level of human awareness."

Somberly, EL-Athu went on to state, "Representatives of varying planets, along with the elders of Ma-Mu, formed a council to decide what was to be done next. It was decided to place another electromagnetic force field higher above Ma-Mu to contain the effects of the energy infraction so as to not disturb any other surrounding tonal compositions. Prior to this energy field being placed, each of us had to make a decision to stay on the planet or leave, escaping the cyclical deterioration. Oeans and our sons Ata and Tuam decided to leave, while our daughter Muaura decided to stay. Ma-Mu was her home. I also stayed behind to assist Ma-Mu's elders in creating a new normality on the planet and to search for my son EL-Gene. I never found him. I left Ma-Mu, never certain if EL-Gene left the planet or stayed behind," he expressed sadly.

Removing the graphs in front of him, EL-Athu went on. "Every so often, the council opens a portal in the electromagnetic force field that surrounds your space, allowing those who consciously remember and are able to do so to return to their original planets. However, we discovered that leaving Ma-Mu by choice became difficult for most humans. Their consciousness had become enmeshed with the new tonal composition. Humans now believe that the only way to exit Ma-Mu is to lay down their physical form in death. The cyclical deterioration has become their reality."

"Thinking we could remedy this disease that was spreading within the consciousness of Ma-Mu," said Oeans, "the same portal the council opens to allow those to leave also gives other humans entrance back onto your planet. The restorers of the life force from Opiyu returned to Ma-Mu to set up centers around the planet. These healing structures were designed by the EL and encoded with Ma-Mu's original tonal composition. In the beginning, the centers appeared to help. That is, until our fellow humans tried to control those who would benefit from the healing centers. Chaos ensued, and many lives were lost. It became clear to us that it was in the best interest of all to withdraw from the planet. The healing centers were shut down. We had to stand back and wait for Ma-Mu to cleanse herself."

"The surface of your planet is under the new tonal composition of E-A-R-T-H," EL-Athu pointed out. "While the core of your planet continues to quietly pulsate, singing the true tonal composition of MA-MU."

The recording device zoomed out, returning to a full view of the room. Oeans and EL-Athu walked back to the positions they'd held when the transmission began.

"In her time, Earth will be released from quarantine status," Oeans said. "She will once again take the place within her universe that she held before the energy fraction. We just hope the consciousness of the humans on your planet will be ready for the shift. Our descendants stay safe." Then the transmission ended.

The black mirrored surface returned, and Kitchet faced everyone in Samantha's bedroom.

"My father's ancestors came from Elphiam," Kitchet said. "And my mother is what many now call elfin—those who live among the woodland kin. Elfins were among the first humans on this planet. My mother's ancestors came to Ma-Mu from a planet called Pan-AEL, which is where all fae humans originated. I don't mind being called an elfin. *Elf* is part of *self*, if you get my meaning," he said, laughing at his own joke. "Elf, dwarf, gnomes—my family has been known by all of these words. But truly, these are simply labels. We really are just another form of a human being."

"Like Kitchet's mother, many of my ancestors and I were born here, having arrived from Pan-AEL," Bess shared cheerfully. "I am full woodland folk, or elfin."

"Wait a second. How old are you all? And if you're an elf, where are your pointed ears?" asked Zen.

"We age at a different rate than most humans. Some of us can even regenerate, as all humans were once able to do," Rhiannon said, still leaning up against Gypsy with her hands tucked behind her. "I'm only 315 years old—younger than most here in this room. Oh, of course, not younger than you all," she corrected herself, pointing toward Samantha's family. "And hey, Zen. Look what I can do." Rhiannon extended the top of her left ear into the customary elfin point as Samantha had seen many times in movies and read about in books.

"All right! I wanna do that!" Zen said, running over to get a better look at Rhiannon's ear.

"So, elfin folk aren't born with pointy ears?" Samantha asked.

"No. We only started making our ears bigger when we hid in the woods from the tall ones who went mad. With these ears, we heard their big feet coming from yards away," Rhiannon explained.

Addiwan said, "It is felt that the woodland humans' energy flows along an alternating frequency, similar to that of the tree folk. All tree folk go through a seasonal deterioration process. Some never go through the process and live a very long time, like the ones on this property. It appears that the energy infraction created many alternate energy streams. I have escaped deterioration. I suspect there are others like me somewhere across this planet, but they would keep on the move to not be noticed.

"When did your ancestors arrive here, Addiwan?" Samantha asked.

"Shortly after Oeans and EL-Athu arrived. My ancestors, like EL-Athu, are from Elphiam. I chose to stay here on this planet when they left," he stated.

"Why?" Samantha asked. "Why do you stay?"

Addiwan's whole expression changed after she asked him the question. The always articulate Addiwan stood frozen, staring off into space. *Did he hear me?* Samantha wondered. As she waited for his answer, her room became uncomfortably quiet. Then, for an answer, the tall man turned back toward the window and chose not to reply.

Staring at his back, Samantha felt as though a heavy door had closed all around him, locking out her and everyone else in the room. *Something must have happened or hurt him very deeply*, she told herself. Even though she'd known him for only a short time, she got the impression that his action was out of character.

"Who are the core people?" Aunt Sam asked, breaking the silence.

"The core people are a population of elfin folk—humans from varying planets, like your ancestors, and tree folk. Some have always called the inner core their home, while others decided to stay in the inner core after the energy infraction," Bess answered, casting a concerned glance in Addiwan's direction.

Then Samantha remembered seeing something in the transmission that she'd seen before. "EL-Athu drew two circles moving in opposite directions. I saw something like that behind the old clock at the center of the village."

"That clock was built by my grandfather," Kitchet said

proudly. "He tried in vain to reverse the energy infraction's damage to Ma-Mu. That contraption, that clock, was his final attempt before he died a very, very old man. His name was Samu-EL. I, Sam, and even you, Samantha, and other Fairlands before you carry a variation of his name. Back on Elphiam, he was known as EL-Sam-U the Elder."

"Why do Fairlands carry his name, Kitchet?" Samantha asked.

"Because Samu-EL is a blood relative of yours," Bess said quickly.

"Bessie!" Kitchet gasped.

"I have to tell them," she said. "Arborden, Muaura's husband, was our son. So, you're our grandchildren. Of course, you're many times removed. But you're our grand-children just the same," she rushed on to say before Kitchet could stop her.

"I never knew!" Aunt Mayra said with surprise.

"The last person to know was Nanna's mother," Kitchet said.

"Our grandparents," Samantha said softly to herself. Then, much more loudly, she proclaimed, "I have ancient elfin grandparents. Wow!"

"I shall call you both Old Pa and Old Ma," Zen said jokingly.

"Or you can call them Oma and Opa," Aunt Mayra said. "They sound very similar, and they mean *grandmother* and *grandfather* in German."

The room became a flurry of people talking over one another and asking more questions. And, for the first time in a long time, there was laughter. Samantha stepped back, wanting to get a better view of them all gathered around the warmth of her fireplace. She had always seen herself and her family members as a kaleidoscope that reflected the faces of people from around the world. This evening, she had looked into the eyes of ancestors who stood on a distant planet and added elfin folk to the branches of her family tree. She couldn't help but giggle when a question popped into her head, asking, *How would Nancy Drew handle this?* Then, from the corner of her eye, she caught sight of Addiwan quietly slipping out of her room. A few seconds later, she heard the front door below open, then close behind him.

I really want to know what he's hiding.

CHAPTER 32

A GENTLE, BRAVE WOMAN

Samantha sat in her window seat, all ready for bed and holding the photo of Ameara sitting under her favorite tree. She had brought it down from the attic a couple of days before and kept it on her nightstand. Ameara's face was the first she saw when she woke in the morning and the last before she fell asleep at night.

A week had gone by since Samantha's family had visited the core people and gathered in her bedroom to listen to the message from Oeans and EL-Athu. Since that day, she'd spent most of her days in the flower shop with her mom and helped her dad set up his office. After two days, Aunt Mayra returned to New York. Peter Lin stopped by on his way back to Maynard to pick up his belongings. His plan was to move to Hearthshire to be closer to the Fairlands. Zen spent his days close to home, hoping to catch up with Addiwan, whom no one had seen since the gathering in Samantha's room. Even though his parents told him Addiwan wasn't allowed to teach him to shift his energy pattern, Zen was still determined to turn into something other than what he was.

"I miss speaking with her," Terrance said to Samantha as she continued to stare at the picture of her Grandma Ameara.

"What was she like, Terrance? Was she like my mom?"

"Oh, yes. She had a gentle essence that glowed all around her. Your mom has the same energy."

She ran her hand over the glass in the photo's frame. Looking into Ameara's warm brown eyes, she could see the gentleness Terrance said she'd radiated. Then a disturbing image popped into Samantha's mind of her grandma running through those same woods where she and Zen had run for their lives from Kenneth and Emily Randall. "Do you think she was frightened at the end of her life, all alone in those woods?"

"She was not alone, Samantha," Terrance said softly. "My sisters were with her in the end. They say she was quite brave and determined till the end to make sure her family was kept safe."

"Gentle and brave. I hope I grow up to be like her."

"You are well on your way, Samantha."

Headlights lit up the driveway, and she saw her grandpa's old green station wagon pulling into the garage. It was her parents and Zen returning home from dropping off Sam and Junzo at the airport. Several moments later, her mom entered her bedroom.

"I thought I saw your light on as we drove up. Were you just talking with Terrance?"

"Yes, we were talking about Grandma Ameara."

Taking the photo from Samantha's hands, her mom said. "You remind me so much of her."

"Yeah? Really? In what way?"

"Oh, your smile and your eyes are just like hers. And

when I was with my mom, I always felt comforted, just as I feel with you."

Samantha swelled with pride at her mom's words.

"Okay, time for bed," her mom said, handing Samantha back the photo. "Good night, Terrance."

"Peaceful night, Anna, Samantha," he called back.

"I've noticed that when we go into the village, you've stayed far away from your favorite place—the library," Anna said as she pulled down Samantha's blanket and took a seat on the edge of her bed.

"I will never step foot in that library again," Samantha declared sternly as she placed Ameara's photo back on the nightstand and climbed under the covers. She hadn't had another nightmare about Ms. Emily, but she felt she couldn't walk back into that place again without thinking of that woman and her son.

"I understand your feelings, Samantha. Ms. Emily had us all fooled. However, don't let it keep you from doing the things you love. And you love spending time in the library. Remember, Ms. Emily's deeds harmed us. It wasn't the library itself."

"I know. I'm just not ready to go back in there."

"Well, I didn't want to show you this. It was to be a surprise. But I guess I'll have to. Hopefully, this will change your mind about visiting the library." Then her mom took a yellow flyer out of her jeans pocket and handed it over for Samantha to read.

Hearthshire Public Library Presents:
Joanna Taylor
Author of
The History of Nancy Drew
A Collector's Story

Saturday, March 9th, at 1 p.m.
Come join this fun-filled afternoon and meet our new librarian!

"I hear Ms. Taylor will be displaying some of her rare Nancy Drew—"

"I'll be there!" Samantha squealed.

"That was easy. We'll make it a family affair, with an early dinner afterward."

CHAPTER 33
THE NEW LIBRARIAN

It had been nearly three weeks since the whole village learned that their librarian, Ms. Emily, and her son, Kenneth Randall, were responsible for the twenty-five-year-old murders of Nanna and Ameara Fairland. Many of the locals stopped by the flower shop to express their sympathy. "Case Closed" was the lead headline in *The Hearthshire Ledger* for two consecutive days. Thankfully, Chief Bevin was able to keep Samantha and Zen's involvement out of the paper for their privacy.

That afternoon, Samantha and her family attended the library's special event that would announce the new librarian for the Hearthshire Public Library. There also would be a guest speaker, Ms. Taylor—author and Nancy Drew collector. It was Ms. Taylor who Samantha was most interested in meeting.

Bouquets decorated the windowsills, and a basket of cookies had been placed at the information desk.

Well, the new librarian sure has changed the mood in this place, Samantha thought. She also noticed the large number of people gathered. "Everyone must be here because of the guest speaker."

"Yeah, but they're all older people. There's no one here our age," Zen pointed out. "I thought Nancy Drew was a kids' book."

"A lot of these older people probably grew up reading Nancy Drew, Zen," Anna explained. "These books have been in circulation for a long time."

"I'm gonna go and get some cookies," he said, eyeing the basket. "Then I'm gonna find a nice, quiet place to take a nap."

As Zen walked off, Kitchet joined them.

"Where's Bess?" Samantha asked, noting her absence. In fact, she'd noticed that her oma hadn't been around the house much lately.

"She'll be here soon," Kitchet promised.

"Samantha, let's go meet Ms. Taylor before her presentation begins," Craig suggested.

Ms. Taylor looked to be in her thirties and smiled warmly when Samantha and Craig approached her. She had her table set up with several copies of Nancy Drew books that Samantha would have loved to get her hands on.

"Ms. Taylor, I'm Craig Keen, and this is my daughter—"

"Don't tell me," Ms. Taylor said, stopping him. "This must be Samantha."

"How did you know?" Samantha asked.

"The librarian told me."

"The librarian? But how did she know—"

Just then, Mayor Jasper started talking, welcoming everyone to the library.

"Come back and see me after my presentation," Ms. Taylor said. "I have something for you."

Grinning from ear to ear, Samantha hurried to look for a

seat. They all seemed to be taken until she spied an empty chair next to a young girl about her age. The girl waved to Samantha to come sit by her.

"Go ahead. Take it," Craig said. "I'll go stand in the back with your mum and Kitchet."

On her head, the girl was wearing a knitted pink-and-white pageboy hat. And she had it on backward. It had a white star crocheted on the side and covered the girl's shoulder-length, raven hair. Her hair was so black, in fact, that it made her steel-gray eyes shine like headlights and her fair skin appear alabaster. The girl was wearing matching pink track pants and a long-sleeved white T-shirt. She grinned at Samantha and said, "Hi, I'm Laney. What's your name?"

"Samantha."

"I was sure glad to see you when I came in. I thought I was gonna be the only kid here."

"That's what my cousin thought too."

"There's another kid here? Where is she?" Laney asked.

"It's a he. His name is Zen. He's off somewhere ... eating."

"Cool. He likes Nancy Drew?"

"Not exactly. Zen does not—"

"Oh, wait. I think the mayor is about to announce the new librarian. I hope she's nice. That old librarian gave me the creeps." Laney peered at the mayor, then sighed. "Oh, not yet. Sorry I cut you off. I didn't mean to be rude."

"That's okay. I didn't think you were being rude."

"My friend Jocelyn isn't here today. But she's always telling me how I can be rude sometimes."

Samantha's first impression of Laney was that she liked her right away. Then again, maybe she took to Laney so quickly because she was the first girl she'd met since moving to Hearthshire, and she was starting to feel desperate to talk to any kid other than Zen.

"She's going to introduce her now," Laney said, craning her neck to see past the people sitting in front of her.

Samantha sat up too. She wanted to know who this librarian was who seemed to know so much about her.

Mayor Jasper said, "I am happy to welcome a woman who came highly recommended by our local florist."

"My mom?" Samantha said.

"Your mom's the new librarian?" Laney asked.

"No, my mom's the local florist."

"Oh."

"Bess Kitchet," Mayor Jasper said as everyone in the room began to clap.

Bess Kitchet? Samantha turned and looked at her parents, who were smiling and clapping. *Well, that explains the baked cookies and the touch of flowers everywhere. I'm gonna live in this library!*

"Thank you, Mayor Jasper," Bess said, beaming. "I am thrilled to have been invited to be Hearthshire's new librarian." Bess was wearing a pretty rose-print dress that complemented her rosy cheeks and rosy disposition. "I hope everyone stays after the presentation to look at some of the new books I've added to the shelves. There's a suggestion box near the basket of cookies for anyone who wants to ask for books that are not already here at the library. Thank you," Bess finished, waving to Samantha.

"She seems to be very sweet. Do you know her? She seems to know you," Laney said.

"Yeah, Bess is my oma."

"Oma? That's *grandma* in German. I speak German. Do you speak German?"

"No. *Oma* and *opa* are the only words I know."

"If you like, I can teach you German. Your oma, huh? That's way special. I'll have to make a point to come to the library more often," Laney said in her rapid way of speaking. "I'm sure I'll see you here, too, since your oma is the librarian."

"How many Nancy Drew books have you read?" Samantha asked.

"Well, I've only read one of them so far. It was *The Case of the Twin Teddy Bears*, but I really liked it."

"Oh, that's a newer one. Released in 1993. It's a good one."

"Boy, Samantha, you really know your Nancy Drew books. I love to read too."

Yeah, she's nice. I think we could become good friends, Samantha thought.

During the presentation, Samantha pointed out the Nancy Drew books she owned that Ms. Taylor had on display, and Laney told Samantha about other books she'd read.

"Thank you all for coming, and I hope I get new Nancy Drew fans signing onto my website," Ms. Taylor said as she ended her hour-long presentation.

This was the best day Samantha felt she'd had in a long time. A crowd gathered around Ms. Taylor, so Samantha went to look around for Bess.

"Where are you heading, Samantha?" Laney asked. "Don't you want to go up and talk to Ms. Taylor?"

"Yeah, but I wanted to find my oma first. You want to come and meet her?"

"Sure."

They found Bess behind the front desk, telling people where to find the new books she'd added.

"Nice surprise?" Bess asked when she spotted Samantha coming her way.

"Yep. Did everyone know except me?"

"You and Zen were the only ones who didn't know. We didn't want him to tell you."

"This is Laney," Samantha said, pointing to the girl by her side.

"Nice to meet you, Oma Bess," Laney said as she plucked a cookie from the basket at the counter. "You'll be seeing a lot of me in here. Hey, I'll catch up with you later, Samantha. I see my father over there. Or my vater, as it's said in German."

"Nice meeting you, Laney," Bess said as the girl disappeared into the crowd.

"Can we go eat now?" Zen asked, coming up behind them and reaching for another cookie.

"Zen, you cannot be hungry." Bess pushed his hair away from his forehead to get a better look into his eyes.

"Ignore him," Samantha said. "He always looks for food when he's bored. Come on, Zen. The crowds thinned around Ms. Taylor." Before taking off, Samantha stepped behind the information desk to give Bess a hug. "Thanks! I love you."

Bess stared off after Samantha and Zen, rubbing a bit of moisture away from her eyes, before turning to greet more people.

"Can you imagine, Zen? A signed copy of Ms. Taylor's book, *The History of Nancy Drew. A Collector's Story*. And she said after Bess told her I was a collector too, she gave me this! A first edition of Nancy Drew's *The Witch Tree Symbol*. Ms. Taylor said she wanted to add to my collection," Samantha gushed as they walked through the crowd.

"Big whoop. More books. I thought you were done reading those."

"Samantha! Hey, Samantha!" Laney called, hurrying over.

"Laney, look! A copy of *The Witch Tree Symbol*," Samantha said, holding up the book.

"Whoa, can I come over and read it with you?"

"Not another Drew head," Zen said, sighing loudly.

"What's the matter, kid? Don't you like Nancy Drew?" Laney asked.

"No. And I'm no kid."

Swaying back on her heels, Laney laughed. "Sorry. I didn't mean to insult you."

"Laney, this is my cousin, Zen," Samantha said.

"Nice to meet you, Zen." Laney stuck out her hand.

"It's Alexzender," he corrected.

Samantha rolled her eyes.

"Sorry again, Alexzender." Laney smiled. "Hey, I want you to meet my father."

They followed Laney to a man standing off by himself. As they got closer, Samantha recognized him as Officer Roberts out of uniform.

"Samantha, Zen. How have you both been doing?" he asked.

"Officer Roberts is your—" Zen started to ask.

"My father," Laney finished.

"Officer Roberts, fancy seeing you here. Are you getting caught up on your Nancy Drew reading to help solve your next case?" Craig teasingly asked as he came over.

"I'm more of a Sherlock Holmes bloke myself. When I stopped by the flower shop, your wife told me that Ms. Taylor would be here today. I'm here with my daughter,

Laney. She's a new Nancy Drew fan, as I see Samantha and Zen are."

"Not me," Zen said. "I live mystery and adventure. I don't read about them."

"I see." Officer Roberts arched his eyebrows. "I hope you're talking about mountain biking or hiking adventures and maybe a game of Clue for a little bit of mystery. Remember, Zen. Leave the real mystery-solving to the police from now on."

"Of course, Officer Roberts, sir. I always leave the real hard crimes in the fine hands of the Hearthshire Police Department." From his tone, Samantha couldn't tell if her cousin was being sincere or sarcastic. Judging from how long it took the police to solve Ameara and Nanna's murder case, with the help of her and Zen, she thought he was being sarcastic.

"So, this is your daughter Laney, Officer Roberts?" Anna asked, coming to join them.

"Yep, this is my Laney. And please. You can call me Zachariah or Zach. I'm not on duty."

Samantha observed how relaxed and friendly Officer Roberts appeared to be out of uniform and away from Chief Bevin.

"That's why she acts like a know-it-all. She's a cop's brat," Zen whispered, standing directly behind Samantha.

"She's nice," Samantha replied.

"You'll see. She has bratty girl written all over her," he warned, waving in wild circular motions behind Laney's back.

Samantha didn't understand why Zen was acting so weird. "Stop that," she whispered back at him. "What's wrong with you?"

"What are you doing?" Laney asked, spinning quickly.

"Is that some form of martial arts? I take martial arts classes."

"He doesn't know martial arts, Laney," Samantha said. "Zen was just being ... a boy."

"Did you say you take martial arts, Laney?" Anna asked.

"Yes, ma'am. My mom teaches here in the village."

"'Yes, ma'am'? Who does she think she's fooling?" Zen said under his breath.

"Craig, we should sign Samantha and Zen up for classes," Anna said.

"I don't think Mom would approve of me taking those types of classes, Aunt Anna," Zen protested. "She doesn't condone violence of any kind."

"No, Zen. It's all taught in a safe environment," Officer Roberts explained.

"I think I may be too busy to fit in more classes, but thanks for the info," Zen said through a forced smile. He then faced his aunt and uncle and asked, "Is it time for dinner?"

"Yes, we should discuss this over dinner. Would you and Laney like to join us, Zach?" Anna asked. Samantha noticed that her mom didn't pick up Zen's hint that he was trying to get away from Officer Roberts and his daughter. "I'm sure the kids would like that. We're just going over for pizza."

"Oh, can we, please? I want to talk to Samantha some more about her book collection," Laney said.

Zen plopped himself in a nearby chair, letting his head drop back like a rag doll. By the look on his face when Laney mentioned her book collection, Samantha knew dinner was going to be torture for him. Leaning over him, she said, "Come on. She's not that bad. Besides, the pizza place has game machines. I bet Laney won't talk too much about books if we get her playing games."

"All right," Zen said, stomping to his feet.

"Here's my wife now," Officer Roberts said. "Let's just check with her about dinner."

Samantha saw that Laney's mom was a tall, lean woman with pale-blond hair. But she shared her daughter's steel-gray eyes

"Leeza, this is Anna and Craig Keen, their daughter Samantha, and their nephew Zen," Officer Roberts said. "They've invited us for pizza."

"It's nice to meet you, Mrs. Roberts," Anna said. "If dinner is no good for you today, we can get together another time. I wanted to ask you about your martial arts classes for the kids."

Displaying an even set of perfectly white teeth, Laney's mom answered. "I would love to join your family for dinner. But please call me Leeza. I don't go by my husband's name. I've kept my maiden name. It's Simms. Leeza Simms."

ACKNOWLEDGMENTS

I would like to thank my husband Alexander for encouraging me to write, for reading my endless rewrites, and for giving me his love and support, which carried me through this wonderful journey of storytelling.

Thank you to my daughter Alex for listening to my story repeatedly and for her wisdom and input.

Thank you to my son Ian for giving me the title of this book and for his advice on description.